When Bunnies
Go Bad

Books by Clea Simon

The Pru Marlowe Pet Noir Mysteries
Dogs Don't Lie
Cats Can't Shoot
Parrots Prove Deadly
Panthers Play for Keeps
Kittens Can Kill

The Theda Krakow Series
Mew Is for Murder
Cattery Row
Cries and Whiskers
Probable Claws

The Dulcie Schwartz Series
Shades of Grey
Grey Matters
Grey Zone
Grey Expectations

Nonfiction
Mad House:
Growing Up in the Shadow of Mentally Ill Siblings
Fatherless Women:
How We Change After We Lose Our Dads
The Feline Mystique:
On the Mysterious Connection Between Women and Cats

When Bunnies Go Bad

A Pru Marlowe Pet Noir

Clea Simon

Poisoned Pen Press

First Edition 2016

10 9 8 7 6 5 4 3 2 1

Library of Congress Catalog Card Number: 2015949172

ISBN: 9781464205330   Hardcover
      9781464205354   Trade Paperback

Poisoned Pen Press
6962 E. First Ave., Ste. 103
Scottsdale, AZ 85251
www.poisonedpenpress.com
info@poisonedpenpress.com

Printed in the United States of America

For Jon

Chapter One

There are many uses for a knife, and just then I wasn't thinking of my steak. In fact, I was letting a perfectly good T-bone grow cold, white droplets of fat solidifying on the plate. My appetite—normally quite healthy, thank you very much—had been quashed. Not by that fat. I'm a carnivore, and cholesterol comes with the territory. But by another useless waste of space. The large, obnoxious diner at the next table.

"What's the matter?" He wasn't talking to me. If he'd dared to glance over, he'd have known better than to take that tone with me. "You're the one who wanted to come here."

I couldn't see the face of the woman he was addressing. Just the back of her rich auburn hair, head bowed low. I'd seen her when they came in, though. Wondered at first if she was his daughter, so perky and bright—a shiny brass penny next to his dull, dark mound.

Dull dark dollars, most likely. The man with the suspiciously thick black mane had started in on the maitre d' right away, complaining about the parking and the conditions of the road. We don't do valet parking here in Beauville. This time of year, we're lucky to get through. And that was the next problem. Hardware—Main Street's nicest eatery—was packed. This was the first Saturday in five without a major storm, the latest thaw seemed to be holding, and a bunch of us had had the same idea. March in Massachusetts, as the worst winter anyone could remember ground to a halt, and we all had cabin fever. When

Jim Creighton, my main squeeze, had called to say he'd snagged a table, I didn't hesitate. Too much time on my own had made me a little crazy, and Hardware's grub was better than anything I could manage on my own. Only Mister Money, here, didn't get it. He'd graced the little café with his presence, and he let it be known that this commanded star treatment.

"That's it?" Right from the start, he'd been trouble, looking at the two-top by the window as if it were dirt. He didn't realize how lucky he was to get it. "Don't you know who I am?"

Maybe the maitre d' did. At any rate, he'd had the sense to make the kind of low, soothing noises I'd use on any irate animal. But even the double martini—"Ketel One, I'll know"—hadn't made things easier.

"Get this out of here." He'd grabbed the waiter as he came by—with our steaks, mind you—handing him the bread basket.

"Sir, the brioche is a—" He didn't get a chance to finish.

"Cheryl here has the self-control of an alley cat." He nodded to his date. I couldn't see her face, but I'd bet it was as red as her hair. "Going to be as fat as one, too, she keeps this up. And get me another one of these." With his other hand, he waved his cocktail glass, sloshing the remaining contents onto the floor. "She'll have water."

The waiter had nodded, grabbing the offending basket as soon as he'd placed our plates. The service professions are used to jerks like these, and the best you can do is defuse them.

"Teddy…" I heard her plea. The TV over the bar was on—this was Beauville, after all—but the sound was low enough for conversation. Underneath its sweet entreaty, her voice was tense. A combination of embarrassment and rage, I thought. I would have inclined toward the latter. "Baby, please…"

Creighton saw me lean forward and smiled, a bit rueful. He couldn't blame me for eavesdropping, not after that display. Everyone in the place had heard that exchange. One beefy dude had even turned from the tube and was frankly staring, the news—some suits at a podium—less interesting than the drama up close. It didn't matter. The woman had dropped her voice below what I could pick up. But if I couldn't hear the rest, Jim did, his grin spreading across his face.

"You find that kind of thing amusing?" I speared a hunk of meat, and addressed my own date, keeping my voice low. "You think I should make all nicey-nice when you're in a mood?"

"Wouldn't dream of it." Creighton kept his eyes on his own plate, wise man, though his dimples did give him away. "How's your steak?"

"Quite tasty, thank you," I replied as he refilled my wineglass. As I've said, Creighton is a smart man, and a lot better mannered then the big guy at the bar.

The TV had switched focus to a painting—a woodland scene, with a rabbit in the foreground. The caption read "TRAIL GOES COLD." But before I could ask my beau about it, he sat up with a start, bottle still in hand.

"Teddy, baby…" The woman behind him sounded near tears. That wasn't what Creighton was responding to, though, as he stood and started to turn.

"Excuse me, sir." He had on his cop voice. I put my cutlery down. "You can't speak to a woman like that—"

"She's my concern." The red-faced man wasn't backing down. "Bought and paid for, and if you think I'll be taken by a little ski bunny that way—"

"Please." The redhead was standing now, too. Facing Creighton with her hands up in a placating gesture and eyes big with tears. "Please, sir. I'm sorry. This was my fault."

"Come on, Cheryl." Teddy slammed a twenty down on the table and started to leave.

"You don't have to go with him, Miss." Creighton can be old school. "We'd be happy to escort you anywhere."

"No, I—I do." Her voice was a stage whisper, the pleading note in it hard to miss. "He's not usually like this."

Ducking past the waiter, who had arrived with the second martini, she trotted after her date in impossibly high heels. Between her gait and the short fur jacket she had grabbed from the maitre d', she did evoke a bunny. Though a wild rabbit, like the one in that painting, would have more sense than to follow a wolf out into the dark.

"Well, that's not going to end well." Creighton craned to watch her hop away after her date before reclaiming his seat.

"Maybe she'll get fed up." I topped off his glass, willing the evening back toward normal. "The bunny turns, and all that."

"Maybe." With a shrug, he tore into his steak, and our conversation moved on to more congenial topics: the wine, my latest client. Over at the bar, the story had shifted, too—the stolen painting replaced by a celebrity divorce. I knew the scene was weighing on my guy, though, much as it stayed with me. None of us likes to see one human dominate another, and the tired formula of a moneyed older man using his wealth to manipulate a beautiful young woman was as depressing as the month-old snowbanks.

Neither of us wanted to see that couple again, though Beauville is small enough that I suspected we would. Neither of us knew that would happen as soon as the next morning, or that Cheryl the ski bunny would be the obvious suspect when Teddy Rhinecrest was found dead, stabbed in the front hallway of his Beauville love nest.

•

Chapter Two

I should have known I'd run into him again. After all, one of my gigs here in this hick town is de facto pest control.

I should explain. I'm not an exterminator. I've got little love for vermin of any species, and less sympathy for the human kind than most others. And I live in an omnivorous world, where predator and prey have been doing the survival polka for eons—and will be, long after I've become food for whatever organism finally gets me.

But the mice in your pantry? They're just trying to get through the winter, and if you're going to provide shelter and a good supply of edibles, well, they're smart enough to take advantage. No, I'm not the gal you call to lay down poison or traps.

Partly, that's 'cause I've got a sensitivity—a gift, some might call it—that makes this kind of one-sided slaughter particularly painful. You see, I can hear what animals are thinking. Not what they're saying, per se. They don't talk to me, like some Doctor Doolittle fantasy. No, what I have is the ability to eavesdrop on other species like I did on that mismatched couple. And like with that couple, I don't always get everything—every word or thought. What I can usually glean is what an animal is feeling: the fear, the lust, the hunger. The pain, too, if I let myself—which is why I won't wittingly allow myself to be the cause of it. But it does help me deal with the various creatures that my fellow citizens here in Beauville interact with on a daily basis. Because

I can usually figure out what they really want—or why they're scared or acting a certain way—I can intervene. Make peace, even. Not that I'd want any of my human colleagues knowing how I get my results.

This time out, I'd been called because of the rabbits. Well, Ronnie didn't call them that, not exactly. What he said was that there was a problem out at The Pines. And since his job is to take care of problems, he did what he does best—he called someone else.

I should explain. Ronnie is a caretaker. Not in the sense of a nurturing person—more like a glorified janitor. Through some old high school connections—Beauville being, as I have said, a small town—he'd gotten himself hired at the new development. Condos—townhouses—thrown up in a hurry before the crash and now largely rented out to vacationers as eager for privacy as for the smell of evergreens. Set back in the woods, The Pines featured condos angled so that none of the entrances faced each other. Despite the fancy cedar shingles, the construction had been so shoddy that I was sure the occupants could hear each other, loud and clear. But then the development was usually half empty, so maybe that didn't matter much.

As caretaker, Ronnie was jack of all trades there—plumber, carpenter, and groundsman. When the job wasn't too complicated, I suspected he acted as the resident electrician, too, though I didn't like to think about that. It wasn't that he was industrious—far from it—but he knew that he'd been hired by the owners because he was local and he was cheap. Besides, the residents were primarily out-of-towners. City folk, and that meant they tipped. So when he phoned Albert, our local animal control officer, asking for me, I knew he had a real problem.

"It's one of the renters. He's been complaining about rodents. Said rats were eating through his wires. He could hear them." Ronnie said when I took the phone. I'd dropped by Albert's office hoping for some work. It's nice to be treated, but a girl likes to be able to buy her own steak sometimes. "I've already done some repairs for him."

I'd kept my mouth shut. Rabbits were more likely than rats, out here. But if the place had been built properly, a hungry rodent or two wouldn't have been a problem. Besides, this late in the season, I was feeling the pinch—and the folks who stayed at The Pines could pay.

"Will you be around later today?" That was all I asked. I'd learn more about what was going on by checking it out myself than through anything Ronnie could tell me. Beauville men tended to fall into one of two camps: smart and shifty, like Mack—my ex—or big and dumb, like his buddies Vince and Earl, who both tended to think with their fists. My father had been the former. From him, I get my brains, as well as my taste for bourbon. Ronnie was the latter, as was his buddy Albert, although both were too lazy or too stupid to get in much trouble. But also unlikely to think through a problem by themselves. Which was good in that it meant more work for me. Yeah, there was a reason I was with Jim Creighton.

"Uh, not too late?" Of course, Ronnie and Albert were drinking buddies too.

"Before happy hour." I hung up and turned around, quickly enough to watch Albert blush and sputter. It might not yet be spring, and my jeans were nowhere near as tight as that ski bunny's, but Albert is a simple animal. Not that I cared about his response.

"Frank here?" I eyed Albert's down vest, which would be part of his wardrobe until July. "I didn't see him when I came in."

"Oh, yeah." He looked relieved that I'd asked a question he could answer. "He's here." A fumble with his desk drawers, and the masked triangular head of a ferret popped up. Frank, nominally Albert's pet, reached two pale paws up to the desk top and began furiously sniffing the air.

"What's up? Where's it hidden? Who's there?" The pink nose twitched as the curious little beast caught up on the news.

"Have you been keeping him locked up in there?" As I turned on Albert, I tried to query the poor ferret. *"Has he?"* I asked silently, visualizing Albert locking the small creature away in the metal desk. It didn't help my temper.

"No sense in fighting." The ferret fixed his black eyes on me, his advice forming into words in my head. *"None at all."*

"What? No." Albert pushed his chair back, as if afraid I would lunge. It wasn't a bad reaction on his part, and for a moment I was distracted. It's good to know I can inspire fear. "He's just— he's been acting weird lately. Kind of—frisky."

That turned my attention back to Frank, who by now had climbed to the desk top, and the strong sense I was getting from him—a feeling I could only translate as "make love, not war."

"Well, spring is in the air," I said out loud as another thought hit me. "Frank's not neutered, is he?"

"I—uh—I don't know." The round patches of cheek visible above the beard turned scarlet as Albert turned away. "He— maybe—at the shelter…"

"Got it." I hadn't known how the fat animal control officer and his sleek pet had first hooked up. There was no point in beating up on Albert, though. I do try to be gentle with dumb animals, and so I knelt in front of the desk. In the guise of making nice with a cute pet, I'd have a chance to greet the only other intelligent creature in the room.

"What's up, Frank?" I held out my hand for him to sniff, a move as polite as it was wise. Frank's sharp nose and even sharper eyes had frequently provided insight into my life.

"Dog, dog, that cat again…" His busy nose trembled over my fingers. I'd started my day with my usual dog-walking gigs, but underneath it all, I had no doubt the ferret was picking up the scent of Wallis, the tabby who shares my life. *"Wait, wait…a bunny?"*

That one surprised me, and I could feel the smile starting. It didn't matter. Albert would think I was amused by his pet. In truth, I was impressed. I hadn't noticed any rabbits this morning. But before I'd gone out to meet Growler, the bichon with whom I had a standing date, I had made a lame attempt at dismantling the snowbank beside my front porch. It was shrinking, but not quickly enough, and the forsythia peeking through was looking bent and battered. What remained had melted and refrozen often enough to be nearly solid: a dense reminder of the winter mess. There had been a handful of small brown pellets on top of the snow—the local rabbits had found my poor forsythia, too.

"Yeah, rabbits." I kept my voice low. Albert was keeping his distance, but I couldn't take any chances. My reputation was shaky enough in this town without talk about me communing with a ferret. "Just trying to get by, I figure."

"This is a dangerous season." The black button eyes looked up at me. *"Not everyone survives."*

◇◇◇

I took the mustelid's words to heart as I drove over to the condos. Driving is one of the great pleasures of my life. The chief consolation for leaving behind the city and returning to the small town of my birth was trading in the subway for a '74 GTO with a retro engine and a custom paint job. And while I've reconciled myself to the added expense that my baby blue baby costs in gas and maintenance, I have to constantly remind myself that my muscle car wasn't made with modern safety features—or designed to handle the black ice that invariably followed a thaw. So, as much as I wanted to open her up, let that massive engine roar, I held back—at least on the shadowed streets—as I made my way over to meet Ronnie and his rats.

"Hey, Pru!" I found him in front of the development office. Tall and heavy, he complemented the build of an autumn bear with the personal style of the awkward teen he must have been some two decades before. As he looked up, I wondered once again how someone who spends so much of his time outdoors could have such an unhealthy complexion. Some of it seemed to be a blush. I'd startled him, as he was digging through the work box in the back of his pickup. Looking for cigs, most likely, or maybe something more potent, from the way he stood with a start. As long as he wasn't feeding anything to an animal, I didn't much care. "You're early."

"You've got rodents?" As I've said, Ronnie—like his buddy Albert—isn't necessarily the brightest tool in the shed. And if

I've learned one thing from working with animals, it's that the closer you can keep on message, the better results you'll get. Not that my professors in animal behavior could have guessed just what kind of beast I'd end up training.

"Yeah. I think so." He was actually standing up straighter as he came toward me, wiping his hands on his flannel shirt as he did so. Training 101: Ignore the behavior you want to discourage, and reward the behavior you want with attention. I did so, shaking his outstretched palm. It was disconcertingly moist, but at least he was trying to act professional. "The tenant in number six complained."

"And?" I looked at him, curious. Usually someone in Ronnie's position would put down poison and hope to get the credit—and any reward—himself.

He shook his head. "And nothing." A shrug. "I set some traps—the good kind, of course." Humane ones, he meant. I doubted it, but I didn't interrupt. "But I didn't get anything. And then this morning he called me from the road, saying something had eaten through his wires."

"Did you check?" What he was saying wasn't completely impossible. A winter like we'd had was rough on wildlife. You think you have trouble driving to the store when the drifts top three feet? Try digging through the ice pack to get at the last of the acorns or the tender bark of a sapling. As I knew from the scat by my house, anything that can be gotten at is fair game by February, and although the weather had eased up on us with the opening of March, the recent melt hadn't made edibles more accessible yet.

"Yeah, sure. I looked at where the wires come in and everything." Another shrug. "He didn't want to hear it."

"Fine." I was here. I was going to bill anyway. "So, is he here now?"

Ronnie swallowed, his wind-reddened cheeks going pale. "You don't believe me?"

I sighed, audibly. Not that it would do any good. "If there's a problem, I need to eliminate the obvious," I explained. "Like that your tenant kicked the plug out or something."

"Okay." He didn't sound happy. "Just—the guy has a temper."

I followed him down the walk, which looked like it had been cleared barely enough to avoid complaints. On either side of the concrete, the crusty snow had been piled thigh-high, but that was lower than it had been a week ago, and dark, damp patches of earth could be seen in the sunnier spots. Soon, I hoped, the crocuses and snowdrops would be peeking through. I'm not sentimental about spring—I'm not sentimental about anything—but even I craved color after the endless, dreary freeze.

"Hello!" I was still examining the snowbank as he yelled into the mail slot. Inside, a small dog was yelping. "Anyone there?"

As he knocked, I crouched to examine the pitted side of the melting drift, a possibility suggesting itself. It was hard to tell from where I was looking, but what Ronnie's tenant had suggested could happen. The larger animals—deer and rabbits—had been scrambling, but the smaller ones—moles and voles—made good use of the snow cover. They'd be burrowing under the drifts, safe for a time from many of the local predators. I'd heard of mice that had tunneled into storage sheds under cover of snow and made off with a season's worth of feed, unseen by hawk or human.

"Hello!" More yapping. To me it sounded like, "*Rat! Rat! Rat!*" I didn't take it as evidence of a rodent infestation. The high, sharp bark sounded like toy of some sort, and they're excitable. The doorbell and knocking were as likely to have set him off as a four-legged intruder.

I stood and turned toward Ronnie. "Should I send you my invoice, or…?"

"Hang on." He fumbled at his belt, as I'd hoped. Sending Ronnie an invoice would be about as sensible as sending one to those mice, and that impressive ring of keys had to be more than cosmetic. Sure enough, a moment later, he had the front door of the condo open. "Hello?"

His voice was an odd mix of scared and hopeful. Me? I don't work at the beck and call of wealthy vacationers. Pushing the door open slowly, I tried to calm the dog, forming the thought

in my head: *"friend, treats, friend."* Even from here, I could
see evidence of Ronnie's sloppy handiwork: one panel of the
wainscoting had been replaced, a bent nail pounded flat. Out
loud, I announced myself: "Pru Marlowe, animal behaviorist.
I'm here about—"

And then I stopped. Because right inside the condo's front
door, sprawled across the glazed tile entranceway, lay the body of
the man I'd seen the night before, his eyes already dull with death.

Chapter Three

"I can't believe she did this." Ronnie was hyperventilating by the time the cruisers arrived. The EMTs who followed were too busy to deal with Ronnie, but I'd found him a paper bag to breathe into and suddenly we were best friends. "I mean, she was so nice."

"Oh?" I'd recognized the body, despite the damage. The mop of hair, an unnatural dark brown. It was the wealthy guy from the restaurant—the one who'd been so rude. Knowing that he wasn't polite to the help—or to his date—didn't mean he deserved to die. Didn't take the edge off the shock of finding a body, either. But nasty surprises don't make me go all soft. The opposite, actually. A trait Wallis, my tabby, approved of. "You mean his date?"

"Date? Girlfriend." Ronnie took a hit from the bag so naturally I wondered if he was hoping to find some glue inside. "She came here with him. I mean, he was the renter but they were, like, a couple, at least."

I nodded. That fit with the conversation I'd overheard. But even though that had grown heated, it was a long way from dinner table nastiness to murder. And murder it was. Of that I had no doubt. People die. That's natural. But very few fall on knives, and the handle that had been sticking out of the tenant's gut didn't look like a fashion accessory. What I didn't understand was why Ronnie had brought up the girlfriend—Cheryl, I remembered her name was.

"And you think she's involved?"

He shrugged, his shoulders sinking heavily, his face downcast. The cops had told us not to go anywhere, but they were leaving us alone for now. We were sitting on the steps of unit five. Right next door but angled in such a way that we didn't have a view of the action at number six, we were being left in relative peace. Except for the flashing lights glaring off the snow, and the slight green hue of Ronnie's face, you'd never know we were feet away from a crime scene.

"Ronnie?"

"She—they fought," he said finally. "A lot. I mean, I don't blame her. Cute thing like her. What's she doing with an old guy like that?" I bit back my answer. If he didn't know, he was dumber than I thought.

"People fight, Ronnie." It had sounded like an old grievance to me. Him taking out his issues on someone weaker and more dependent. "That doesn't mean she killed him."

He shook his head, his mouth set. "I don't know, Pru." I looked at him, trying to size him up. Animals, I get. They have a thousand different ways of showing you who they are and what they want. They have no problem with letting you know where they stand—and where you stand in their universe. People, though. They can be difficult. I hadn't thought Ronnie was that complicated.

"Ronnie?" Sometimes the simplest thing is to ask. "What aren't you telling me?"

"Well, for starters…" his voice dropped down low. Not that anyone was going to hear us. "I think he was married."

I made an effort not to roll my eyes. Beauville is exactly the kind of backwater you take your little chickie. And these condos? "That's reason for his wife to go after them, Ronnie." He was staring straight ahead, his mouth set in a grim line. "You honestly think she could have done it?"

I wasn't going to be swayed. I was curious about his reasoning, though. Besides, I was stuck here, for a while anyway.

"You don't know." He gave me a baleful glance. "You didn't see her."

"Ah." I got it. Women are evil. Especially the pretty ones. He and Albert would have explained away every crime in New England on the females who had spurned their advances, if the law let them.

"No, honest, Pru, you don't understand." I fixed him with a cool stare. Living with Wallis has taught me the advantages of not blinking. "She's been planning it. Planning on getting rid of him. She's been meeting with another guy."

"You've been watching her?"

He had the decency to blush, but still, I didn't buy it. Not that he hadn't been spying on the girl. I knew Ronnie. I only hope she kept her shades drawn. What I didn't see was why.

"Come on, Ronnie. You said it yourself, he's married. What does she get if he dies? More likely it was the wife." I was talking to fill the time. I had no dog in this fight, but I do prefer logic in my conversations.

"But I've seen her. More than once."

It was my turn to shrug. Maybe the girl *was* in on it. Bait to trap a cheating husband for one final time. Maybe—but before I could speculate further, the cop in charge interrupted our relative privacy. Ronnie was ushered off by one of the uniforms, but I was taken to the front seat of an unmarked car for some heavy duty questioning.

I told the detective in charge all I knew. The call, the bunnies, the locked door. There wasn't much to it, but I know better than to hold back anything in a criminal investigation. Yes, I'd been the one to suggest opening the door. No, I had no reason to suspect anything unusual.

He looked at me as I'd looked at Ronnie, as if I were hiding something. Granted, he might have had some reason for this, usually. But not today, and I bristled. Some would say I bristled easily. Finding a dead body hadn't been great for my mood, however, and the tone this cop was taking with me wasn't making me feel much better.

"What?" I could hear the snark in my voice. At that point, I didn't care. On top of everything, I'd been left sitting outside for close to an hour, and despite my parka and the car's heater, I was still cold. I was also hungry, and I had other mouths to feed before I could settle in for my own evening. "You going to cuff me?" It was uncalled for. I didn't care. "Tie me up?"

"Tie you down, more likely," growled the detective, in a low voice intended for only my ears.

I had to grin. Officer Jim Creighton was not only the top cop in town, he was also its most attractive male human, despite a buzz cut that made him look like a superannuated boy scout. I'm not monogamous by nature—another trait I shared with Wallis—but it was more than the lack of viable alternatives that had kept us pretty constant through the winter.

"Hey, you're my alibi," I replied. It wasn't a non sequitur, not with the way he was questioning me. "Or don't you remember?"

He smiled for real, then. But it didn't last. "No, Pru. I'm not."

"Ah." I nodded. I got it. "So he wasn't killed until this morning?" That's right—he'd called Ronnie. And Creighton had left my place before dawn. This is a small town. Everybody knew we were what my mother would have called "keeping company." But Jim likes to keep up appearances.

"Pru." That growl again, warning me off.

"Do you have a time of death?" Now the brows came down, glowering. "Hey, you know Ronnie thinks the girlfriend did it. Can't say as I—" I was about to say "blame her." Make a joke out of it. But I'd seen the damage and the words stuck in my throat. "Where is she, anyway?" I could hear my voice tightening as I thought of that blood. We hadn't gone in to explore. "She's not…"

"She's not in there." He reached out. Only then did I realize my hand was on the door. I'd wanted to bolt, to race back to the condo to look for her. "She's probably off skiing. That's why they were here, supposedly."

I sat back, recalling something from the night before. "Skiing? Her, I could see. But him?"

Creighton shook his head. "I gather he spent his time in the lodge, playing cards. She was some kind of expert—tried out for the Olympics supposedly. And he liked to watch."

My eyebrow went up at that, and Creighton's grin came back. But another question soon knocked the innuendo from my mind.

"If she was such a great skier, why come here?" He tilted his head, not understanding. "I mean, nothing against the Berkshires, but if she's the real deal, why didn't she push for something in the Rockies or Europe? Somewhere they have real mountains and real snow."

"Who knows?" Creighton stared off into the distance as he spoke, his voice going soft. The afternoon light was fading. The EMTs had taken the body away, their taillights glowing in the dusk, and it looked like even the forensics people were beginning to clean up. "Maybe she wasn't after the big slopes. Maybe she had other goals."

"Or maybe he was too cheap to take her someplace nice." In other circumstances, Creighton might have argued with me. He grew up here, too. Unlike me, he never tried to get away. "Maybe she didn't have any say in the matter."

"Now, now," my beau responded. "What would Wallis think of that?"

I froze. His tone had been joking, his words light. But there are some things he doesn't—can't—know about me. It's not that I want to maintain my mystery. I've got plenty enough feminine allure for Jim Creighton. At the very least, he appreciates my appetites, which extend far beyond that steak he stood me for. But I have secrets nobody else can know. At least, no other human.

"I only meant you were being catty, Pru." He sounded wounded. "I know it's been a rough day, but the guy's dead. And he was a human being."

"Speaking of." I forced a lightness into my voice that I didn't feel. "I've got a cat to feed, and you know she's not going to let me hear the end of it." That was probably too much. But I looked outside and made sure he saw me looking. Dusk had gotten later, but it was kicking in, and all those damp spots on the pavement would be slick black ice soon. "Hey," I turned toward him. "If your guys have let Ronnie go, I should still check the wiring. I mean, I can look around the outside. The snow's receded enough."

He was shaking his head. "No need, Pru."

"But if something got through to one of the underground cables, chewed through the line from the transformer to the meter, it could be dangerous."

He opened his door, with the clear intention of ushering me out. "It wasn't the power, it was the phone line."

"Welcome to Beauville, huh? No wonder that guy was annoyed. He's probably not had to use a land line for years." I shrugged, the ghost of a thought tickling my brain. "But still, Jim, maybe I should check it out."

He held his door open. He was waiting for me to do the same. "I said, you don't have to."

I stopped and looked at him, the import of his words finally sinking in.

"It wasn't an animal, was it?" I studied his face. For all the intimacy we'd shared, he was still a cop. His face was as blank as wood. I watched for a twitch. For a blink. "Someone cut that jerk's phone line, didn't he? Someone didn't want him calling for help."

Chapter Four

"What did you expect? That he'd bring you what he knew like a dead vole?" I got home twenty minutes later, still stunned by what I'd managed to piece together. *"He's a hunter, same as I am. Only he's not going to share."*

I was sitting at my kitchen table, a glass of Maker's Mark in my hand. Somehow, the chill of the evening had followed me in. That and the memory of Teddy Rhinecrest's body. The blood like the red wax that dripped down the bottle before me. The handle of the knife like the one stuck in my mother's old butcher block over on the counter. So common, I no longer even saw it, until I reached for it. A kitchen knife, nothing more.

"So, are you going to make some dinner, or what?" I forced myself to look away from the counter and into the cool green eyes of my companion. Wallis was sitting on the table and staring at me. She'd been there since I came home and opened the bottle that was inches from her side. *"Or shall I leave you to—this—"* her ears flipped back briefly as she sniffed at the wax—at the air above my tumbler. *"And fend for myself?"*

"No, I'll get dinner." I pulled myself up, making myself leave the glass on the table as I stood and walked to the fridge. Wallis probably could find her own dinner. The field mice that had wintered over in my basement were still hanging on. But although she phrased her question in selfish terms, I knew she was worried about me as well. I was on my second bourbon on an empty stomach. While I regretted anything that would dull my good buzz, I knew I should balance out the liquid with something solid.

"Chicken?" She jumped off the table and brushed against me, just enough so I knew I'd read her concern correctly. *"Mmmm..."* A rumble, half purr, half growl. *"Bird."*

"As long as I don't have to kill it." I said to myself as much as her, rummaging around in my fridge.

Before long, we were feasting. I'd bought a rotisserie chicken in town the night before, and had only pulled one leg off for Wallis when Creighton had called inviting me to dinner. Now Wallis was making quick work of the other drumstick, one velvet paw holding the bone down while she sank her fangs into the cold flesh. I was gnawing on a thigh bone and, in truth, feeling better.

"Thanks, Wallis." I paused to reach for my drink—water—and to wipe my face.

She looked up briefly but didn't comment. She didn't have to. We both knew that Wallis had saved my life some years before, although how she had done it was a mystery. I'd been living in the city then, indulging in all the vices the city could offer. I'd been studying for my degree, too, at least during daylight hours—qualifying to be an animal behaviorist. But the candle-at-both-ends thing hadn't worked out for me. Instead, it came back at me, making me sicker than I'd ever been—some combo of flu and hangover and general exhaustion that had me in and out of consciousness.

Wallis had been my only companion in my sickness. Whatever man I'd started the first night with had either left or dropped me off before the fever hit. And it was Wallis whom I heard, going into what I found out later was the third day, telling me I had to get up. Had to drink something. Or else I might die.

That voice—solicitous, insistent—had done the trick. Only once I had gotten myself to the bathroom and drunk my fill straight from the tap had it hit me. My cat had talked sense to me. My cat. And I had understood her. What followed was an episode neither of us liked to remember. I'd gone straight to the nearest ER. The doctors' IVs had rehydrated me and their antibiotics brought me back to life, but when I then checked myself in for observation, I pushed the line. I didn't like being in a cage any more than any wild creature would, and when I came home to one very hungry cat, Wallis and I had words. I'd packed us up then, determined to get away from the city and from all its attendant craziness.

The voices never went away, though. And while I had come closer to accepting what had happened to my life, I knew better than to share it with anyone. I never wanted to go back to the psych ward again.

And so I try to listen to her now, as much because of that history as because of the tone she takes with me. Besides, dinner was a good idea. I like to think I'm tough, but finding that body had unsettled me. With some food in my stomach, I had a better chance of sleeping. By the time I finished cleaning up and dragged myself to bed, Wallis was already there, curled into a disc of fur on the bed. I didn't expect any other company. With a case like this, Creighton would be working late. But despite choosing my most comfortable flannel against the early spring chill, I slept restlessly, tossing and turning to the point where Wallis jumped to the floor, leaving me to my visions of knives and bunnies going bad.

Chapter Five

They say the economy has recovered, but you wouldn't know it from Beauville. The Massachusetts Miracle passed us by back in the '80s, too, though my mother managed to hold onto her job at the state hospital through it all. In fact, Beauville hasn't seen any real industry here since water power was upstaged by coal and gas.

These days, the best we get are the leavings of city folk, here for the foliage or the Hills, the ski area just outside of town. But as I'd pointed out to Creighton, even that's not much, our mountains as old and tired as the rest of the state. Even Hardware, our one upscale joint, relies on the bar traffic and that one wide-screen TV, not to mention Spaghetti Sundays in the off-season.

The Hills was aptly named, with its gentle slopes and icy, damp snow. Our one advantage over Aspen or Gstaad is location. We're close to New York and Boston, and the marketing folks play up the convenience, when the charm doesn't sell. When I woke the next morning, the dull throb of a hangover playing behind my temples, I thought about location in terms of the man who had died yesterday and the ski bunny I'd seen him with. New Yorkers, most definitely. And despite what I'd said to Creighton, I understood. The dead man had acted like he had money, but it takes serious bucks to sneak off to Switzerland for a weekend. Coming up here, maybe he could convince his wife he was on a business trip.

I sat up with a start. The wife. I knew Creighton would be on it. His people had undoubtedly already been in contact. She'd probably take the little yapping dog back to Syosset with her. But I should check, after—I'd just seen the clock—I made my morning rounds.

The fresh air cleared my head, even as it cooled the coffee in my travel mug. Spring wasn't here yet—not for real. But for the first time this year, I'd opened the window as I drove and let the brisk wind and the early morning calls of birds and beasts— *"we're back, let's nest!" "my turf, mine!"*—blow past. Wallis had not made an appearance before I left, but that didn't worry me. She took it personally when I slept badly. I disturbed her rest, she'd tell me, but I thought it was more that any wakefulness on my part worried her—brought back too many echoes of the bad time. Either way, I'd make it up to her. In the meantime, we were both independent adults.

Luckily for me, most creatures aren't. I'm not talking about the animals, per se, but their people. Although I'm trained as a behaviorist—almost have my degree, even—I make my living in a more prosaic manner, picking up the chores that most humans don't want to do. In addition to those nuisance calls, like the one from yesterday, I walk dogs. I also clip nails and clean tanks. Work, as I've explained, is sparse in Beauville. Which is why I was gearing up for the harridan of the Berkshires.

"No, Mrs. Horlick." I mentally rehearsed the scene to come. Tracy Horlick mainlined gossip like a junkie does horse, only her sources never ran dry. Before I'd be able to take her beleaguered bichon, Growler, out for his daily walk, I knew I'd have to answer the old lady's questions. Accusations, more likely, since she considered me responsible for almost everything that happened in Beauville, particularly when I withheld information. "Sorry, Mrs. Horlick," I muttered to the wind. "I don't know anything."

A crow, flying overhead, cawed in protest, and I laughed. He wasn't haranguing me. He was caught in his own domestic troubles. But the bird and the hour made my first job seem even more grim than usual. Pressing on the accelerator, I decided to follow that crow—at least so far as a short detour.

The road was empty and clear. The black ice of the night before seemed to have melted, and although I didn't give the accelerator quite as much pressure as I'd have liked, my mood improved considerably as I crested the hill on the edge of town and surveyed the highway before me. Off to the right lay the conservation land and, closer than that, the condos where Teddy Rhinecrest had died. To my left was the turn back to the older part of town and Tracy Horlick.

With a sigh, I decided on the left. Poor Growler deserved his break, too, and the sooner I ran the gauntlet of his person, the sooner he'd get it. But as I leaned in, letting my muscle car absorb the turn, a flash of color caught my eye. Red—bright, and too big for a cardinal. I didn't dare turn around, not at this speed. But I made a mental note: a red sports car, I was pretty sure. Heading toward the development I had visited only the day before.

◇◇◇

"Well, if it isn't the angel of death." Ten minutes later, I was standing on the stoop of a rundown Cape Cod, trying to contain my temper.

"Good morning, Mrs. Horlick." I forced a smile, knowing that it would annoy the harpy before me.

"Is it?" She took another drag on her cigarette and leaned on her doorframe. Behind her, I could hear Growler, frustrated, scratching. She'd locked him in the basement again. "Not for Mrs. Teddy Rhinecrest, I imagine."

"I wouldn't know." I made a point of staring over her shoulder. "Is that Growl—Bitsy I hear?" I could have kicked myself. Although I preferred to use the tough little dog's chosen name, I was doing neither of us any favors by forgetting the cutesy tag Tracy Horlick had given him.

"He wasn't growling." She misheard me, for which I was grateful, even as her painted lips cracked and twisted into a pout. "My dog is well trained."

"Of course." I worked to keep my tone even. Anything else might reflect back on the poor beast. "But I bet he wants to go out."

She turned into her house to free her small captive, and I heard the scrabble of claws as he dashed for the door.

"Hey, Bitsy." I snapped his lead on, all the while trying to make eye contact.

"Don't engage." His soft whine forms words in my mind. *"Never engage, walker lady. Don't start a fight you can't win."*

"Yes, yes." I patted his fuzzy head and smiled up at his person. "Okay, back soon!"

"For dog's sake." Growler was still muttering as we rounded the corner. He watered a tree that has recently lost its mantle of snow and sniffed at a fence post, where crocus shoots were beginning to poke through. *"Doesn't anyone think these things through anymore?"*

He might have been commenting on my behavior. By engaging, I delayed his brief daily freedom. Then again, he might simply be taking in the neighborhood news. That fence post was a favorite spot. Either way, I didn't respond. Growler gets little enough respect at home. I try to make up for that as I can, giving him his privacy unless and until he invites me in.

"Crazy bitch." I bit my tongue as he shook, his tags rattling in emphasis. Growler used the term in the technical sense. Still the little dog has reason to dislike females, especially of my species. *"Doesn't have the sense of a…"*

A particularly ripe spot stopped him, sparking a sense memory so strong even I got a whiff of it through his doggie thoughts. Several animals had relieved themselves here, through the autumn and early winter. The heavy snow had preserved the pile, which was only now growing fragrant and soft in the melt.

"Always something, if you look." That was another of those stray thoughts that came my way. This time, I was pretty sure he was referring to the brown pile. *"Always something to hide."* His black button eyes looked up at me. *"Would you know where to hide, to protect your own, if you had to?"*

I had no answer to that one. We kept on walking.

◇◇◇

"I hear you met the girlfriend." Tracy Horlick has clearly been working the phones during our walk. I ran through who else was at Hardware two nights ago, wondering who talked—and what they said. "I hear she was stepping out on him."

I bent to unhook Growler's lead and to compose my face before responding. As I did, he looked up at me in mute sympathy.

"Thanks, little guy." I lay my hand gently on his fluffy head. His tail wagged twice, then stopped. We both knew we couldn't avoid his person forever. But as I stood, trying to formulate a response, she started talking again.

"There was some big guy—looked like a surfer—asking around about her, you know." Her stare, through the smoke, made me think of a snake or, perhaps, a dragon. "I wouldn't be surprised if they never find her body."

I sighed. I couldn't help it. She took that as encouragement. "You do know he was mobbed up, right?"

"Mr. Rhinecrest?" She'd startled that out of me. "I thought he was here on vacation."

She smirked at my non sequitur, smoke spurting from her nostrils. "Like anyone comes here for vacation."

This was too close to my own thoughts for me to argue. Besides, I'd learned my lesson. With as bland a voice as I could manage, I made my escape.

"See you tomorrow, Bitsy." I called as I backed away. "You too, Mrs. Horlick." It was easier to be nice, knowing I was leaving, and I needed to get away fast. I wouldn't ordinarily give any credence to old lady Horlick's gossip, but what she had said made me think again about that flash of red I'd seen on the road—and of a particular gentleman who drove a sportster the color of blood.

Chapter Six

I didn't have time to dwell on that car just then. My next client was a new one, and I wanted to make a good impression. I'm not that worried about the human part of the equation. I'm clean and presentable—at least by Beauville standards—and I show up when I'm supposed to. But for the animals I commune with, I've got a whole other set of requirements.

For starters, I needed to wash—and thoroughly—and so I swung toward home, where I could change my shirt for good measure. But although I watched the road for anything unusual—the first robin, for example, or any other interesting plumage—the melting snow only gave way to shades of gray and brown.

"Prey animal, is it?" Wallis sauntered into the bathroom as I gave myself a quick towel bath over the sink. The way her whiskers were pitched forward, I knew she was taking in whatever odors I'd carried in. *"Must be something timid to be afraid of that little braggart."*

"Growler's not a—" I caught myself. For all I knew, his scent was telling my cat things I couldn't even imagine. "He's in a difficult situation," I said instead.

Huh." With a little chuff, half grunt, half snort, she walked off. I don't think Wallis is anti-dog, entirely. More likely, she didn't respect an animal who couldn't control the people in his life. Not that she had complete control over me…

"I could've left, you know." The thought reached me from the hallway. *"I still could."*

Cats. Autonomy matters to them. Maybe that's why we get along so well.

I didn't bother to seek her out before I headed off again. It's usually wise to let her have the last word. Besides, I didn't want to be late. New clients aren't that common, and yesterday's job hadn't panned out as I'd hoped.

The new gig sounded curious, to say the least. But I found myself thinking about Teddy Rhinecrest as I drove. Not the way I'd seen him last—though that image was hard to banish—but the man I'd encountered at the restaurant the night before. Even if I hadn't lived in the city, I'd have known the type. Dissatisfied, despite his money. Desperate to buy youth and beauty, but determined to bully it once he had it in his life. He was the kind who would keep a pretty thing locked away, just because he could.

A shadow crossed the street, interrupting my thoughts. A mourning dove, flying low. I recognized the shape and the flutter, and I knew that if I looked up, I'd see a hawk—a redtail, probably—cruising the sky above. Down here, the smaller animals cowered. I thought of the redhead as the round dove made it under the trees. What was her name again? Cheryl?

But Teddy Rhinecrest was no hawk. Mobbed up, Tracy Horlick had said. And while it was tempting to dismiss anything that shrew spouted in her vitriol, I couldn't stop thinking about the flash of color I'd seen on the road. Teddy Rhinecrest seemed like the very opposite of a gangster. He'd seemed powerless—impotent—with an edge of desperation that made him mean. But old Horlick's thoughtless comment and that glimpse of red made me think. I knew a man who drove a Maserati that color. An older gent with impeccable manners, who I had reason to believe was more deadly than any raptor and who had eyes just as cold.

I did my best to banish any thoughts of hawks or their ilk as I turned into one of the older subdivisions of Beauville. Built after the town's heyday, the tract houses here didn't have the grandeur of my mother's Victorian—a drafty old pile that cost as much to heat as I could afford—but they were neat and well cared for. And if the cookie cutter Cape Cods were less showy than the condo development I'd been at just the day before, they were sturdier—built before the boom, and before the economy had gone totally bankrupt.

I had a good feeling as I pulled up in front of Marnie Lundquist's, with its well-groomed shrubs and neatly shoveled walk, and, despite my earlier funk, found myself smiling quite naturally as I lifted the shiny brass knocker on the front door.

"Good morning." The woman who answered my knock fit the tremulous voice I'd heard on my answering machine. Seventy, if she was a day, five-two tops, and small-boned with white hair tied back in a neat bun and eyes made larger by her oversized glasses. "You must be Pru."

"You called about a rabbit?" As I entered, my eyes scanned the floor. House rabbits weren't common out here, but back in my old life I knew at least one who had the run of a Lower East Side apartment and the punk name of Scar.

"Yes, yes." The tiny old lady looked around her, following my gaze, and as her white bun bobbed I felt my grin widening. Here was living proof that we either choose the pets that reflect best who we are or we come to resemble each other over time. "Now, where is he?"

I got down on my knees. Although I wanted to make a good impression on the client, it was more important to bond with the bunny. I'd done what I could to avoid carrying any scent of a predator. Now if I could just make myself appear harmless to what I was guessing would be an overweight white…

"That's not a house rabbit." I sat up with a start.

"Henry!" The old woman clasped her hands together, the noise startling the creature before me, who turned up toward her, nose twitching. "There you are!"

"But—" I paused, unsure how to proceed. I was looking at an Eastern cottontail, its dappled brown coat smooth over a compact, well-muscled body. "That's not a domestic animal, Mrs. Lundquist." There, it was out. "That's a wild rabbit, and legally…"

I sighed and shook my head. Somebody had sold the old lady an illegal pet. And while I knew the state fish and wildlife had other concerns than one contraband bunny, I also knew that wild animals make notoriously bad pets. Rabbits, in particular, since the heightened sensitivities that help them to survive in the wild make them extremely vulnerable to stress and disease.

"Where did you get this rabbit, Mrs. Lundquist?" While the sensitive ears—black at their tips—turned every which way, taking everything in, the little creature's liquid eyes stared at me. I resisted staring back—some animals consider a direct gaze threatening—and instead tried to blank my mind, opening it to whatever the animal had to communicate.

What I got was vague: *"Who?"* was the best I could put it. *"Are you family?"* the rabbit seemed to be asking me. *"Are you safe?"* The overall tone was appraising, rather than afraid, despite a vulnerability that was enhanced by the long, delicate lines of the fuzzy face. Almost like a fawn. Or no, I corrected myself, like a doe I had come across once, face-to-face in the forest. *"Who?"*

"Henry, please." For a moment, I was startled, stuck in my memory. Then I realized, she was talking about the bunny. "He's my granddaughter's, and, yes, I do understand that he is not supposed to be a pet. Only, she found him, injured, in the yard last autumn. The college groundskeepers had just been through and—well, I gather the rest of his little family did not survive. She took him in and has cared for him since. Only now she's traveling, and I said I would baby—I mean, rabbit-sit him. And, well, I'm beginning to think he's more than I can handle."

"And you want me to take him off your hands?" I was already running through my list of wildlife rehabilitators. It's a short one, especially out here. And if this rabbit had been living in captivity for that long, his odds of making it back in the wild weren't good. "Perhaps a rescue organization?"

"What? Oh, no. Not at all." She turned toward me, her eyes exaggerated by those glasses, and the resemblance between the two hit me again. "Cara would hate it if anything happened to Henry. Only, you see, I had been keeping him in his crate, until Cara called and told me that was cruel. And so I've been letting him have free rein of the house, but I fear I need a bit of help to make sure everything is safe."

With a sigh of resignation, I sat back and listened to the old lady speak. Her granddaughter, she explained, was a vet tech and had done some wildlife rehab. Probably not licensed—I decided not to ask—but certainly experienced. She had hand-raised this particular orphan, just as she had brought up squirrels and birds before. Her parents had supported her passion and indulged her before their death, and Cara was going to veterinary school in the fall. First, however, she was taking a year to trek around Asia, leaving Henry in the care of her widowed grandmother.

"She'll probably come back with an orphaned yak," I said, when the old lady was done.

"Yes, I wouldn't be surprised," she replied, with a warm smile. "So, you can see why I want Henry to be happy and healthy during his stay with me here in Beauville. And why I need your help."

I did, and once I abandoned my scruples about him being a wild rabbit, my work was fairly straightforward. Despite her advanced years—"eighty-four this summer, my dear"—and apparent frailty, the old lady was fairly spry. While I did the kneeling and bending, she pointed out all the wires and other chewable hazards the little leporid was likely to find. As far as I could tell, they had already been rabbit-proofed, either encased in the kind of tubing that even those determined nibblers couldn't get through or raised high enough to be out of reach.

"Yes," she agreed, when I pointed this out. "I may take a while to get back up again, but I do like to think I can still function."

Before I could ask, she showed me both the litterbox—little Henry was well trained—and the bin of fresh grasses she kept to vary his diet from the store-bought pellets too many rabbit owners rely on and to keep him fit and trim.

As we went through the house, I was constantly aware of the little fellow. Although he kept his distance, he hopped along after us, and his large dark eyes were always on me. And although I reached out in my way—both with a handful of timothy grass and with the open, questioning mindset that sometimes persuaded even wild animals to respond—I got only that vague sense of concerned questioning in response. Henry wasn't afraid of me, per se. He'd been a pet too long to retain his utter terror of people, confirming my suspicion that the rabbit could not return to the wild. Plus, the way he purred—there's no other word—as the white-haired old lady gently stroked him showed bonding of the highest order. But even if the little creature had lost his natural prey reaction to the deadliest species on the planet, he didn't trust me.

I didn't take it personally. I was a stranger, and I probably carried some residual cat on me—if not on my hands and clothes then in the mental images that came up as I admired his smooth brown fur and the curious tilt of his whiskers as he sniffed where I had sat.

"Henry's making up his mind about you." Marnie Lundquist's soft voice made those long ears twitch back.

"He seems quite calm." I looked up from the floor. The phone jack had also been well protected.

"We are quite peaceful here," she said with a smile.

"So I see." I smiled back, but I was no longer entirely easy. In fact, I was beginning to wonder why she had even called me here. I'm not in the habit of turning away paying customers, but I was also not going to rip off an old lady.

"It seems like you have everything under control." I sat back on my own haunches. Henry was eyeing me from Marnie Lundquist's side.

"He's such an inquisitive little fellow." She caught me watching him and turned toward the bunny, as if seeking his approval. When her white bun bobbed, I assumed she had received it. "I find him a pleasure to have around. Only…"

She paused and I waited, realizing what was happening. The old lady was as timid as the bunny. She had been watching me much as he had. Waiting, before she would reveal the truth about why she had called.

"Yes?" I used the soft voice that usually calms the most fearful client, dipping my head slightly in a manner Growler would recognize.

"It's nothing." A sigh barely strong enough to stir a leaf. "I'm an old worrywart is all. Henry means so much to my granddaughter—" She paused. This was it. "I'm just so glad you think everything is all right here."

"I do," I said. "But if you have any questions, any concerns at all…"

"No, you've been wonderful," she said with an emphasis I hadn't heard before. "And Henry is clearly taken with you, too. Now, may I pay you with a personal check?"

"Of course." I got to my feet, my curiosity unabated. I considered various options as Marnie Lundquist fished a checkbook from her bag and carefully filled one out, but I could find no excuse that didn't sound pushy. Pet people were like their pets, and whatever the underlying issue, I wanted her to feel comfortable calling again. Because one thing I was sure of. Even as I slid the check in my jeans pocket and took her proffered hand, I knew. The rabbit lady was hiding something.

◇◇◇

I was still musing this one over as I drove off, startling a squirrel who cursed me soundly in the chittering manner of his kind. I hadn't noticed any behavioral problems with the little creature. The house appeared clean, and the litterbox was being used. And either the old lady or her granddaughter had done a better-than-average job of making the small house safe for both the little leporid and his white-haired keeper. I have scruples about wild animals kept as pets, but it was too late to act on them at this point.

No, what was bothering me was something different. It wasn't only the old lady, either. That bunny didn't trust me. I could have understood if he simply hadn't introduced himself to me. Most pets have names for themselves that differ from the ones we humans give them—names like Growler that more accurately reflect their rich inner lives than any cutesy handle—but naming is a human affectation. Often, I've found, wild animals do without.

There was something going on here beyond the small creature's silence, and I couldn't shake the feeling that I was being weighed and considered. Still, he seemed quite comfortable with his human companion. And she with him, I saw, as I took an easy turn. Whether or not she would have chosen this particular beast for a pet, the way she had stroked him—a gentle hand moving in the direction of his fur—and the soft purring grunts he gave in response, displayed a comfortable affection that revealed more than anything either of them could say.

And yet, there was something. People don't hire a professional without a reason, and I spent much of the afternoon running through the possibilities—each getting more and more farfetched. When my cell rang, I discarded the latest—that the old lady had a secret yearning for a cat, only she knew how the presence of a predator would unsettle Henry—from my thoughts and answered.

"Hey, beautiful. Miss me?" It was Creighton, in a good mood. I let myself smile, knowing he—like any attentive animal—would hear my pleasure in my voice.

"I figured you'd be working late." It was the truth.

"That's not what I asked," he teased.

"Well, then, yes." I've tended to keep Creighton at a distance. Only that distance had been growing shorter. "Is that what you called to hear?"

"Maybe." The uncertainty made his voice interesting, and my ears pricked up. "Maybe that's why—or maybe I just know you, Pru. And I knew you'd want to know," he said. "We located the deceased's friend, one Miss Cheryl Ginger."

"Cheryl Ginger?" The name was too good to be true.

"That's how she identified herself, and she had a New York driver's license to back it up. It's legal to change your name, Pru." This was in response to the half-snort, half-laugh that I didn't try very hard to suppress. "Women do it every day, as a matter of course."

"And you found her where?" I knew what Creighton was leading up to with that name nonsense. I've been letting him get closer to me. That did not mean I was the marrying kind.

"At the ski lodge, chatting with the staff." He took my cue, returning to the matter at hand, his tone growing businesslike if not exactly cool. "Turns out, she was skiing all day yesterday. She was positively identified by the Hills lift operator and members of the ski patrol as being there from the opening bell."

"They have a bell?" I kind of missed the playful Jim.

"You know what I mean." He, I gathered, did not. "At any rate, I knew you'd had a bad shock, finding his body like that, and also that you'd wondered about the girl, so I thought I'd let you know."

"Thanks, Jim." I meant it. "I appreciate you telling me this."

"Not a problem." The humor was back in his voice. "Not protocol, exactly, but for you..."

"Does this mean I might see you tonight?" I let him hear the warmth in mine.

"Possibly," he said, and I waited. There was something else going on here. "But it will be late. I have some business first."

"That business wouldn't be a redhead with a stripper's name, would it?"

I expected a laugh. I didn't get it. "I'll try not to be too late," was all he said.

"Okay, then." I started to hang up, before I realizing I had a question. "Hey, Jim, What's the deal with the dog? Is this Cheryl going to be able to take care of it?"

I didn't want to ask if she was in custody or being questioned. I would respect Creighton's boundaries. The animal I had heard barking, however, was another matter.

The answer, which came after a moment's pause, was not what I expected.

"Dog?" asked Creighton. "What dog?"

Chapter Seven

I didn't have time for this. I really didn't. Never mind that my day was a little too light on appointments to make me happy, I never have time for the kind of careless nonsense that Creighton was displaying.

"What do you mean?" My first reaction had been disbelief. Followed shortly after by anger. "Couldn't you and your crack team hear barking and deduce that maybe there's a dog on the premises?"

"Pru, come on." He was going to say "that's not fair" or something of that ilk. But I was no longer in a mood to be accommodating.

"Look, either one of you let the poor creature out and left him out." I couldn't believe I had to spell this out to someone who claimed to know me. "Or you've locked him in, alone with nothing to eat or drink." With a sigh that I intended to be fully audible, I slowed enough for a U-turn. "I'm on my way to that condo now. And there had better be someone to let me in."

Maybe it was the rabbit. After all, the March weather—while cold—wouldn't necessarily be fatal for a small dog, left out overnight. It was more the hungry habitants of our local woods I worried about. Not only that hawk, whose presence had made the mourning dove fly so low, but all the terrestrial creatures from fishers to coyotes who would be out and about, looking for food in a landscape still largely covered by snow—some already with hungry kits back in the nest or on the way.

Wallis would have asked me why I cared. She's always quick to point out that she and I both dine regularly on the flesh of other living creatures, and that my hypocrisy runs as deep as any in my species. I'm not sure I could have explained it. Maybe it was that I had heard that agonized bark and not followed up on it. Maybe I was simply looking for an excuse to fight with Creighton—or to meet up with him in the middle of the day—and the poor canine was nothing but a prop. Wallis would certainly have a field day with that theory, but out here on the road, I had to admit it wasn't the least likely option.

Not that it mattered. As I pulled up to Teddy Rhinecrest's condo, I saw that my guy had taken matters into his own hands. His unmarked was nowhere to be seen, but Ronnie's truck was there, its owner slouched in the front seat, looking like he'd gotten an earful already.

"Hey, Pru." He slid out and walked over. "I got the call to let you in."

"Thanks." It wasn't Ronnie's fault if I'd missed something—or if Creighton had. "Everything okay?"

He shrugged as he sorted through his ring of keys. "I guess. It's just, I was kind of planning on taking today off."

I nodded. "The cops kept you late yesterday?"

"Yeah." He led me over to number six. "Wanted to know what I'd seen."

"What you'd—" I stopped as I remembered. "You mean, about the girlfriend having someone on the side?"

A nod. "I should never have said anything," he said softly. "Rule number one…"

He slid the key in the lock, but I stopped him, putting my hand over his. "I didn't think you were serious about that." I was telling the truth. Guys like Ronnie and Albert always cast women as the bad guys. It lets them off the hook from having to deal with us. "That you'd seen something."

"I was. I did." He turned to look at me now, meeting my eyes with a directness Albert couldn't have managed. "But, Pru,

I didn't mean anything by it. You think maybe you could talk to your boyfriend? I mean…"

He looked down again, his face gray, and I felt a wave of pity for the poor guy. "It's okay, Ronnie. Creighton's not a brute."

"I should have known." He sighed as he opened the door. "When did a cop ever buy me drinks?"

"Drinks?" That didn't sound like Creighton's style.

"Yeah." Ronnie swallowed. "We closed Happy's." Happy's being our local dive, I wasn't surprised Ronnie was there. That had been my father's hang, too. But Creighton? "At least, I think we did," the big man mumbled.

Working late? That's what my father used to say, too.

"Anyway," Ronnie's voice interrupted my memories as he pushed the door open and stepped back. "There you go."

"Thanks." I turned toward him before stepping inside. "Are you going to be around?"

"I'll be in my truck." He sounded like he'd been sentenced to hard time. "I'm not supposed to leave. I've got to lock up after you're done."

I managed a smile before he turned and walked off, then I walked into the condo, closing the door behind me. And then I took a deep, deep breath.

There's something about a space where someone has died. Something too still in the settling of dust or the lack of even the faint air currents that a silent, but living, occupant will stir. Something other than just the staleness of an unoccupied space—a deserted house or empty apartment. Something inherently sad.

Now, I'm not a jumpy kind of girl. I don't spook easily, never have. And even my special sensitivity has become pragmatic, a new sense to manage—to tune out or turn a deaf ear to when other humans are around. This was something else again, something dark. I don't mean in a supernatural or even a moral sense. From what I saw of him, Teddy Rhinecrest was no great shakes alive. I doubted he'd come back to haunt anybody, and he certainly had no beef with me. I hadn't even taken the time to let him know what I thought of him, bullying his girlfriend like that, not to mention the waiter. But I've spent enough time around animals to know that there's much in this world that we are too dull to comprehend.

Animals don't react to death the way we do. They don't dwell on it or worry about it. Sure, they feel pain. They work as hard as they can to stay alive, and in some cases, they'll sacrifice themselves, usually for their young. But dead is dead to a cat or a dog. They have no mythologies to weird them out. What they do have are more acute senses, and, more important, they have the ingrained wisdom to trust those senses. It's something I've tried to learn—and I suspected that was what I was doing now. I might not actually smell the blood that still stained the entry floor. I don't have Growler's or even Wallis' nose. But at some microbiological level, I was picking up its scent—and probably that of the pheromones poor old Teddy had cast off as he struggled with his killer.

What I did know was that being in this place, alone, was creepy. And that I wanted to do what I'd come for, and get out.

"Puppy?" I hadn't bothered to get the barking dog's name, but I figured a generic word and a friendly tone would do the trick. "Here, doggie!" Contrary to what most people believe, our pets don't pay much attention to what we call them. Not unless we stumble upon a name they'd choose for themselves. If they come when called, it's because they've chosen to respond to a voice: a beseeching upward tone, the pitch of a familiar call. "Puppy dog!" My words were more for Ronnie, or anyone else who might be listening in. Not that they'd do any good.

I might not know how I could tell I was in a house of death. I did know that I was in an empty dwelling. Unlike a person, a dog won't ignore you. This place was too still. The dog was gone.

I made the rounds, looking at the back of closets and cabinets, in case the little fellow had gotten frightened and hid from the commotion of the crime and then the follow-up of the cops. If I've learned anything from the animals in my life, it's that I'm fallible. And besides, it was fun. Once I'd gotten over the whole murder-house thing, I enjoyed peeking through the high-tech ski wear—hers—and the designer name lounging outfits that he seemed to prefer. In the back of the hall closet, I found their luggage, his and hers, that I bet he'd bought when they made their travel plans. These were empty, except for a pair of high-end binoculars, the kind professional birders use. If this was a robbery gone bad, the perpetrators had missed out on some of the biggest loot. I wondered if Creighton would recognize their value? He probably noticed the wires leading to the blank space on the desk. A laptop or tablet that could be anywhere by now.

What I didn't find were the corollary doggie toys. Don't get me wrong. Fido will get as much pleasure out of a cheap chew toy as a Gucci gewgaw. A pair of Italian loafers at the back of Teddy's closet attested to that fact. But usually when pet owners splurge on themselves, they get a little something for the creature they identify with, as well. And yet, while I found kibble and dishes, that was it. No squeaky toys, no nothing.

"Hey, Ronnie." I found the manager dozing in his truck. He jumped when I rapped on the window. "Tell me about Teddy Rhinecrest's dog."

"It wasn't his." He confirmed my suspicion. "It was hers. Why?"

"I don't know." He looked a little less green now. It could have been the air. "She came out here with him, right?"

A nod. "A rental. For the week. I know—the cops had me check."

"And she brought the dog with her?" It wasn't just the lack of toys. "You saw her with it when they arrived?"

"Nah, I—I didn't." He shrugged. "But, you know, sometimes with the rentals…" Of course, pets probably weren't allowed. Not that Ronnie was authorized to turn away a paying client.

"Did they have any friends around here?" I looked past the door to number six. No signs of life. "Did she know the neighbors?"

Another shake of the head. "They kept to themselves. A lot of people do, up here." His voice dropped and he leaned toward me. "Except, well, the guy she was meeting. I saw that. I really did."

"I believe you, Ronnie." Not that it mattered. I hugged myself against the cold as I thought that through. A woman cheating on her sugar daddy wasn't likely to give her dog to her man on the side. Only I was having a hard time imagining where the dog had gone—and why I hadn't found a traveling case for the animal anywhere on the premises.

"Maybe she smuggled the dog in one of her suitcases?" I was thinking out loud. Trying out the idea. It didn't fit with the woman I'd seen. She was much more the designer carrier type, but people are odd.

"Maybe." Ronnie seemed amenable. "I didn't hear any barking when I took their bags in, though. Come to think of it, that dog didn't bark that much."

"Honestly?" I kept hearing his frenzied yap.

Ronnie nodded. "Yeah, he never barked when Cheryl went out to meet the other guy."

That was damning, if it were true. "You tell Creighton that?"

"It wasn't him. It was this other guy—a Fed, I think. He was all over me. What did I see? When did I see this? Where was I watching from? He seemed really pissed off."

That was curious. I didn't think anyone would give much credence to Ronnie's stories. Then again, the guy interrogating him wasn't a local, so maybe he didn't know about the tendency of certain locals to insert themselves in the story. There wasn't a good way around it. Besides, it was chilly out here.

"Did he accuse you of anything?" I wouldn't put a lot of things past Ronnie—peeping tom. Minor theft. Hunting or fishing without a license, for sure. But murder?

"No." He shook his shaggy head. "More like he was just pissed at me for living."

"Well, I'm going to ask Creighton about that." I was, not that I'd be likely to share what I found out. Still, it was curious behavior—and if there was an outsider asking questions about anyone here in Beauville, I wanted a heads-up. "But meanwhile, I've got to find that dog."

"Can I leave now?" He had the forlorn look of a kid kept after school. "I mean, if you're done with the condo."

"Well, no, not if I find him." I can't help it. I feel sorry for dumb creatures. "Look, leave the keys with me. If he turns up, I want to get him indoors and get him fed, while we figure out what's next."

"But, Pru. I mean—I..." He stuttered a bit, and it occurred to me he'd been instructed not to loan the keys out.

"Look, you can stay if you want." I turned to stare at the woods around us. The day was already fading, the mercury dropping.

"No, no." He fumbled at his waist. "Hang on," he said, handing me the keys. Fifteen minutes wasted. I slapped the roof of his truck and he drove off. Leaving me to hunt for one lost dog.

The woods are never quiet. Unlike the inside of that condo, the second-growth pine forest that surrounded the development was bustling with life, even if it wasn't obvious. I walked across the drive that circumnavigated the cedar-shingled complex and onto the thick bed of pine needles that the recent melt had exposed. I was listening—taking in as much of the environs as I could, without becoming overwhelmed.

I've gotten better at this. At first, after I got out of the hospital, I'd thought my head would explode. Hearing my cat talk to me was bad enough, even though her advice—to drink some water, to get out of bed—might have saved my life. Coming home after my three days in the psych ward, only my intense aversion to locked doors kept me from going back. It was the pigeons that did it. Those most urban of birds are a pest at the best of times, fouling cars and statues and unlucky passersby. But with my new ability manifesting itself, they became aural polluters as well. There had been a nest in the cornice of my building, not far from my bedroom, and the coos and twitterings that had formerly faded into the background—white noise covering the traffic of the avenue—were suddenly a nonstop stream of inanities. Domestic issues of the most trivial, complete with rivalries and jealousies that would make a cheerleading squad proud. And when it came to me that the low-level headache was actually the result of the rats in the subway, muttering about their lot in life—and how much better their peers down by the docks had it—I knew I had to get away.

That was when I'd packed up Wallis and a few possessions and hightailed it back to Beauville. It might not seem like it, but the animal noise here in the Berkshires was quieter than in the city. Partly because we had space here; in the city we'd truly been living cheek by jowl. Partly, I suspect, it was also that the wildlife had its own agenda out here. Animals that don't interact with humans on a daily basis might not live longer or more peaceful lives—in fact, the opposite. They do tend to be less neurotic, however. And for that relief, I was grateful.

Over the last few years, I've also developed some skills. While I can't completely block out the sounds I pick up—the cries and hopes of creatures on the edge—I am learning to control them. Wallis says this is a talent that the youngest of kittens soon masters. Maybe she says that to put me in my place, but I take it as a challenge. One of these days, I'll be able to turn this power on and off. At least now, I've found the volume control.

As I walked between the tall, spindly trees, however, I wasn't trying to turn it off. I had no idea where that little dog had gone—and without having ever met him, I wasn't even sure what I was listening for. What I did know was that a small domestic animal must have gotten out. And that as a representative of the species responsible for his safety and well-being, I had to try.

"Hello?" I voiced the word softly, turning as I did. A flock of starlings was fussing over nesting sites off to my left. I could hear the bickering, even though I could not see them.

"Anyone there?" A chipmunk crisis—something to do with the scat of a bobcat—had disrupted the peace, off to my right. The cat itself was nowhere near—I'd have heard it, I believe, even if it were still asleep—but chipmunks are not known for their levelheadedness in the best of circumstances, and this particular family had been stressed to the limit by the extended cold of the winter.

"Anybody?" The field mice, much more sensible creatures, were being cautious. They were one of the few creatures that had done better with all the snow. With their burrowing capacity, they'd been tunneling under the white stuff since the first heavy fall, making a system of paths between their nests and their food caches, all safe from the outside world. Now, however, they were aware of being exposed. Someone—a relative, perhaps, or maybe just another small rodent—had been scooped up by an owl last night. The story was spreading still.

Those were only the main discussions, multiple animals sharing their news and concern. All around me, life pulsed—something was eaten, something else died. A mother sought a safe place for her young. What I didn't get was the panic or fear of a domestic animal lost in the woods. I also wasn't getting anything from any alpha predators. Though, if the little dog had been on his own since yesterday, any coyote or larger raptor might already have been and gone. Or a human, I had to amend my thoughts. Although the development was far enough off the highway to blunt the sound of traffic, I was dimly aware of the road, not a quarter mile away. Close enough to be a factor in an animal's life, especially a naïve one that had given up its fear of my kind. If I didn't find something soon, I'd wander in that direction. Already gruesome images were beginning to form in my mind.

"Caw! *Watch!*" One of the grackles took off. For a moment, I thought it had picked up on my mental imagery—a sad, if unspecific vision of roadkill. *"Intruder!"*

The harsh cry meant something else, however. And while my simple mind heard it one way, I stopped myself. "Intruder" could mean another bird or any predator. It could refer to me, I realized, as I suddenly stopped walking and froze in place.

"Where? Where?" The cry had gone up in the avian population, and I scanned the sky for a hawk. The pines didn't provide much cover, but I couldn't make out anything. Down by the road, a late model sedan, the windows flashing in the fading light. I caught a glimpse of something light-colored. Maybe blond hair, maybe the reflection of the fading sun. At any rate, it was gone before

I could get a good look, and so instead I started casting out my thoughts at ground level. From the birds' response, a predator was more likely. A fisher or even an opossum could be a threat to a nest, climbing to get the eggs.

"Where is she? Where?" A new voice had joined the cacophony—and this one I did understand. What I heard as a question was the sharp bark of a small dog, racing toward the development—and me.

"Hello?" I called out loud. A domesticated animal wouldn't fear a human voice, and this little fellow must have been lost and hungry. "Good boy! Here, boy!"

A rustle in the woods marked the creature's passage. I could feel him listening for me—rushing toward the condos. "Good boy!"

At the same time, I heard another sound—a car, driving up to the development.

"Where? Where?" The barking was growing louder, and I turned. It would be a sad circumstance if the little dog were hit by a car just as he emerged from the woods.

"Hey there!" I called out and raised my hand, stepping back into the road. "Watch out!"

The car—a silver Honda—braked to a halt and a redhead—Cheryl Ginger—stepped out. As tall as I was, at least in those heels, she had an athlete's trim hips, although the short fur jacket implied curves above. "Did you hear him?" she asked. "Is he here?"

Without waiting for an answer, she trotted to the edge of the woods, hampered by those shoes. "Pudgy!" she called, cupping her hands like a megaphone. "Pudgy! Are you there?

"Here! Here!" A flash of white and brown among the trees. Ears flapping, the dog—a spaniel—came flying.

"Pudgy!" The woman beside me knelt as the dog—a Cavalier King Charles spaniel, from the size and silky coat—leaped into her arms. "I've been looking for you everywhere." She was talking to the dog, but I saw her glance at me as he reached up to lick her cheek. When she caught me looking, she turned to work a small twig out of her pet's jeweled collar. "Where have you been?"

The dog didn't answer. Then again, I had the feeling her line of questioning had actually been for me. I wasn't sure what this pretty ski bunny was about, but I knew a staged scene when I was placed in one.

Chapter Eight

The dog was the giveaway. Despite his wagging tail and the way he had jumped into the redhead's arms, he wasn't entirely thrilled. I'd heard this little fellow before—he was a talkative guy—but there were none of the chuffs or grunts that serve as the canine equivalent of purring. The pint-sized pet was glad to be out of the woods, I had no doubt, and that twig must have been annoying—even more than the ostentatious collar. But he'd leaped into this woman's arms more like it was a trick he was completing rather than her embrace being the reward. It was an act, and he was a bad actor. That was my cue for the next line.

"I'm glad you came along when you did." I was talking to the woman, and I wasn't working very hard to hide my sarcasm. "I've been looking for this guy for about an hour now."

"An hour?" Big green eyes blinked at me, almost as expressive as the dog's. "But why? How did you know he was out here?"

"I heard him, yesterday, inside the condo. But the cops told me that the condo was empty by the time they left."

"You heard? Oh." The meaning of what I'd said hit her and she blinked again, more rapidly this time. "It was you who… You found Teddy."

"Yes." I watched her face, waiting for something I didn't see. "I'm sorry for your loss."

"Thank you." Her brows furrowed, her lips puckered, but she came across more bothered than distraught. "I—" She ducked her head, burying her face in the dog's curls, as if to hide her tears. "I can't believe it."

The spaniel was whining. I couldn't get a read on him, his distinctive markings masking his big dark eyes as he hid his mistress'. She pulled back at that, attaching a leash to his collar, and setting him down on the ground. When she looked up again, her eyes were full. Her makeup, however, was undamaged.

"Thank you for finding Pudgy," she said. Chin up, her tone that of a lady addressing a servant. But I don't do submissive, and I was willing to bet I knew more training tricks than she did.

"Pudgy, huh?" I bent and held out my hand. He sniffed it curiously, his black leather nose twitching. But when I tried to hear what was going on behind his wavy locks, all I got was a polite refusal. *"Working,"* was the best translation. Well, so he was. "Had him long?"

"Only a few months." She'd stepped back, ready to go, but the dog wasn't through checking me out, and she seemed hesitant to command him to heel. "Come on, Pudgy." She pulled on the leash briefly, as if it were a horse's rein.

I switched my attention from the dog to her. "You know, a well-trained dog is a happy dog." I wasn't sure what was going on here. That didn't mean what I said wasn't true.

"Pudgy is trained." She emphasized the last word. She'd misunderstood me.

"I don't mean housebroken." I couldn't get a read on her either. "I mean, in terms of not running off when a door is left open." Nothing. "Or following your commands without you having to yank on his leash."

"I didn't…" She caught herself, and her hand dropped to her side. With the sudden slack, Pudgy came over to sniff my boot. I looked down at his caramel and white fur, but all I got was professional curiosity, for lack of a better term. This dog wanted to know who I was and what I was about. I confess, I felt the same. "I don't know that much about dogs," she said, finally.

I tried not to roll my eyes. "Was Pudgy a gift?" I thought of the dead man. For all I knew, the multicolored gemstones on the collar were real and this little spaniel was as expensive as the condo. Although this woman and her late flame had seemed a mismatch, I still held out hope that she and the dog could get along better with a little prompting.

"Yes." She seemed quite sure of that and nodded for emphasis. "From a friend."

"Mr. Rhinecrest?" I lowered my voice slightly. That's as gentle as I get, but I needn't have worried. There would be no more tears from Cheryl Ginger. Although her face puckered up again slightly, her full lips pursing, the effect was more one of dismay than of sadness.

"No, no," she said quickly. "Another friend. Earlier." The way she tacked that last word on made me think of what Ronnie had said about another man. Though if she were here on Rhinecrest's dime, it would have been pretty ballsy of her to bring her other lover's gift along. "From long ago."

"Ah," I nodded and waited for her to realize her mistake. She did, pretty quickly. Whatever else the redhead was, she wasn't dumb. Instead, she blushed and waved one hand in the air, as if swatting lies. "I mean, from a few months ago. Before I met Teddy, of course." She looked down at the dog as if for confirmation before raising those striking eyes to mine. "I've just been turned upside down by all of this. I left for the day to go skiing and I never thought…." She swallowed and nodded. It was good. So good, I was confident she'd rehearsed.

"I still can't believe he's gone." Tight smile, more blinking. "And I was off, having fun."

That's right. Her alibi was that she was skiing. "When did you find out?"

She shook her head. "He took off. He did that sometimes. He had a temper." A sigh that could have shaken the pines. "When I came in for a break, one of the lodge attendants found me. Teddy had been playing poker, so I thought he'd be happy. But I guess it didn't work out, and he'd left me a note."

I waited.

"'Enough's enough,' it said." Her voice had sunk to a near whisper. She'd gone pale, too. "Enough's enough."

As we stood there, the woods around us fell silent as well. So silent, the distant hum of traffic came through.

Pudgy, however, seemed to hear more. He went on the alert, his face—no, his entire body—directed back toward the woods.

"What is it, boy?" I bent to the dog again, placing my hand on his back. He was trembling with eagerness. Spaniels were gun dogs originally and have been bred to accompany hunters as far back as the eleventh century. Their original work function shows in their lines, those broad muzzles housing sensitive noses, and their muscles compact and strong, no matter their size. Even the toy breeds, like Pudgy here, have it in them still, the urge to be steady and attentive during the hunt. Now, watching him point toward the trees from where he had recently emerged, I could have sworn he was waiting—for a call, for a shot to be fired, his keen face alert to where game might be.

"Waiting…" I didn't need my special sensitivity to pick that up. The slight tremble as he held his pose would have told me that. *"Waiting for…him."*

And with that, he shut me out. His training had him so focused on one person—his hunter—that anyone or anything else would be viewed as a distraction. This was what he was born for. However, it didn't bode well for his future with the recently bereaved redhead.

"You know, you should try some obedience classes." I looked at her sidewise as I crouched by the dog's side. After what I'd seen in the restaurant, I wondered if she'd wince at the word "obedience." She didn't disappoint. "These dogs bond tightly, and if you're going to keep him…"

I left the question open. This was her cue to mention the "other friend" again. *Enough's enough*, indeed. No wonder she had gone white.

"I would take Ms. Marlowe at her word." I stood with a start. That low voice, as soft as gravel, had come from not ten feet behind me.

At my side, the spaniel whimpered softly, his focus disrupted. I, too, had been staring off into the woods. I had heard a car— cars?—but I hadn't seen the red sportster that I associated with that voice.

"She's not only the best animal behaviorist in Beauville, she may well be the finest I've ever met."

The words were courtly. Smooth. But even before I turned, I knew I would be looking into the slate-colored eyes of a stone-cold gangster.

"Gregor Benazi, as I live and breathe," I said, those two functions suddenly very dear to me. "How kind of you," I added. "Do you know Ms. Cheryl Ginger?"

I wasn't sure what the play was. The dog whined in frustration.

"I'm not sure I've had the honor." He reached out and, mesmerized, she gave him her hand. "I have, however, heard so much about you. The pleasure is all mine."

Chapter Nine

It must have been the smile. As a pretty young woman, Cheryl Ginger must be used to avuncular types. Older men who are drawn to her youth and beauty—or who use their age as an excuse to get close, whatever their darker purpose. And Gregor Benazi did not come across as sleazy in any way. The suit he wore, the dull sheen of silk showing beneath his cashmere overcoat, was well cut and classy, a steel gray that played well against his still-thick hair. The way he took her hand, too, was gentlemanly—his fingertips gripping hers lightly for only a moment before release. No, it had to be the smile.

"Oh!" Her response was little more than the exhalation of air, but Benazi's smile broadened as if she had greeted him in French.

"Mr. Benazi." I turned toward the dapper intruder, noticing once again how short he was. Strangely, he never seemed small when I thought of him. As I spoke, Cheryl Ginger withdrew her hand and stepped back. "What brings you here?"

"Ms. Marlowe." The tip of his head was a courtly acknowledgment that I had broken his spell. I had a fleeting thought that this must be what it feels like to step between the cobra and its small, furry prey.

"Don't tell me you were simply in the neighborhood," I said, keeping my voice level. Benazi scares me, don't get me wrong. I didn't know anything for sure—it would be dangerous to know too much about this man—but I had reason to believe he had killed at least one woman. Not that she didn't deserve it. Still, I had a strange kind of détente with him. Part of that was mutual respect: he saw me as someone like himself, I believe. Someone slightly outside the lines of civil society. Also, I'd helped him adopt a cat once. It's a long story. At any rate, I felt I could talk to him. I could certainly do more than the woman standing mute beside me.

"I would never dissimulate with you, Ms. Marlowe." My eyebrows went up at the ten-dollar word, and his smile grew a fraction wider. "No, I am here on business, as you doubtless imagined. I'm an old acquaintance of the late Mr. Rhinecrest." At this he turned toward Cheryl and nodded once. "And I was hoping to pay my respects."

"The funeral is going to be in the city." Cheryl's voice was little more than a whisper, a quavering whisper at that. Still, it took nerve for her to respond. "I'm not—It won't be here."

"Of course." Another nod of the head confirmed that he knew about the wife, now a widow. "Only, Mr. Rhinecrest and I had had some dealings recently, you see, and I was hoping to tidy up some outstanding business."

I looked from him to her. She had gone whiter than before, if that were possible, her pretty lips pursed tight. "I stayed out of Teddy's business," she said. "We came here to ski. For me to ski," she corrected herself, stumbling over the words. "He liked to play cards and watch me on the slopes."

"And I'm sure you both liked to be alone together." Benazi looked around, as if he were seeing the trees for the first time. "In such a bucolic setting."

"Yes, well." A blush crept up her cheeks, turning them an itchy red. "That, too."

For a moment there was silence, and another image hit me. Benazi wasn't a snake, he was a hawk, about to swoop down. He even leaned in slightly as if gauging the distance between some lofty height and his prey on the ground. But before I could interrupt—this wasn't nature; this was humanity at its worst—I was beaten to the punch. Pudgy, or whatever the little dog's name was, had begun to growl. Smart dog, I thought, as I looked down. No matter how inexpert Cheryl Ginger's care of him might be, he knew a threat when he smelled one.

Only the spotted spaniel wasn't at her feet, when I looked for him. Nor was he facing Benazi, for all his menace. Instead, the dog was at the end of his lead, facing the woods. And the soft whine he emitted was accompanied by a slow, sad wag of his tail.

"Cheryl?" I put my hand on her arm, both to turn her toward the dog and away from Benazi's mesmerizing stare. "You might want to see to your dog."

"Oh! Pudgy!" She ran the few steps to him as if he had been lost for ages, scooping him up once more into her arms. "No, Pudgy." She stroked his silky ears, cooing. "You're staying with me from now on."

"Good idea," I said. Not that he was much of a watchdog. "I heard him in the condo yesterday, but I gather the police must have let him out."

She nodded, murmuring into the back of his head. "Poor baby. Out here all alone." With her free hand, she worked the skeleton of a leaf out from his curls, smoothing his fur as she did so. The dog hadn't had too hard a time, I thought. Not only had he survived, his coat didn't look too matted down with mud or burrs. "My poor, poor Pudge. My little love." His tail beat against her side.

I cleared my throat to interrupt the reunion. "It's probably been a long twenty-four hours for him. You might want to take him indoors. Give him some food and water. Check him for ticks." I was watching Benazi as I spoke. He kept his eyes trained on her face. "It's early in the season, but you can't be too safe." I didn't dare offer more of a warning, but I wanted her out of there.

"I'll leave you to it then." Benazi took my cue, even if she was still standing there, stroking the dog's head as if she had just discovered him. "Since you are both so busy. I do hope you take Ms. Marlowe's advice, Ms. Ginger. As I've said, she is the best in the business."

I nodded at him. I knew I ought to thank him, but I wasn't sure I could.

"I'd like to come around later, however." He kept talking. "I believe you are staying at the Chateau now?"

She blinked in acknowledgment. The Chateau was the nicest hotel around, and I seriously doubted Cheryl Ginger would want to stay in the condo where her boyfriend had been murdered, even if Creighton and his crew would let her. So it wasn't a bad guess. Only, I didn't think Benazi ever said anything he wasn't already sure of, whether phrased as a question or not.

"I bet any business you had with the late Mr. Rhinecrest could be taken up with his family"—I stopped myself from saying wife—"or with the cops. You know Officer Creighton, I believe." I didn't know why I was interceding. Cheryl Ginger was as false as they come, and Benazi and I had our truce. Maybe it was the image of a hawk and a bunny that had sprung into my mind. Wallis would say I was weak that way. Wallis would, as usual, be right.

"A simple matter of clearing up some paperwork," he said. The way he accented the last word made it sound arbitrary, although I thought it made Cheryl shiver. "Perhaps the *bella donna* will find my services useful." With that he reached out once more to take her hand. She shifted the dog, who was still staring into the woods, to extend it as an offering. And then with a nod and another smile for me, one that seemed to have a trace of warmth in it, he walked off down the path that led between the condos. This time, I heard the deep growl of his car starting and the rustle of gravel as he made his way down toward the main road.

Paperwork: that was the word he had emphasized, and it had had an effect on Cheryl Ginger. What had struck me was another phrase, however. He had called the redhead *bella donna*. It meant "beautiful woman," of course. But Benazi had never used Italian around me before. He knew my interests. He knew I was well versed in the many dangers of the natural world. Like the plant belladonna—better known as deadly nightshade and the source of atropine. Poison.

Chapter Ten

As soon as the sound of his car faded, I grabbed her so hard she squealed. "I don't know what you're playing at," I hissed at her. "But you do not want to get on the wrong side of that man." I was holding her so close I could see the blood vessels in her eyes, even as the daylight faded. Benazi had taken his leave and—strange as it might sound—I didn't think he was the type to double back in order to eavesdrop, but I wasn't going to take any chances. Besides, this little bunny needed to know I was serious. "He's a predator."

"But…but…" She stammered, holding the dog closer. The spaniel whined in response. But if I expected him to squirm free, I was wrong.

"He's gone." Distracted, I looked down. The little beast turned to meet my gaze with his large brown eyes. *"He was here. My person."*

That broke me. Here I was, bullying the woman while the dog was mourning. Then again, I was hoping to save her from a similar fate.

"How do you know Benazi?" I didn't believe that little pantomime, but even as I focused on her I backed up slightly, trying not to let the dog's low whine distract me.

"He's gone." It wasn't working. Even the dumbstruck redhead heard that soft, high-pitched cry.

"Are you okay, Pudgy? My little love?" His vocalization gave her an excuse to ignore my question and she took it, tilting her face toward his and getting licked in return. To do her credit, she laughed.

"I think he's sad." I interpreted. I confess, I liked her better for that laugh. A lot of women—hell, a lot of people—would have spit and sputtered after such a kiss. That didn't mean I was going to let her off the hook. If anything, I had more reason to want her safe. "Upset, I should say, over your friend's death."

I couldn't see her eyes anymore, but I thought she shook her head, as if in denial. An odd response when someone mentions your recently murdered lover.

"You don't think so?" There was something going on with this woman.

"They weren't that close." She finally looked up at me. "Teddy didn't like animals much, and I think Pudgy knew it. Didn't you, my little darling?"

"Huh." I nodded. It could have been that the dead man didn't like his mistress hanging onto presents from former boyfriends, but this didn't seem like the time to point this out. Instead, I tried to pivot back. "Maybe he was upset by Benazi, then." The dapper gangster loved animals. I was betting Cheryl Ginger didn't know that side of his personality. "And you know him how?"

"I don't." She was staring off in the direction he had gone and shaking her head slightly. Her eyes, I noticed, were clear and free of tears. "Or, only slightly. Teddy met with his friends sometimes, while I was skiing."

"Friends?" I remembered what Creighton had said about the dead man. How he tended to hang out in the lodge while she hit the slopes. I wondered how much more he could have told me. "Did you meet these friends?"

"Some of them, in passing." She shrugged before turning back to me. "Teddy tended to compartmentalize his life. And he could be prickly."

Now it was my turn to be struck dumb. This redhead was smarter than I'd given her credit for. At least, in terms of her late lover.

"So you must know what they say about Teddy." I still hesitated before saying too much. "About what he did—his friends."

She nodded. "I know he was maybe not all on the up and up." If she saw my eyebrows rise, she didn't acknowledge it. "So, yeah, I'm guessing some of his friends weren't either. But you didn't know him, Miss—"

"Marlowe. Pru Marlowe."

"You didn't know Teddy Rhinecrest the way I did," the pretty redhead said. "He could be very generous."

I couldn't help it. I rolled my eyes. To do her credit, she colored slightly, although this time the blush formed a becoming tint, filling out the apples of her cheeks.

"No, I mean, in little ways." I imagined small checks. Discreet diamonds. She must have read my thoughts, because she kept talking. "He gave me fun things, too, like a monogrammed ice cream scoop. And he could be sentimental. A few weeks ago, I thought I'd lost a stuffed animal he'd given me, and he got very upset."

"I bet." I'd seen that side of the man. "And Benazi?" I waited. Nothing. "You do know he's a dangerous guy, right?"

Another shrug. "I can't help who Teddy's friends are—were. I didn't know anything."

We were going in circles. "Look, I'm sick of mincing words. Somebody killed your boyfriend, and Gregor Benazi is a dangerous man. If he's taken an interest in you, you should be worried." She opened her mouth, but I raised a hand to stop her. "You have to be. He may seem courtly, but I would not want to cross him."

She shut her mouth and nodded. As I'd thought, she was smarter than she looked.

"Do you have someplace you can go? People you can be with?" I didn't know why I felt protective of her. Maybe it was the dog.

"I can't leave," she said. "Not yet, anyway. The detective…"

Of course, even with the best alibi in the world, she would have to be questioned.

"But I have Pudgy!" She hoisted the little spaniel, who looked from her to me and back again, the question clear on his face. *"Are we going? Will we see him soon?"*

"He's not exactly a guard dog." And this woman was not exactly grounded if she thought any dog—even a pitbull—could defend her against Benazi. "But I'm glad we found him," I added.

"Me, too." Still cradling the dog, she turned to walk toward her car.

"Wait," I called, hit by a sudden thought.

She turned, but I could have sworn I saw a flash of annoyance pass over her face. "Yes?" Her voice was as sweet as ever.

"You're staying at the Chateau?" I knew that hotel. Not that I'd ever had occasion to stay there. It was supposedly popular with honeymooners and the kind of leaf peepers who prefer their bucolic escapes to come with a well-stocked bar.

"For now." She looked past me at the condo. The condos at The Pines weren't cheap, but they weren't the Chateau, either, and I remembered that when I'd first seen her in the restaurant, her lover had accused her of complaining. Had she found the time-share tacky? Had she found a new friend—or reunited with an old one—who would spring for room service? "I would—most of my stuff is still in there." She spoke as if she were reading my mind. "Only the police…"

"I understand." Who was I to blame the girl if she decided to splurge a bit, after what she'd been through? If that was indeed what was happening. If she was indeed treating herself…

And I had my in: "Only, you might have a problem." I kept my voice level. She looked at me, waiting. "Pudgy," I said. "I don't believe the Chateau allows pets."

"Oh," she looked down at the dog. Sensitive to her mood—or to something—he started whining again. "I hadn't thought…" She bit her lip, and the whining picked up. *"Is he coming back? Are we going to see him?"* I wanted to comfort him. At least he seemed to miss the dead man.

"Mr. Benazi said…" Her face was hopeful, in an odd juxtaposition to her words. "You don't do boarding, do you?"

"No." It was odd what stuck with this woman. Though it did mean she'd heard some of what was said to her. "I'm a behaviorist.

I train animals. For instance, I could help you with Pudgy. Teach him to heel—and not to run away."

"That might be useful." She bit her lip, giving the problem more thought than I'd expected. "I guess I can't leave him here overnight." She looked up at the condo, which was secured with yellow crime tape.

"Definitely not." I didn't care what Creighton would say. I was thinking of the spaniel. While it might help him to smell what had happened—animals recognize death—leaving a small, socialized creature alone in an empty building for that long would be cruel.

"Well, I'll just have to smuggle him in then." She smiled at her own answer, and wrapped her coat around the dog. "What are they going to do, kick me out?"

I had no answer to that and could only shake my head as she walked back to her car. Women like Cheryl Ginger usually do get what they want. It's the ones around them who pay. And what hit me as I watched her drive off into the dusk was not that she seemed so unmoved by the murder of her lover. It was that she was so, well, cavalier toward the fate of the little spaniel, the one creature she had professed to love.

Chapter Eleven

"You're surprised?" Wallis was bathing. *"Really?"*

In response, I simply looked at her. She avoided my eyes by reaching down, removing some unseen bits of her dinner from what appeared to be a spotless white bib. The question was rhetorical, anyway. That didn't mean I didn't have to think about the answer.

I had come home after that odd interaction, chilled to the bone and still wondering about the day's two mysteries. The first—and less urgent—concerned that bunny. I'm happy enough to take money from a client without any heavy lifting. But I didn't see why Marnie Lundquist had hired me, and I was frankly curious about what had caused that basic unease I had sensed in her presence. If it had only come from Henry, the rabbit, I would have understood—him being a prey animal, and an undomesticated one at that. But the nice old lady had seemed both competent and kind, and I'd shown up at her invitation. Well, that one, I'd decided, would sort itself out.

More pressing was the question of Cheryl Ginger. I had little doubt she would be able to manipulate the management of the Chateau. For starters, the high-end tourism the developers expected had never materialized, despite the so-called recovery, and the redhead seemed to have money of her own. Add in that she was, in fact, a nice-looking lady, and, well, I doubted they would kick her out for having a dog in her room.

But if she thought she could twist Benazi around her finger, she was in for trouble. She didn't seem stupid. If anything, she acted like she was distracted. Rather like the spaniel, come to think of it, although at least the little dog appeared to miss the man who had been killed only the day before.

"Not surprised, then." I answered Wallis finally, my own thoughts coming clear. I'd made a point of eating, too, though it was the bourbon that was warming me now, as I sat with my feet up on the kitchen table. "Just…concerned."

Wallis looked up, and I nodded in acknowledgement. This wasn't like me.

"Maybe I just don't want to see Benazi in action," I admitted. Wallis had never met the man, but she had picked enough from me.

"Nothing here you aren't used to," she said now, resuming her tongue bath. *"Nothing you can't handle. He's a hunter. Same as you or me."*

"I'm not—" I stopped myself. It was true that I went for what I wanted. Recently, that had landed me in hot water. I tend to get involved in other people's problems and with my sensitivity, I'm often able to, well, ferret out things others miss.

"Now she's talking about that weasel." The thought came to me with the taste of fur. I sighed and took another sip of my drink. It washed the fuzzy feeling from my mouth and gave me a moment to think. Wallis is not the most social of creatures, and she has a little respect for most other species—my own included—but if she was on my case about something, it was worth figuring out what.

"You don't think I should be asking these questions, do you?" She swiped a white mitten over her ear. "You want me to stay out of this?"

"You said it yourself." Another swipe at the ear. I took another drink. *"That man may love cats, but he's a hunter. And you don't come between a hunter and his prey. Besides…"* Another swipe. More fur, followed by more bourbon. *"Don't you have better ways to spend your time?"*

I should have known. Wallis' hearing is better than mine, and I often think she has other senses at work, as well. While I was digesting that last remark—and refilling my glass—I saw the headlights out front. For a moment, I confess, my stomach tightened. I caught my breath anticipating the appearance of a low, red car and a cool-eyed killer. But the engine that pulled up my driveway wasn't anywhere near as powerful as Benazi's, although regular tuning had made it hum like the purr that now emanated from my tabby.

"I said you would have no reason to go out seeking what you want." She'd stopped washing and instead tucked her front paws under her snowy breast. *"Information, that is."* Her eyes closed with the satisfaction of being right. *"No problem at all."*

"Jim." I met him at the door. He was used to my whiskey kisses. "Want one?"

"I can't drink tonight." He smiled back, reading me like a book.

"Not even a beer?" I stepped back to let him in. He stepped inside, but no further, not following up on that initial embrace.

"Pru, that still counts as drinking." He not only looks like a boy scout, he can act like one at times.

"Whatever." I gave him my most Wallis-like shrug. "I gather you have to go back to work?"

"Mmm-hmmm." Even his assent was close-mouthed, and so I waited. "Probably won't be able to come back later, I'm afraid."

"Yeah, I figured." I leaned against the doorframe, trying not to look curious. I failed. "And so you came by—why?"

"Look, Pru, this is a small town and we both know you've been a real help with some of the things that have happened around here. You've really put yourself out at times." It was the vaguest thanks I've ever gotten, but I started to smile anyway. Started to—as I processed his words, it occurred to me he wasn't necessarily thanking me. "And this time I have to ask you to stand down." He cleared his throat. "Just because you and I—well, you have to keep out of this, Pru. Trust me."

"Oh?" I packed a cooler of ice in that one syllable. I'm not big on trust in the best of circumstances. When a man I'm intimate with asks me for it, without offering an explanation, my internal alarms go off. If I were Wallis, my fur would be standing on end.

"I was there with you, you know. I heard Teddy Rhinecrest haranguing his girlfriend, too." Creighton went on the offense. It was the smart move. "But you can't automatically align yourself with Cheryl Ginger. This is a complicated case—more facets are involved than you know."

"Really." I let the ice begin to drip. If he'd asked, I would have told him about Benazi. Probably. I might even have shared the redhead's curious lack of reaction to the old gent.

"We know you've spoken with her." He was sounding all matter-of-fact now, ignoring my freeze-out. "We know you're going to be working with her dog while she's still here. And we know—*I* know—that means you'll probably have access to some information that might take us longer to get by our more conventional means."

He paused, waiting for that to sink in.

"Please, let me—let us—handle this case." It wasn't a question, but he looked at me as if waiting for an answer.

"Sure, Jim." I managed a smile, and I kept it in place until he kissed me again—close-mouthed this time—and drove off.

Then, trembling, I retreated to the kitchen and poured myself another bourbon, swirling it around in the tumbler while I thought through what had just happened.

Ronnie had mentioned being questioned by the Feds, but I'd discounted it. Usually, murder cases go to the state, although out here, Creighton pretty much acts as a point man for the Massachusetts troopers. Still, if Rhinecrest was, in fact, mobbed up, it made sense that his murder would be much more than a local matter. Bigger even than the Commonwealth.

No, what was troubling me were the other things—the smaller things he had said. He must already have spoken with Cheryl Ginger, I realized. Ronnie had driven off by the time she and I had our talk, and I hadn't seen anyone else around the condos. Which meant that he must have met her at the Chateau. Maybe checked her in. That would be fine. Sure, my hackles rose a bit at the idea of that pretty redhead spending any time with a man I considered mine, but she was a prime suspect in a murder case. And unlike some men I knew, Creighton would most likely consider that a turn-off.

No, what bothered me was that she had apparently been so free with my name. Telling him we'd spoken. Using me, almost, like a get-out-of-jail free card, without ever having responded directly to my offers of help. That woman had something going on, and I didn't think it had to do with her spaniel.

But I could deal with the redhead. I knew her type. What worried me more was what Jim had said in an almost offhand way. He knew, he said, that I had "access to information." Jim Creighton wasn't dumb, and we'd been spending a lot of time together. If I'd let my guard down about hearing animals' thoughts, I might very well be sunk.

I didn't think he'd have me committed, and Massachusetts hadn't burned anyone as a witch in quite a few years. But I knew that a small town could be a cruel place for anyone who didn't fit in.

I'd fled here once. I didn't want to have to run again.

Chapter Twelve

I was up early, but I wouldn't call myself rested. All night, I'd tossed and turned, weighing the possibilities and the threat. Creighton cared for me, I knew that. Whether that meant he'd be less likely to doubt my sanity—or to have me hospitalized "for my own good"—I couldn't tell. But he was also a supremely rational man; it was part of his job, and so I doubted he could ever let himself accept my sensitivity, even if I tried to explain. No, if he knew—if he suspected—at least part of my comfortable life here—the part where he came over several nights a week, sometimes bringing pizza—would be over. And things would be strange enough so that I'd have to move on. Rather to my surprise, that idea made me sad.

"Not much fun, is it?" Wallis met me as I made my way into the kitchen. *"Not having control over where you live or how."*

I could feel her cool green eyes on me as I rummaged around the refrigerator. For me, coffee came first, but I didn't want to argue with my cat. Not in my current mood.

"Here." I dropped a pat of butter on a plate for her, even before I slapped some into a pan. "Peace?"

"Huh." Her dismissive grunt soon gave way to lapping, but as I left the eggs to fry and set about making coffee, I couldn't miss her jab. *"Has a nose but not the sense to use it."*

I gave Wallis all the eggs. I had no appetite anyway, and as soon as I filled my travel mug, I set off on my day.

"I hear you've landed yourself a new client." Tracy Horlick greeted me, if you could call it that, with a blast of smoke and a question that sounded like an accusation.

"I'm always open to new clients." Even after my coffee, I didn't want to engage. "How's Bitsy today?"

"She's a strange one, isn't she?" Drawing on her cigarette, the old witch eyed me and waited. I tried not to sigh audibly. It was already one of those mornings.

"Mrs. Lundquist?" I wasn't going to badmouth a client. I also didn't see any point in hiding. "She's quite sweet, actually, taking in her granddaughter's pet while she travels."

"Not her." The cigarette dropped to the stoop and she ground it out with more force than I would have thought necessary. "The redhead—the one who killed her boyfriend."

"Cheryl Ginger?" I recognized my mistake as soon as I saw the smile. Well, Tracy Horlick would have learned her name at some point anyway. "She's not a client." I paused, remembering. Creighton had said something similar. "Not that I wouldn't take her on."

"Birds of a feather." The old gossip reached into her housecoat for another smoke. I didn't know whether to be insulted or flattered, which made it easy to keep my face a total blank. The morning was chilly, and it only took a few moments of silence before the old bat turned back into her house and freed the poor dog she'd ostensibly hired me to care for.

"Hey, Growler." As soon as we were down the walk, he'd stopped to relieve himself. "How's it going?"

Conversation wasn't the bichon's forte. He had an understandable grudge against humans—especially female humans—but it seemed rude not to observe the social niceties, no matter how unsocialized his person was. I let him set the pace as we moved along the quiet street.

"Simpson, my boy, you've got to watch it…" He paused to sniff a particularly well-used hydrant. *"Roger, you old dog…"*

I stared off into space. It was wrong to eavesdrop, even if I had no choice. When he was ready to move on, I focused on the trees around us. Even with snow still on the ground, they were beginning to bud. Spring usually makes people hopeful, but I couldn't stop thinking about Creighton—and about the questions Cheryl Ginger had raised only the day before.

"You've got a nose." A grumpy voice broke into my uneasy reverie. *"Use it."*

I looked down, struck by the similarity between Growler's words and Wallis'. Black button eyes stared into mine.

"I'm talking to you, walker lady." The low whine, punctuated by a sharp yap, came through quite clearly. *"And I'm no cat."*

I shook my head. "I don't understand."

The whine got louder, and Growler broke my gaze to stare off down the street. *"Don't you want to know what he was looking for?"*

"Creighton? Or—no—Benazi?" A chill ran through me. No, I didn't want to get any more involved in the suave gangster's business than I could help.

"Stewie, silly." He looked back at me, a hint of impatience in the way he tilted his white, fluffy head.

It took a moment. I'd been thinking of the redhead. Of the scene outside the condo and her reaction—or lack thereof—to Benazi. Then it hit me. Her dog—the one she called Pudgy—had been focused on something or someone in the woods. Where it seemed he had spent the night.

"And don't you want to know?" The little tail started to wag, as I got it.

"Yeah, thanks, Growler." I kneeled to scratch him behind the ears in gratitude. "I do."

If we were going to do this, we would have to move quickly. But even as I thought up a plan, the little white dog quickened his steps, taking me across the street and back toward my car. I was glad then that I hadn't parked directly across from Tracy Horlick's house. I'd told myself that I would need a little breather, after her smoke-drenched hostility. I'd also wanted to dissuade any comments on my choice of wheels or my driving. That reticence paid off now, as I ducked into the driver's seat, opening the passenger side door so Growler could hop in.

"We'll only have a few minutes," I said, as I rolled down the window. It was still cold out, but the bichon was doing me a favor. The least I could do was make the ride fun for him.

"*Yup!*" He yapped, putting his front paws up on the door. Partly because of the time and partly to give the little guy a thrill, I hit the gas hard, making my way to the condo development in less than ten minutes.

"Here we go." I'd rolled to a stop a few hundred yards short of the development. I had no excuse for being there, and I sure didn't want to have to explain why I'd brought a client's dog. Growler didn't care, and hopped out as soon as I opened his door. In fact, as I watched him bounce off into the woods, I had a moment of panic. What if the bichon had manipulated me into helping him escape? I had no doubt that life with Tracy Horlick was horrible, but I didn't have any illusions about how long a bichon frisé would last out here—or how vindictive the old lady would be toward me, his purported keeper.

"Growler?" A lump crept into my throat.

"*Hang on!*" One bark as he bounded forward, and I walked to the edge of the woods, waiting, his leash in my hand.

"Ms. Marlowe." The voice was soft, but it sent ice up my spine as I spun around. "What a pleasant surprise."

"Mr. Benazi." I swallowed, my mouth suddenly dry. "You came back."

"You did, too." His eyebrows rose as he smiled, waiting. "With a dog."

"I wanted to bring Growl—Bitsy for a run." I forced my own smile. "His owner doesn't let him out much."

He nodded, and I remembered. Gregor Benazi seemed to have some special senses of his own. "I'd say that fellow deserves a bit of a run. Shall we?"

My mouth was too dry to respond. I had reason to suspect that this man had offered similar invites to others. Reason to suspect that they never returned.

"I only want to share some thoughts," he said.

I caught his eye. It might not have been difficult to guess at what I'd been thinking. Then again, I couldn't be too careful with this man.

"I don't have long." I managed not to choke out the words. "I didn't exactly tell the dog's owner I was taking him here."

"So much the better." A smile creased his face. "He looks like a dog who wants to break the rules."

With one last look at the woods—Growler had disappeared among the leaves and hillocks—I nodded and followed Benazi as he walked up toward Teddy Rhinecrest's condo. Ronnie's truck was nowhere to be seen. The development was quiet. Deserted, I would have guessed. I would not, I told myself, go inside with him.

"I am wondering if you can help me with a problem," he said, finally, as we approached number six. "It's a delicate issue, and I believe a woman's touch may be useful. Especially," he paused to look back at me, "a woman of your particular sensitivities."

I nodded. His use of that word sending another chill down my back.

"I would be most grateful." He gave the last two words extra weight, and I began to breathe again. Perhaps this was a promise, rather than a threat.

"You may have heard that the late Mr. Rhinecrest had dealings with," a pause—a brief look of distaste passing over that craggy face—"unsavory types."

He waited again for confirmation, and I nodded. There was no sense denying what we both knew to be true.

"That's as it may be, of course." Benazi waved off his words, as if he were shooing a fly. "But it is possible that in the course of some of those interactions the late Mr. Rhinecrest may have become involved with some, well, shall we say keepsakes?"

"Sure." My curiosity had gotten the better of my fear. "So you're looking for a way into his condo?"

"Oh, no, my dear." A low chuckle. Of course, bribing Ronnie would have been child's play for a man like Benazi. In fact, he probably would have sent an underling. No, if he was here, there was something larger afoot. "You see, the keepsake seems to have gone missing. And Mr. Rhinecrest's family—his legitimate family, back in New York—would very much like to have it restored. As a remembrance of the man they lost, of course."

"Of course." I stopped short. "You think Cheryl Ginger has it."

"No, not at all." He shook his head. Of course, her belongings would have been searched as well. "But she may have some awareness—some vague recollection that could help us locate it. Only, she is refusing to work with me."

"Hey!" I turned, distracted by a sound. A bark. A ball of white was bouncing toward us, breaking away from a patch of snow and over the browns and blacks of the sodden woods. Growler. *"Come on, walker lady!"* More yaps, the sounds of an excited pooch. *"Old smoke teeth is going to bust a gut. And I may have found something!"*

"Go." Benazi raised his hand as if in benediction. "But if you would keep my request in mind, Ms. Marlowe, I would be more than grateful."

Chapter Thirteen

It was a tactical retreat, nothing more. I had little to gain from lingering, and if Benazi thought I was on his side, well, that might give me a little leeway. Besides, Growler was right. I needed to get him home before his absence was noted. And I wanted to hear what he had found.

"Come on, boy." I opened the passenger door and called. Not that Growler needed my urging. "Come on."

"*Huh.*" He jumped up with a soft chuff. "*There's no fooling that one. You know that, right?*"

"A girl can hope," I said, as much to myself as to my fluffy white companion. With that, I floored it, bouncing toward the main road at a speed my suspension would pay for.

It wasn't until we were on the highway that I turned to look at my companion. Growler had his nose out the window I'd left partly open, sampling the wind.

"*Crows, grackles, nests and eggs…* " A proper catalogue of wild-life occupied him, and through the list, I could sense his pleasure. "*White tail fawn, early yet. Raccoons and possum. Bobcat?*"

"Better you enjoy that from in here." I took advantage of his momentary surprise. Growler might know a bobcat's scent from his genetic memory—the size and ferocity of the creature, however, had set him back.

"*Like you're so tough.*" He turned, and I sensed a touch of embarrassment that he'd been caught out.

"It's always smart to avoid alpha predators." I thought of another small but fierce creature. "As you said, there's nothing to be gained from engaging."

"*Huh.*" The bichon shifted on the seat, settling down in the leather bucket. "*That's not what I heard going on.*"

"I had to say something to him." I couldn't believe I was explaining myself to a dog. "I didn't agree to do his dirty work."

"*You think I'm talking about the little gray man?*" He paused to scratch his ear, nearly losing his balance in the process. I'd have to check him for fleas and ticks. "*He's not the one who's been hunting in those woods.*"

"Cheryl Ginger?" I visualized the redhead—and the image of her late boyfriend followed hard on that. It wasn't like she didn't have motive. "Is that who you smelled out in the woods?"

"*Huh.*" He shook, rattling the tags on his collar. "*Humans… after the hunt. He was on a trail! The one who follows!*" In his excitement, the little dog's thoughts became excited yaps. "*Tracking!*"

"A tracker?" As he turned back toward the window, I realized my mistake. "You mean a retriever?" I racked my brain. Surely, the bichon would recognize different species, different talents. Unless that was a human distinction. "Do you mean the spaniel? What was his name, Stewie?"

"*Bird, squirrel, squirrel…*"

"Was he the one hunting?" Nothing. "Growler, please."

"*You were on the track, walker lady. Now leave me be.*"

We were nearing his home, and he could smell it. As I turned off the highway, I saw his perky ears begin to droop. Animals experience time differently than we do, but the bichon knew his morning of freedom was drawing to a close.

But I had given him that morning. "I thought Cheryl might have gone out there for a reason. To meet somebody. To meet a man." I tried to remember precisely what Ronnie had said about clandestine meetings. I wasn't sure how his words would translate to the altered male on the seat beside me, but surely the intention would come through. It was spring, and some behaviors are universal.

"One-track mind." He was staring out the window again. I was slowing. The street we were driving down was residential, but it was more than that. I felt Growler's resistance—his resentment toward the woman who was more jailer than friend. *"Women…"*

"I'm sorry, Growler." I meant it. I was.

"No, stupid." He turned, pinning me with his wide black eyes. *"I don't care about old smoke-teeth. I get my own back."* An image of something gnawed—a trunk, I thought—and of a quilted robe stained with urine—flashed before me. *"I mean, you. Not even in heat."*

"There you are!" Despite my pace, we'd reached Tracy Horlick's house, and as I coasted up to the curb, the old lady was marching down to meet us. "I was about to call the cops. Not that the Beauville police would take a helpless old lady's side against you!"

I opened my mouth. Tracy Horlick was the last person I'd have called "helpless." But Creighton could defend himself against her insinuations, and I needed the steady gig.

"Especially with the company some of them have been keeping." She squinted at me, waiting to see if her dart had hit home.

"I'm so sorry." I ducked out to open the passenger side door. That made it easier to ignore whatever it was she was insinuating. "You see, Bitsy's usual play space is all muddy because of the melt, and so I wanted to take him someplace where he wouldn't mess up his coat."

As I lied, I bent to stroke his white curls. Silently, I apologized. *"If she takes this out on you, I'll make it up to you. I promise."*

"He's in great shape." I kept my eyes wide as I looked up at her from the dog's side. Along with the smile, I was signaling submission. "And after the winter we've had…" I waited, the unfinished sentence my version of the tentative tail wag.

Her eyes narrowed as she reached into her pocket. For a moment, I worried. Did she have a gun? A knife? But she only fished out a pack of Marlboros and proceeded to light up.

Growler barked. *"Hey! Answer her!"*

I smiled down at him in gratitude.

"I didn't authorize any additional outing," she said at last, smoke leaking from her nostrils. "Unlike your detective friend."

"No, you didn't." I was not going to be baited. "And there's no extra charge. My treat," I added, in case she missed it.

"Huh." Her grunt sounded so much like the little dog's, I looked at him in surprise, even as she took the leash from my hand.

"Thanks for the run, walker lady." He looked back at me as Tracy Horlick started back toward her house. *"I'll track for you again, but you've got to listen!"* A short, sharp bark as he jumped up the steps. *"Listen!"*

I stood there smiling until old lady Horlick closed the door, partly to continue to allow her dominance and partly because I was trying to figure out what Growler was trying to tell me. I wasn't going to listen to the old bat's taunting, so it had to be something we'd found in the woods. I'd tried to picture the scene Ronnie had described to me—Cheryl Ginger meeting a secret lover—but Growler had seemed to reject that scenario. Instead, he talked about a hunter. Had that hunter been the pretty redhead? She was still the likeliest suspect. Unless, perhaps, her other man had done the deed. Maybe she'd let him in. Maybe they'd set up the wealthy Teddy together.

Or maybe I had misunderstood the little dog entirely. For all I knew, he'd been referring to that bobcat, whose scent had so shaken him. A hunter—or a retriever? Or both?

When my phone rang, I was almost grateful. "Hello?" I didn't recognize the number.

"Pru? Pru Marlowe?" The number was unfamiliar. The voice warm and decidedly feminine.

"Yes?" If this was about selling me a time-share, I was going to enjoy venting.

"You said to call you, you know. If I needed some help." My ears don't prick up like Wallis' do, but I confess my curiosity was piqued. Cheryl Ginger—I placed that honeyed voice—calling me for help.

"I said I would be happy to take your spaniel on as a client." Always good to set your boundaries from the start. People or animals, it didn't matter.

"Of course." There was a chuckle in her voice. This chick knew what I was doing. She even seemed to respect me for it. "That's entirely what I meant, Ms. Marlowe."

Ms. Marlowe. Well, she'd heard me and raised me one. I waited.

"Pudgy and I are staying at the Chateau for, well, the foreseeable future. Only I do think he needs to have someone who can work with him regularly. All the changes…"

"Yeah." "Changes" wasn't the word I would have used. But I got it: the little dog was acting out. Having your master murdered and then being uprooted will do that to you. "I may have some time free this afternoon." I ran through my mental calendar. It was pretty empty. "How about three?"

"Looking forward to it." She signed off, leaving me wondering. That poor spaniel could use a sympathetic ear, and if I could ease his pain, I'd be doing good work. But as I considered the dog's grief, I couldn't help but notice the contrast. The long-haired dog might be acting out, but Cheryl Ginger seemed to have quite recovered from her boyfriend's murder.

Chapter Fourteen

"When I referred to a nose, I did not mean that stunted, little..."
The rest of Wallis' comment was smothered, as she bent to wash her bottom. It was a significant gesture, I knew, adopted from a life spent with my species.

I'd gone home after my morning appointments: running a potential guide dog through his paces and clipping the claws of a particularly spoiled Siamese, who allowed my weekly visits as a form of obeisance. The break gave me a chance to drink more coffee and to do a little passive snooping via the Internet. But the bitter brew—I'd reheated the remains of the pot—reminded me I'd skipped breakfast. So as my old laptop booted up, I'd sat down for a turkey sandwich with Wallis. She skipped the bread, though she did lick delicately at the mayonnaise, and listened as I debriefed her on my run-in with Benazi.

"Growler did say he'd gotten something." I said, assuming she was referring to the bichon as the stunted, little... Wallis had more respect for the gangster. "Only, I'm not sure what. At any rate, I'm going to see that spaniel again, so maybe I'll be able to find out what he was searching for."

"Huh!" She'd moved on to her tail, smoothing the fur with long strokes of her tongue. *"Probably an opossum in heat, stupid, little..."*

"No, I don't think so." Growler had rejected my initial suggestion that a romantic—or sexual—liaison had taken place.

At the time, I'd assumed he was responding negatively to me and to his female- and hetero-dominated world. Now, I wasn't so sure. "But maybe I can find something on Cheryl Ginger."

Nothing showed up for the redhead. Nothing at all, which was odd. Most people, you get at least some old Facebook reference or a mention from their high school paper. Then again, Cheryl's name sounded enough like a *nom de strip club* that I shouldn't have been too surprised. When I tried the same for Benazi, with similarly blank results, I toyed with the idea that this name was also assumed. It wouldn't be the first time. The old gangster probably had plenty of tricks up his tailored sleeve. The only shocker was that the old gent was Web savvy, as well as smooth enough to avoid leaving even a virtual fingerprint.

The deceased was neither so skilled nor so lucky. With only a few clicks, I found a photo of one Teodros "Teddy" Rhinecrest and recognized the prominent chin and those beady little eyes. Seems Cheryl's late ex had skated on a federal charge—an art heist from some big-name museum—several months before. The site showed that same picture I'd seen on the TV news, a woodland scene called *Berkshire Forest*.

Now that I had a chance to examine it, I understood the name. It could have been painted around here, although those old-growth trees were now mostly gone. In the painting—"circa 1858," the report said—they stood tall and proud. Beeches, probably, their bark silver in the shaft of sunlight that centered the picture's composition. I remembered that slant of light from the TV, the way it illuminated those majestic trunks and the rabbit that sat there, grooming. Because of that tiny figure, the white belly fur picked out by the lighting, the painting had acquired the nickname *Bunny in the Sun*, the article said, listing a value that made me whistle. No wonder they were still looking for it months later. That bunny was worth more than Beauville.

I skimmed over the painting's history—Hudson River School, blah, blah, blah—to get to the case. As of this story, the investigation had gone stale. The only one of the crew they'd gotten had been the driver, some kid named Paul Gittelson. Even in the bad perp-walk photo, Gittelson looked like a fall guy, scrawny and pale with a brush of freckles across his face that made him look like he was twelve years old.

"Good luck to that poor loser." I couldn't help voicing my thoughts out loud. Where he was going, I didn't expect he'd have any.

Wallis refrained from commenting, and I looked over at the clock. I had renovated recently—a house fire had taken out the entrance hallway and badly damaged the stairs that ran up to the old house's third floor—but the kitchen, off to one side, remained pretty much as it was in my mother's day. The gas stove was old but functional, sturdier, really, than most contemporary appliances. The refrigerator was on its last legs, but I didn't keep much food in it. And this old wood table, scarred and notched, served as my center of operations. My mother would have had words for Wallis, who had finished her toilette and now sat, inches from my plate, eying the dab of mayo on its rim. She'd tried to discipline me too, back in the day. But my mother wasn't here, and that old clock was reminder enough.

"Go for it." I pushed the plate toward Wallis. She gave it a ladylike sniff before lapping up the drop. I contemplated more coffee—and maybe adding something to it. I had a few hours to kill before my appointment with Cheryl Ginger, and the day loomed long. I'd told her three p.m. at random. It never hurts to have a potential client think you're busier than you are. If the weather were just a little warmer, I could've started out back. The trash from the demo was still mostly piled there, exposed by the recent melt. As much as I wanted to ignore it, it wasn't going away, and I didn't have the kind of money to pay someone else to deal with it.

I was saved by the bell. The ringer on my phone, actually, though when I picked up and heard the panic in Marnie Lundquist's voice, I almost wished I hadn't.

"Ms. Marlowe? It's Henry." It took a moment before I realized she was talking about the rabbit. "Something's wrong—something's very, very wrong."

"Mrs. Lundquist, I'm not a veterinarian." I used the low soothing voice I would for any spooked animal. "If you have a medical emergency, I recommend calling—"

"It's how he's acting," she said, her voice high and tight. "I fear—I fear I made a mistake."

I had to make another attempt. "Mrs. Lundquist, often if an animal is acting strange, there's a physical reason—"

"No, no, it's not that." I heard a sigh, and for a moment I expected tears would follow. They didn't. Marnie Lundquist was tiny, but she was tough. "It's—I believe it is something I did. Please, could you come over?"

Cursing myself silently for not sticking to my position about wild animals as pets, I grabbed my keys and made ready to go. Wallis, I could tell, was watching, her eyes curious and wide. When I poured the rest of the coffee down the sink—it wouldn't take another reheating—she jumped down and came to brush against me. As bothered as I was, the warm pressure was a comfort, as I was sure she knew full well.

"Thanks, Wallis."

The low rumble of her purr and one word—"*family*"—and I had to go.

Not that there was any reason for me to rush. In the twenty minutes that it had taken me to get to Marnie Lundquist's neat little house, it seemed the crisis had passed. I entered to find the older woman pink-cheeked with relief, and the small brown rabbit happily sucking up a blade of grass from the small pile before him as if it were fresh pasta.

"Look at him eat!" She clasped her hands before her. "Doesn't he look lovely?"

"Yes, he does." I answered slowly. Maybe this old bird wasn't the model of stability I had assumed. "But you called because you had a problem?"

She nodded. With her hands before her and her lips tight, I could almost feel the tension. Marnie Lundquist was holding something back.

"He's not himself," she said finally.

"Do you want me to examine him?" I waited. "As I said, I'm not a vet..."

"I know, and, yes, please." I took a step toward the small brown creature before she reached out to me. "Only, please, be careful."

"Of course." I knelt on the floor, trying to make eye contact with the little leporid. He was too busy eating to mind me, but at least I didn't pick up any of the fear I might have expected. Wild animals are fundamentally different from those we've domesticated. Their instincts are keener, their senses sharper. And that meant that my usual sensitivities were often useless, confused, or came to me hopelessly late in an interaction. Still, Marnie Lundquist was not only a client but a nice enough woman. And the rabbit was frankly adorable. With a slight shiver of trepidation, I held my hand out. This was my customary overture: hand low, palm up. Friendly, nonthreatening. My only concern was what Henry would find on my outstretched fingers. After all, I'd only given my hands the most cursory wash before leaving.

He paused in his nibbling to reach his brown head toward me. I held my breath, wondering too late if Wallis' parting contact was meant more as loving gesture or as her claim.

The quivering nose came close enough for me to feel his warm bunny breath.

"*She's your female?*" The thought hit me so hard I jerked back.

"Did he go for you?" Marnie Lundquist had stayed behind me, but I kept my eyes on the rabbit as I responded.

"No, I simply—I lost my balance." It was lame, and I got a wave of something from the rabbit that bordered on amusement. "Why? Did he try to bite you?"

"Not exactly." Henry lifted his active nose once more in my direction, taking in the air around me, and I got a quick rundown on my own day: "*dog, cat, bird, fish?*" But it wasn't Henry I was waiting for. Marnie Lundquist wasn't paying for a house call simply to have me confirm her impressions.

"He, well, he growled at me earlier," she said finally. She looked down at the floor, her hands clasped, as if embarrassed.

The rabbit paused in his meal to gaze up at her. "It was unmistakable," she said.

That was curious, but not unprecedented. "How old is Henry again?" I spoke as softly as I could. As softly as I imagined the bunny would.

She tilted her head, her white bun bobbing as she thought this through. "Cara found him in the fall, so perhaps five or six months?"

I nodded. Although this bunny might look like a cute toy, I was betting he was in the throes of adolescence. "It could be spring fever," I explained. "I could probably tell if our little guy here is sexually mature if he'd let me examine him…" I paused. Technically, I knew how to examine a rabbit, but it wouldn't be easy. Bunny bodies aren't as obvious as a human's, and I'd have to flip the little fellow onto his back to get at the openings that shielded his private parts. He would feel vulnerable. Exposed.

"Oh, I don't think he'd like that." Marnie Lundquist echoed my thought, adding her own trace of embarrassment. "And he seems fine now. Doesn't he?"

"Yes, he does. But still…may I?" I was speaking out loud to the woman, but I focused my thought on the rabbit before me. When neither objected, I reached out for the creature. He didn't struggle, and I got no notes of panic as I gently stroked him, my hand cupping his round body. Instead, I was flooded with pleasure. This little fellow was as soft as anything I'd ever felt.

"Family, nursing…young…" I couldn't help it. I've never been one for the young of my own kind, but I longed to cradle the rabbit to me as if he were a child.

"He likes you." Marnie Lundquist came closer and sat in front of me.

"He does seem quite content." I was aware of how fast the little heart was beating, but I wasn't getting fear or pain. Though there was something…a rumble. A stirring. I reached my other hand toward him. If I could just flip him, I could—

Too late, the little rabbit kicked—I could feel the strength in those hindquarters as he hopped away. When he turned, those big eyes stared at me, wary.

"Have you taken him to a vet?" I thought about making another attempt. His nose twitched, as if to say, "*just try it.*" And I sat back on the floor. I know when I'm defeated. "If just to have him neutered." I was talking to his person now. "It might be a good idea."

"No, I haven't." She shook her head. "I don't believe I should, not until Cara gets back. After all, if the veterinarian felt compelled to report him…"

She didn't have to say any more. Henry was an illegal pet. And while the law—certainly in our neck of the woods—has other problems, if someone brought a wild animal in to Doc Sharpe over at County or any other reputable vet, little Henry would probably be reported and confiscated. Or worse. I might not know what was going on with this little fellow, but I wasn't going to make any more problems for Henry or the kindly old woman who loved him.

Chapter Fifteen

I was going to be a bit late for my appointment with Cheryl, I realized by the time I got back on the road. Marnie Lundquist had dragged out the visit, asking me questions that she appeared to know the answer to as if reluctant to let me go. It was odd behavior for a woman who seemed so competent, reminding me of the questions I'd had after our first meeting. But I didn't know the old lady well, and some animals do put up a brave front at first, as a defense against attack.

I finally got out the door by promising her another visit. Henry had moved on by then, hopping slowly over to his nest of paper shavings, which he proceeded to dig at in an almost feline manner. Watching him, I was reminded of how little I recalled about the family Leporidae. My school days were a few years behind me at this point, and I made a mental note to bone up on rabbit behavior. This little guy seemed to be the picture of health, both mentally and physically. But I couldn't discount what his petite caregiver had said. Nor could I dismiss that feeling—a sense of stirring—that I had picked up, however briefly, when I had touched him.

I tried to dismiss my worries as I drove to my next appointment. The day was doing its best. While the March air still held the hint of frost, the freshness that Growler had enjoyed had warmed up. Add in the additional daylight—only a month ago, we'd have been nearing dusk—and the drive was a joy, the road dry and dappled by the afternoon shadows. Granted, the folks at the Hills wouldn't be so happy about the thaw. I wondered if Cheryl Ginger was considering sneaking back to the ski area for a last few runs. For the rest of us, spring couldn't come soon enough, and it was with a stab of regret that I saw I was approaching the upscale hotel and my next appointment. The biggest problem with driving fast is that too soon the ride is over.

"Cheryl Ginger, please." I hadn't thought to get a room number, but the desk clerk jumped to attention at the name. Some behaviors don't need training, not in spring.

My initial impression was reinforced by the flush on the young clerk's cheeks as he got off the phone. "You can go up," he said, his voice soft and a little wistful. "She's in the Monadnock Suite."

And suite it was, I saw as she opened the door for me. I'd only seen a room in the hotel once before, and that was a regular room—if you can call a hotel room that was better furnished than my entire house "regular."

"Come on in." Cheryl turned and walked down a hall lined with tasteful landscapes, the carpet thick enough so her heels made no sound. "Pudgy and I were just settling in."

"Thanks." I snuck a look into the bathroom as I passed. It smelled of expensive soap. I resisted the urge to duck in and steal a bar and, instead, followed my hostess into a sunlit back room, where the dog was waiting, front paws crossed decorously as he lay on a deep rose chaise longue. "How you doing, Pudgy?"

Silently, I addressed the dog. "*Stewie*," I tried to direct my thoughts. "*Will you talk to me?*"

"Oh, he's so much better." Cheryl sat next to him, her hand on his back. "I think his night outdoors really scared him."

"I believe it." I continued looking at the dog who, I noticed, was not wearing his fancy collar. That could explain the vaguely quizzical sense I was getting from him. Then again, he could simply have been feeling me out. Still, I had questions of my own. "Though he doesn't seem to be any the worse for wear."

"Pudgy?" She turned to look at him, as if he would answer. "No, he doesn't, does he?"

"But where's his pretty collar?" I smiled, hoping to put her at ease, but it was a serious question. A collar is more than a means to attach a leash—or show off an owner's wealth. It holds the animal's ID, his proof of rabies shots, and more. For a dog to go without his collar would be like Cheryl Ginger not having the latest smartphone.

"Silly me." She looked around. The bling-covered leather was on the end table, and she quickly buckled it on, to the spaniel's evident satisfaction. "I was going to brush him, you see."

I nodded, although I didn't. There was something off here. For starters, I didn't see a brush or any grooming tools nearby. Plus, the way she sat once I'd followed her in was more like she was posing for a family portrait than cuddling with a beloved pet. And although she had brought up the little dog's adventure, she had been surprised when I had voiced my concern. Either she was incapable of empathy—always a possibility—or there was more going on than I could see.

I needed to talk to the dog.

"For a first lesson, I'd like to go over some basic commands," I said. I was using my own basic command voice: low and calm. "I'd like to take Pudgy outside and see how he responds."

"Of course." She jumped up. "Let me get my coat."

I shelved my objections until we got outside, which we did without any fuss, Cheryl taking us blithely down the elevator and out through the front lobby. In fact, from the look on the desk clerk's face, I wondered if she might be slipping him treats. But the redhead wasn't my concern, except as a client, and so once we were out of doors, I led the small dog over to the edge of the parking lot. From here, I could see down into the surrounding woods. The snow had retreated on this side of the hill, leaving only white patches against the dark base of the trees. The day had been sunny, the temperatures—almost clement. Either spring was genuinely on its way, or the money behind the Chateau truly did buy its guests something better and beyond. Either way, I saw an opportunity.

"Come on, Pudgy." I chucked for the dog to walk.

"Are you going to keep him on the road?" The merest hint of distress had crept into the redhead's voice. Of course, those heels.

"I'd like to take him on a trail." Again, my voice was smooth and even, with nothing in it to alarm her. I even smiled as I explained. "See how he reacts with distractions like birds and other animals."

"Oh." She paused, lost in thought, and I looked down at the spaniel.

"What did you find in the woods, Stewie? What were you looking for?" He wagged his tail, but that was all. For all I knew, he was simply pleased at the idea of a good walk.

"It might be better if I take him alone." I delivered the *coup de grace*. "For training purposes." Another smile, to soften the blow. "You see, if he will obey the voice commands of a stranger, that assures that he's well trained."

"I'll just wait here then." She sounded a bit forlorn. If I didn't know better, I would have said she was a nervous pet owner— one who had nearly lost her dog the day before. Maybe that was even the truth.

"Come on, boy." I spoke out loud, avoiding the dog's real name while there was the possibility that Cheryl was still in earshot. I had set out at a slow jog, and the energetic little animal seemed quite pleased to run alongside. "Let's go into the woods, shall we?"

"Collar off?" He paused to look up at me, and I'm afraid I started.

"What? No." We were a good few hundred yards into the woods by then. The lengthening shadows blended with his caramel markings, but I could still make out the puzzled look on his face. "Who let you run without your collar?"

I had intended to interrogate the animal, but this was potentially more serious. Letting a dog run off lead I could get behind—a well-trained dog, that is, who would come when called and not get into too much trouble. Taking the dog's collar off was a different matter.

"*My man. My person.*" He turned to sniff at something—I got a strong sense of rot. A dead squirrel. Long dead. "*We would play.*"

"Teddy Rhinecrest?" The scent of decay seemed to blend with my question, but the little dog didn't answer, his nose buried beneath the leaves. "Here, Stewie?"

I reached for his face, redirecting his muzzle toward me. Not all animals respond the same way, and I can't communicate freely with any except Wallis. I credit our years together for that. She thinks it's because she's a cat. What I do know is that contact helps.

For the spaniel, however, my hand was more than a means to move him. "*Rabbit.*" He buried his wet nose in my palm, and I got an image of brown fur, a white fluffy belly, and big dark eyes. I let him sniff, mentally confirming that, yes, I had been in contact with a rabbit recently. I wasn't thrilled by his interest: spaniels are hunting dogs, and even the toy breeds retain the instinct. Maybe my honesty—the offering of my hand—would prompt him to open up.

After a few moments, I tried again. "What were you doing in the woods, Stewie? What were you looking for? What did you find?" I voiced these questions out loud, but in my mind they were all the same —one query centered on one image: the woods.

"*Prey.*" His nose was still busy, reacting to the rabbit smell, and his thoughts were coming through loud and clear. For the first time ever, I found the wet nose—inquisitive and busy—disconcerting. "*Fear.*" He must have picked that up from my desire to draw back, to block his curious sniffling, unless he was getting something older and more primitive from Henry himself. "*Fear and hiding.*"

From the parking lot, I could hear Cheryl calling.

"What was out there, Stewie?" I held his jaw, tilting his face up toward mine. By doing so, I broke his connection with my palm—with Henry. It was a risk, but I was running out of time. "Please, tell me."

"Hiding?" Those big, dark eyes stared into mine. He was trying as hard to read me, I felt, as I him. For all his toy status, he was a good dog—a working dog.

"In the woods." I didn't want to discourage him. I did want to get him off Henry and the prey angle.

"Family…my man. The man." Despite the distractions, I got a sense of bonding. Kinship. Cheryl's old boyfriend—her man on the side?

"Mating?" If this was going to be multiple choice, I would offer the obvious options. Animals aren't squeamish, and if Cheryl was meeting someone in the woods, I doubted it was to trade the time of day. But all I got was confusion and a mishmash of images.

"Family," he said, as much as thoughts could say anything. *"Hiding. Holding on."*

"There you are!" Cheryl Ginger was coming up behind us, heels sinking into the thick mulch. "I got bored waiting and figured I'd tag along."

"Of course." I got to my feet and handed her the lead. "As I've said, the first lesson is about following simple instructions."

"She can do that." It was the clearest thought I'd gotten yet, and I turned to stare down at the spaniel.

"Is everything all right?" Cheryl yanked the leash up to her chest, and we both turned to her. Her face had gone white, her mouth drawn.

"I believe so. But maybe this is too much for you right now."

"No, no." With a visible effort, she lowered her hands to her sides. "It's good for me to get outside. That's why I'm so glad I have Pudgy."

It was such palpable nonsense I didn't know how to respond. For an expert skier, the exercise a little dog would provide would be virtually unnoticeable. But as she spoke, I saw how the spaniel looked up at her, his dark eyes deep and focused.

"I'm here to save her, and I will," he was saying. *"She's my person now, as well as his."*

Chapter Sixteen

It was none of my business. I'd warned Cheryl about Benazi. I'd told her that he was a dangerous man, and I'd even tried to intervene—asking her about her late lover's business. I'd gone as far as I could be expected, and then some.

Maybe I felt I owed her something for her money. That little dog—Stewie—was as well trained as any animal I'd ever worked with. He might have been a bit overeager, but I put that down to a lack of exercise. No, she was the one who needed training.

I'd had to take her hand as we turned back toward the Chateau. She wasn't dressed for hiking, and the forest floor was soaked through from the day's melt. When I had, the connection had been immediate. Not with me—I found the redhead's touch cool—but with the dog. Although she held Stewie's lead, when I made contact with Cheryl, a jolt of recognition had raced through me. The dog was on alert. Although the spaniel's muzzle barely turned toward the woman at his side, those long ears, that nose were attuned to her every move.

It boded well for the basics I was professing to teach. And so, once we were back on the pavement of the parking lot, I stopped her, gesturing to the lead still in her hand. The problem, I discovered, wasn't with Stewie, but with the redhead. Although I demonstrated the basic commands—heel, stay, sit—she seemed not so much uncomprehending as uninterested. For all the affection she apparently lavished on the spaniel, she had precious little real interest in what made him tick.

It was a problem I've seen before—the poor animal was more valued for what he symbolized than what he was. That's one reason I talk clients out of giving pets as gifts whenever I can, but it was too late in this case. Poor Pudgy—what a name—was going to have to deal with being half-ignored, at least unless the friend who'd gifted him stepped back into the picture. With an animal this acute—and this centered on his person—that was a recipe for trouble. It would only be a matter of time before the animal began acting out.

As I said, I'd done what I could.

What I didn't expect was for Wallis to disagree with me.

"Giving in so easily?" She'd greeted me at the door when I got home, rubbing up against me as I came in.

"I didn't think you'd care about a dog." I was discouraged.

"A dog!" Wallis' tone should have been a tonic. *"And she sounded so interesting, too."*

"I don't know what's up with that woman, Wallis." I shuffled in, closing the door behind me, and let her lead me into the kitchen. "I can't imagine she'll be around for long."

"Really?" The question was muted, as Wallis had her head in the grocery bag. Suddenly the scent of roast meat became amplified, and I couldn't be sure if it was my belly I heard growling or some atavistic sound from the cat. I withdrew the rotisserie chicken—Beauville was becoming civilized, at least to the point of having a full-service deli—under her watchful gaze and started to partition it. When I began scraping the meat off the thigh bone, the growl grew louder. I got the message, handing the piece over.

"What's she got to stay for?" I fetched a beer as Wallis began to eat. The sight of her tearing the cooked flesh apart didn't dampen my appetite. It was the thought of getting nowhere with Cheryl Ginger and her dog that had me seeking liquid solace.

"Well, the dog…what did you expect?" The thoughts reached me through the sounds of satisfied lapping as she licked at the salty skin. *"Those creatures will do anything for anybody."* She sat back up and began to wash her face. *"But the redhead?"*

She paused, as she licked the back of an already spotless paw. I reached to remove a nonexistent tuft of fur from my mouth and then gave up, pushing the chicken breast toward her.

"Go wild." I watched as she sniffed. The meat was cooling but still fragrant. "But share with me, if you will, what you mean."

As I watched, the tabby who shares my life bent over the chicken, her black leather nose twitching as she considered the offering. Finally, she licked at it, her tongue dabbing at the charred skin. When she looked back up, a moment later, without taking a bite, I was afraid she'd rejected the deal.

"A lady can't gather her thoughts?" The question sounded in my head and I took another drink. Wallis' ability to read my mind meant I could take shortcuts—clearly she had picked up something, secondhand, from the scents on my clothes. But it would never stop being disconcerting.

"Only because you insist on thinking in such a…linear fashion." She was translating, I could tell not only from the pause but from the way her ears splayed out, their black tips lying almost flat as she concentrated. So I bit back my impatience and waited.

"You needn't be so angry, you know. The woman is not competing with you." I opened my mouth—and immediately closed it. Wallis knows me too well for me to deny it. Cheryl Ginger was an attractive woman, and I knew how my ambivalence about intimacy had at times pushed Jim Creighton away.

"No, she's after bigger game." I wasn't sure if the idea of money and sugar daddies had a feline corollary, but I trusted Wallis to get the gist. "But I wouldn't put it past her to toy with him." An image of Wallis and an unlucky mouse passed across my mind. She huffed—the half-hiccup that heralds a fur ball—and I looked up. Had I gone too far? But she was already jumping off the table to run down the hall.

"Speaking of…" Her voice reached me as she trotted off. *"But you've got it wrong, Pru. He's only doing what dogs do. And her?"* From the living room, I heard a familiar hack. *"She's frightened."*

I put my beer down to fetch a paper towel, but as I passed through the front hall, I saw headlights swinging up the drive and paused. Creighton, his car almost as powerful as mine but much quieter.

"Hey, stranger." Maybe it was Wallis' words—"*what dogs do*"—maybe it was the beer. My greeting was warmer than I'd planned.

"Hey, yourself." He turned from my kiss, and I stepped back, still holding the towel. "You cleaning?"

"Furball." I smiled. A conciliatory move. Girlish. I shook it off. "Wallis," I turned back toward the living room.

"I figured as much." Creighton sounded a little more like himself, a touch of humor creeping in as he followed me to the other room. "Sorry, Pru, I'm just in a mood."

"Oh?" I knelt to clean, the better to avoid a confrontation.

"Let the man talk." Wallis was washing again.

"I know." I meant to keep my voice low, but Creighton has senses like a cat.

"Hey, you get in foul moods, too." He sounded hurt, rather than angry. There was no way I could explain, and so I turned and stood.

"I'm sorry." To my surprise, I was. I wanted peace. Well, in truth, I wanted more. "I've had a strange day, too. But you first."

"A beer would help."

That got my attention. Creighton didn't drink when he was working. Then again, he didn't come by in the middle of a case either.

"Sure." I bit back my questions as I fetched our beverages. "What's up?"

"Nothing." He looked at the can as if it wasn't what he'd just asked for. "Nothing at all, really."

I watched as he downed most of the beer and then went to get him another. I knew this kind of mood, not that I'd ever seen Creighton in it.

"Here." I handed it over. "But at some point, you're going to talk about it."

Jim Creighton wasn't me. Wasn't my father, either. Instead of downing the second can, he nodded and collapsed on the couch. A little wary, I sat beside him. Wallis, I noticed, had made herself scarce. That could mean there was nothing to worry about. It could also mean she was looking out for herself.

"I know," he said. "It's just this damned case."

"Teddy Rhinecrest." I didn't think there was anything else going on in town. Not this early in the season, and certainly not of that magnitude. He nodded, and I took a breath. "Jim, there's something you should know. I talked to Cheryl Ginger again."

He shrugged.

"Met with her." I couldn't believe he'd forgotten. "The girl-friend?"

"Not any of my business." He was staring at his beer again. I was starting to get jealous. "Not any longer."

"Jim?" I forgot about Wallis. Forgot about Cheryl Ginger and her spaniel. I'd never seen my guy like this.

"They took the case from me." With a sigh like a deflating balloon, he sunk down into the sofa. Only then did he open that second beer and treat himself to a long pull. "I was making progress too. Had a lead."

"So that's why you were out drinking?" I understood the urge. I truly did. But I'd never seen Creighton like that. From the blank stare he gave me, I wondered if I'd misheard Ronnie. "You closed Happy's, I hear."

"That was work, Pru." He looked at the beer as if it would speak up for him. "I was looking for some guys Teddy Rhinecrest may have run afoul of."

I thought of what I'd read about the deceased. "I didn't think anyone around here would mess with someone like Rhinecrest," I said.

Creighton looked up at me, but he didn't argue. "So you've heard. But not everyone here knew his history, and Rhinecrest liked to gamble. Only he didn't like to pay up when he lost. He'd gotten out of the habit, I guess."

"And you thought…maybe this was about money?" In general I trust Creighton's instincts. He's a good cop. "That he welshed on a bet?"

"He'd called someone a cheat. Some other names as well." Another drink, another sigh. "To the folks around here, he was just a rich tourist."

"Could be." I thought about Benazi. About Cheryl Ginger. "So what made you change your mind?"

Creighton shrugged. "I didn't. Didn't get the chance," he said. "It's up to the Feds now."

"Wait." I almost took his beer. When Ronnie had referred to "the Feds," I'd assumed he was confused. Ronnie, as I may have mentioned, is not the sharpest. "The Feds? Not the Staties?" I'd been with Jim long enough to know the protocol. The state police have jurisdiction over any local cop in Massachusetts. In smaller towns, that means they step in when there's a wrongful death case. But the Staties had been overwhelmed in recent years, and in a place like Beauville—where there was a good cop and not much else going on—that jurisdiction tended to become a formality. The commander of the local detective unit, out of Springfield, knew Creighton. Knew that someone who actually lived here had a better chance of closing this than someone who drove over from the other side of the county. Although the paperwork might say otherwise, that meant Creighton was usually left to work on his own.

But he was still shaking his head. "The Feds, Pru. It seems they were quite aware that Teddy Rhinecrest wasn't your ordinary vacationer. They seem to think it was…more complicated."

I nodded. "But why here? Why in Beauville?"

Creighton didn't pretend not to understand. "Maybe he was easier to get to here. On vacation with his girlfriend. Not exactly incognito—but, well, under the radar. He probably had his guard down."

"You think maybe he was up to something?" I caught myself. "I mean, besides being rude to waiters and his girlfriend?"

"I don't know, Pru, and nobody's telling me." He put the can down. It sounded empty. "And it's been made very clear, I'm not supposed to ask. Now, come here."

◇◇◇

For a small town, Beauville has its share of problems. Unemployment, drugs, boredom—they all contribute to keep my guy busy, despite the bucolic appearance of the woods and the hills. But he doesn't often get big cases, the kind that require him to really apply his skills, and even with all the distraction I could provide, I could tell that he was dying to follow up. This is his turf, after all. He's got cop instincts, and it would take more than two beers to dull his sense of responsibility to the small town where we both lived.

He was enough of a boy scout, however, that he wouldn't go against the rules. Not directly. And if he wanted to divert his attention with me, well, I had instincts of my own.

It wasn't until several hours later, when I got up for a glass of water, that I found myself staring out at the frosty night and wondering about the mysteries in my own life. Wallis came up silently, pressing her warm body against my bare legs before jumping to the kitchen table to stare out at the night with me.

I looked over at her, noting how the moonlight reflected off her green eyes, making them almost silver. She must have felt me turn, sensed my shift in focus from the still dark outside to her. She didn't speak, though, and didn't return my gaze, the only acknowledgment a silent lashing of her tail. Still, through her presence, I was able to pick up so much more about the world outside. Out in the woods, animals were moving. The snow that had provided cover for mice and chipmunks was nearly gone, and a hungry owl was watching for movement in the carpet of dead leaves. A mother fox was on the prowl, too, her early kits waiting, hungry, in her den. What other creatures were out there, I could only guess.

"*The rabbits you're so fond of.*" Wallis' voice sounded quietly in my head. "*They're out there, too.*"

"Yeah, but asleep, I would imagine." In the wild, the prey animals tended to be active at dawn and dusk, the safer between-times of the day. It was a behavior that made rabbits better pets than nocturnal hamsters or gerbils, despite their greater size. I thought of Henry and Marnie Lundquist. I hoped for her sake that the fluffy brown creature was safely tucked in and snoozing. "Safe in their warrens," I added for emphasis.

Wallis didn't respond. Instead, she jumped off the table with a barely perceptible thud and set off down the hall. She wouldn't come sleep with me, not with Creighton there, and from the way my cop beau was snoring I doubted he'd be up before morning. Wallis didn't begrudge me my pleasures, though. I knew that from past experience, and tonight I got a sense of hunting—or a trail and of the cautious buildup to an attack. She had her own agenda for the rest of the night, and the less I knew about it, the better.

I filled my glass with water and turned back toward the bedroom. It wasn't until I was halfway up the stairs that I stopped. A faint noise—my old house settling or the dying cry of a small creature—had caught my attention. It had also made me remember. I had told Creighton about Cheryl. I hadn't told him about Benazi, or that the old man was looking into Teddy Rhinecrest's death, too.

Chapter Seventeen

I hadn't forgotten the next morning, neither Benazi nor the bunny. But as Creighton showered and dressed, I kept my thoughts to myself. Creighton knew a bit about the old gangster. I hadn't ever told him the whole story, though, about how the dapper if deadly gent had taken me for a ride—literally—to a secluded house up in the hills. Up there, he'd shared his hawk's eye view with me—both of our town and of certain events that had recently occurred. He'd driven me back to town, too, without anything even remotely like a threat being stated. It didn't matter. I knew without being told that some things were not to be shared with anyone, particularly anyone in law enforcement, and I was glad that Creighton wasn't going to be involved. I'd become fond of the guy.

Besides, I thought as Creighton came out of the shower whistling, why should I spoil my beau's good mood?

"You're looking chipper this morning." I watched as he scouted around for his clothes. "Got somewhere to be?"

"Nowhere at all." He smiled up at me as he put on his socks. "Thought I'd catch up on some paperwork. That's all. And don't you have a dog to walk?"

I took his cue and went downstairs to make coffee. He followed as I was filling my travel mug, and I held out the pot as an offer.

"No, thanks." He grabbed a sip of mine, then handed it back. "I should get moving."

"Paperwork, huh?" I waited, but he only smiled. "And it's pressing?"

"You're not the only one who can keep secrets," he said finally, before leaning in for a kiss. "Stay safe."

"Excuse me?" Wallis' voice broke into my thoughts. *"It's a good thing I know how to take care of myself."*

"Sorry." I shrugged off my musings and cracked open an egg for her breakfast. "I've just never seen him lie before. That I know of." I caught her look and reached for another.

"He's on the hunt, same as you." Her tongue darted out involuntarily, swiping over her chops as she watched me slice the butter. I cut off an extra pat as an appetizer. She licked at it delicately as I cooked the eggs.

"I know, Wallis." A sense of dread hung over me. Creighton wasn't one to be pulled off a case. "That's what I'm afraid of."

"We all have our jobs, you know." Her voice had the rich vibrato of a purr starting. *"Like that dog."*

"Growler?" I looked up at the clock. I'd slept later than usual, thanks to my overnight guest. I slid the eggs onto the plate where the pat of butter had been and went to refill my mug. "Poor guy. He's not going to have any sympathy for why I'm late today."

"You've got a one-track mind." Wallis' words barely reached me. *"And you're focusing on the wrong animal."*

◇◇◇

It wasn't until I was halfway to the Horlick house that it occurred to me that Wallis wasn't simply being snarky. Don't get me wrong—animals have a sense of humor. Pets in particular, since they pick up so many behaviors from the people they cohabit with, and cats specifically understand more about irony than many of us would credit. You live with someone who controls your behavior, you either learn to laugh or you die. But as I drove, I realized that Wallis was referring to one of my other charges—Cheryl Ginger's spaniel.

Something of my thoughts must have shown on my face, because Tracy Horlick greeted me with a more curious squint than usual.

"What's on your mind, I wonder?" She leaned toward me, exhaling twin streams of smoke through her nose. "Who are you thinking about?"

"A dog I'm training." The truth has a different sound to it, and I was hoping to get Growler without the usual fuss.

"Sure you are." The squint tightened. "Just like your mother."

My eyebrows must have shot up at that, because only then did Tracy Horlick lean back with a smile. "Didn't know that about your old lady, did you?"

"Your dog, Mrs. Horlick?" I didn't want to get into this. I knew my mother had her faults, but it was my father who'd been the wandering one.

"Better keep him on his leash," she said. I didn't think she was talking about Growler, but I took the lead she was holding without comment. There was no reason to punish her dog with a further delay. Besides, I didn't think I could win this one.

"Come on, boy," I said, just to break the silence. The fluffy white dog eyed his person and then me and whined softly, making his desire to get going crystal clear. "Let's go."

I wasn't going to call him Bitsy, not even to placate that old hen. Maybe I couldn't prevail against her, but I would salvage whatever dignity I could—for both Growler and myself.

"*Dog?*" The question came to me as Growler led me down the street. I simply shook my head. If he wanted to read my thoughts, he was welcome to. Maybe he could make some sense of them. But I was willing to let them go—along with any idea of closure with that spaniel or with Cheryl Ginger.

I hadn't gotten what I'd wanted the day before, but I didn't have any excuse to go back. And if I felt a bit ambivalent about that, I told myself to let it go. Cheryl Ginger was clearly in several kinds of trouble, and I was better off out of it.

"*As if.*" Wallis wasn't the only animal around me who was picking up on human colloquialisms. Growler's snort only emphasized the disbelief I heard in his words. "*Like a cat with a bone.*"

I eyed the bichon, but his head was down—sniffing at the newly bared trunk of a sapling. Wallis had warned me over a year ago that what I "heard" as words was actually my mind translating amorphous thoughts. Had I superimposed the human-type sayings on the little dog—or had he adopted them for his own purposes?

If that was the case, could I have misinterpreted something the spaniel had been trying to tell me? I thought of him, out in the woods. Clearly he was unfazed by our forests, which was kind of unusual for a city dog. Then again, if he had been a gift from a lover, maybe his presence was more than token. Maybe he was—as Ronnie had said—her excuse for getting out of the condo. Maybe the eager little beast was used to spending time in the woods, his athleticism giving the redhead an excuse for coming back flushed and picking leaves out of her own hair, as well as his.

"Get your mind out of the gutter." Growler was neutered, but he was still a sexual little beast. To have him reprimand me this way had to mean something else.

"What?" I stopped walking, and he turned back to look at me. "Can you tell just by sniffing me what that spaniel was trying to communicate? Or is there some doggie network I don't know about?"

"Jeez." The little pooch snorted. *"I'm just saying you have to think beyond the box. Even if you do cohabit with a cat. Now, do you mind?"*

I had no response, but I did have a responsibility—to Growler, if not the person who was paying me. And so I fell silent and let him lead me onto his usual spots, muttering to himself about a social scene much more relevant to his canine mind.

Out of respect as much as principle, I didn't answer my phone when it rang. This was Growler's time, and even if he didn't choose to communicate with me directly, I owed it to him to be alert. Not only to the subtle cues any animal sends off—even to those with normal sensitivities—but also to the dangers a town like ours can pose to a small creature. I wasn't overly worried about wildlife. Although I had reason to believe there was a large wild cat loose in the nearby preservation land,

I doubted the bichon would be at risk. Growler would be a tasty morsel to some of the larger creatures around—both coyotes and fisher cats would be hungry and prowling after the winter we had—but neither were likely to hunt by daylight, and both would be dissuaded by my presence. No, I was thinking of the more ordinary dangers house pets face: from people, other pets, and, of course, cars.

I was glad for this discipline when I caught the quiet hum of a car approaching a bit too fast for comfort. And as I pulled Growler's lead close and turned, I was doubly glad. The sporty little number that had pulled up just as the bichon had stepped back onto the curb was red and as familiar to me by now as the driver, who stepped out to greet me.

"Ms. Marlowe." With a grace that defied his apparent age, Gregor Benazi sidled across in front of his car to stand beside me, and I had to fight the desire to gather Growler into my arms. "Back to your usual routine, I see."

"What of it?" I don't like surprises. I also don't like discovering that people know more about me than I have chosen to share. "Growler."

The little dog had begun to sniff our visitor's pants cuff. At the sound of my voice, he paused and looked up at me. Benazi, I saw out of the corner of my eye, smiled.

"It's a nickname." I fought back my own urge to growl. Benazi had always been polite to me, and I didn't think it made sense to antagonize him.

"Most fitting," he said, dipping his head, though whether his half bow was to me or to the white dog at his feet I couldn't tell. "But I haven't sought you out to interrupt your duties."

I swallowed, his words banishing any possibility that his appearance was a chance meeting. "Yes?" One syllable was all I could manage.

"Ms. Marlowe." His voice was calm. Soothing. I thought of all the stories I'd heard of snakes that hypnotize their prey. "You know I have the greatest respect for you, and, of course, for your abilities."

I nodded. It seemed some sort of acknowledgment was required.

"I'm also aware that your position allows you a kind of access that not many enjoy." He paused, but I didn't respond. For all I knew, he was talking about my relationship with Creighton. Or could he mean…From the way he was looking at me, I got the distinct impression that he knew what I was thinking. I did my best to clear my mind. To be blank. The man had sensitivities of his own. And with another brief nod, he continued. "As you know, I am in town because of matters relating to the late Teddy Rhinecrest, whose unfortunate demise is now the subject of a federal investigation."

He said that as if it were common knowledge. I swallowed again.

"I have no desire to interfere with the workings of the state, of course." He shook his head, more in distaste than anything else, I thought. "But I did want to follow up on my earlier request and to inquire if in your dealings with Ms. Ginger you may have come across any information that would be useful to me."

"Information?" I licked my lips. My mouth was dry. "I thought you were looking for a keepsake of some kind?"

"One may lead to the other. Perhaps the mention of mutual friend, or a stop made along the way." His voice was calm and soft, as if we weren't discussing matters of life and death. "The kind of small matter that may escape the notice of a more formal inquiry."

"I doubt I'll be seeing Cheryl Ginger again." I found my voice. "In fact, I bet she won't even be in Beauville for much longer."

The old man smiled, a wide, close-mouthed grin that didn't touch his eyes. "Oh, I suspect the resourceful Ms. Ginger will be reaching out to you again, Ms. Marlowe. I believe she will have need of your service and has already learned to respect your particular talents. As have others."

"I'm just an animal trainer, Mr. Benazi."

The old man smiled and bent to pat Growler on the head. "You look out for her, my little man," he said in a voice I could clearly hear. "She's a special one."

I was still shaking as he got back into his car. It wasn't until he drove away, that snazzy red sportster disappearing around a corner, that I realized he'd not left me a phone number or any way to contact him. It didn't matter. I had no doubt he would be in touch.

Chapter Eighteen

My fear had given way to anger by the time I got Growler back home. Benazi had intercepted us more than a block from Tracy Horlick's house, which was just enough time for me to work up a good head of steam. It was not, however, enough time for me to debrief the bichon before we turned the final corner.

"What did you get?" I asked, slowing as we approached the battered-looking split-level. "What was he up to?"

"He's got a cat." Growler seemed confused by that. *"He likes cats."*

"I know, Growler." I stopped in front of the neighbor's lawn. "But, please, can you help me? You were sniffing his leg."

"He admires cats, you know. He sees something of himself in them." The little dog sat and looked up at me, black button eyes bright. *"Something of you, too."*

"There you are!" Tracy Horlick was coming down the sidewalk, huffing with the effort. "I thought maybe you'd stolen my dog."

"Not at all." I conjured my conciliatory smile. I wasn't going to lie on my back for her. "We were just going over some routine commands. Sit, heel."

"He's got no use for that kind of nonsense." Holding her cigarette to her lips with one hand, she reached the other for the lead. "Come on, Bitsy," she said, shooting me a venomous look. "Some of us have lives."

I stepped back before she could push me, and watched as she bundled herself and her dog into the beat-up Chevy in the driveway. I'd never seen the old bat leave the house, although she clearly got her smokes—and her gossip—from somewhere. And while I suspected her hair color and its outdated lacquer finish were professionally done, I didn't quite understand the urgency. It might be spring, but I seriously doubted Tracy Horlick had a date.

"Bye!" I waved, as much to Growler as to the woman who paid me. But he only stared, mute, from the window as she backed into the street and took off.

"People." I was shaking my head as I walked back to my own car, and almost missed the squirrel darting in front of me.

"*Watch yourself!*" The creature chittered at me from the safety of a tree trunk. "*You'd think you're the only one out here.*"

He was right. Benazi's visit should have reminded me to be alert. At the very least, I needed to be more conscious of my surroundings—and my phone.

"Hello, Pru?" I recognized the caller on my voicemail even before she introduced herself. Cheryl Ginger should have been the ideal client. She certainly had the means to pay me. Just then I wished she didn't. "Would you call me back? I'd like to book some more sessions for Pudgy. Starting today, if possible."

Sessions? That dog didn't need training. She did. Besides, I had no desire to get more involved in whatever game Gregor Benazi was playing with the pretty redhead. I didn't like to think of myself as intimidated, simply smart. But as I was about to hit "erase," I caught myself. Maybe the aptly named Ms. Ginger really did want my help with her dog. After all, she didn't seem entirely in control of the little guy, despite his apparent schooling. Or maybe my warning had finally sunk in, and she wanted to talk to me about Benazi.

That should have been impetus enough to delete the call, but as much as I respected the menace cloaked behind Benazi's tailoring, I also felt another, contrary impulse. Who was Gregor

Benazi to threaten me? Or, to be specific, believe he could pressure me into becoming his accomplice?

I hit re-dial. I was not going to be intimidated by the old gangster. And I did need to earn a living. That meant I was going to go about my life as if he hadn't surprised me by the side of the road. I wasn't sure of Cheryl Ginger, but she was a client. If she tried to involve me in anything that didn't feel legit, I'd decide what to do by myself.

"Hello?" Her voice sounded tight as she answered. Taken by surprise, I thought. Or maybe scared.

"Cheryl? It's Pru Marlowe." I used my comfort voice: low and even. The one I use to soothe panicked animals. "I'm returning your call about further sessions with Pudgy." I didn't like that name for the little spaniel, but I needed to make the connection with his person.

"Yes, thanks." I thought I heard her licking her lips. "When can you get here?"

"Is there an emergency?" As soon as the words were out of my mouth, I kicked myself. And rephrased: "If you're having a veterinary emergency, you should take your dog over to County Animal Hospital. Do you want me to call over and tell them to expect you?"

Nine-tenths of training is being clear. Limit the options for the animal being trained. Be as straightforward as possible about the behavior you want. That's it.

"What? No, I—" She was definitely licking her lips. Either she was nervous, or those pretty lips had become horrible chapped. "I was hoping you had some free time today. For an appointment." My tactic had worked.

"I may be able to come by this afternoon." I weighed the words, giving her the reward her behavior merited. With a caveat. "I'll have to check my schedule."

"I'll be here. At the Chateau," she said, as if I'd forget. "Thank you so much."

I was already having second thoughts as she hung up. I'd only returned the call because I didn't want to give in to my fear. If I was going to go out there, I was going to be prepared, I decided. And that meant hitting up Ronnie. The sleazy condo manager had clearly spied on the redhead during her stay, and I bet there was more he could tell me about her than he had.

Pulling away from the curb, I thought about where to find him. At this hour of the morning—it was only a few minutes past nine—he'd probably still be asleep. I didn't mind waking him, only I wasn't sure what rat hole he lived in. No, I decided, turning toward the highway. He would be at work. Maybe asleep, but at the job. Nothing makes owners jumpier than a murder on the premises, and I bet that, at least for the near future, management would be clamping down. I had no desire to revisit the development—between finding Teddy Rhinecrest's body and running into Gregor Benazi, the place was bad luck, to say the least. But I wasn't going to be frightened away from any place on my home turf. Besides, maybe my being there would spark Ronnie's dim bulb of a mind.

The day certainly held no threat. Unfiltered, yet, by any leaves, the sun was bright and surprisingly warm. As I drove through the woods, I caught the play of shadows—trees beginning to bud and the hollows that would soon be filled with fern and jewelweed. In some of those hollows, snow would linger for a few weeks yet, depending on how quickly this spring came in. Under last season's leaves, there were always a few shady spots that were colder than the rest. In time, they'd be a welcome source of water for the smaller creatures out there, the ones who had slept or crept unnoticed under the winter's deep cover.

I thought of such hidden caches as I drove, and of other secrets in the dark. Of whether I could ever explain myself to Jim Creighton. Whether his respect for me, if not his affection, would survive knowing the truth that I kept camouflaged. Perhaps it was the season for secrets to come to light. Perhaps I wasn't alone. After all, Benazi seemed to share some sense of the world around us. He even, he had led me to believe, understood my particular skill.

A shadow on the road drew my eyes up. High above, the distinctive silhouette of a hawk, gliding on the currents of the warming day. On a morning like this, it was easy to think of his flight as a form of relaxation. A lone creature enjoying the sun and the breeze. Even as he soared out of my range, I could see no movement of wing or tail, which made his motion seem effortless. His purpose casual.

But the sharp cheeps I heard as this shadow passed beyond the trees told me another story. *"Watch!"* The sparrows called, a cry picked up by a mockingbird until even a sedentary mourning dove was rumbling her own version. Animals do nothing without reason. Even their play is serious, teaching and sharing the skills they need to survive.

I looked once more for that hawk, but he was gone. And I thought of Benazi, whose own piercing eyes saw me so clearly. Maybe he did understand me better than Creighton. Better than anyone ever could. And maybe, it hit me with a start that had the hair standing up along my arms, he saw other things, too. Like that Cheryl Ginger was going to get back in touch with me. And that when she called, I would answer.

Chapter Nineteen

"Ronnie!" I was banging on the door to the manager's office. My realization about Benazi had leached all the warmth out of the sunny morning, and the absence of the condo handyman did nothing to improve my mood. "I know you're in there, Ronnie. Your truck's here."

"Hang on." Footsteps could be heard through the cheap door, which opened to reveal the sleep-bedraggled man. "I was…working in the back," he said, barely suppressing a yawn.

"Right." I pushed past him, thoughts of the old gangster making me want privacy or at least cover. The office was close and warm. Ronnie hadn't been napping. He was living here. I looked around, unwilling to sit on the Naugahyde couch that still had the imprint of his soft body, and chose the desk chair. "I need to talk with you."

"Yeah, I need to talk to you, too." He started to scratch until—seeing my face—he changed the motion, pretending to smooth a pleat in the rumpled khakis that probably passed for a uniform. "Some lady called."

"Cheryl Ginger? I'm on it." I looked around for a coffee maker until I saw an eighties-era Mr. Coffee in the corner, busted. No matter, he'd be more pliable half-awake. "In fact, she's why I'm here, Ronnie. I need to know what you saw and what you heard. Exactly." I paused, wondering how to play this. "I'll make sure she knows that you helped out."

"Cheryl Ginger?"

Maybe I should have brought him coffee. But, no, he rallied. "She moved out."

"I know." This was going to take time, and I wanted to spend as little of that here, with Ronnie, as possible. "Because her boyfriend was killed." I decided to fill in the blanks. "The one she was cheating on. Cheating that you knew about. And I know you said that you didn't really witness anything, but between you and me and that bear over there…" The white plush toy, incongruous in this setting, didn't comment. "I know you were watching her."

"I didn't…" Ronnie was blushing. Not a good look for him. "I mean…"

"Yes, I know." I cut him off before he could start with the excuses. "You weren't stalking her or acting like some kind of creepy peeping Tom. You just happened to see her or overhear her when she went off to meet her other male friend."

He looked up, blinking.

"And I won't let anyone know how you abuse the perks of your job, like the manager's office. Or your access keys." That was an inspired improvisation, but from the way his color changed—red to white and back again to an unhealthy flush—I knew I'd hit pay dirt.

"Okay, Ronnie." I lowered my voice to the command tone, and continued, speaking clearly and slowly. "Now if you want me to keep your secrets, you have to tell me what you saw."

"It wasn't like that." The room was stuffy, but that wasn't why he was starting to sweat. His face was as red as the cheap valentine I spied on the sofa beside him. Following my glance, he shoved under one meaty thigh. "I only meant to—I liked looking at her."

I nodded. I figured as much, and he was probably too timid to do more, though that valentine made me wonder. "Go on."

"I didn't actually see, you know. Them." His voice dropped. "Going at it."

My raised eyebrows expressed my skepticism. I didn't need to be aggressive to establish myself as the alpha. Simply firm.

"No, really." He was eager to convince me now. To win me over. "In fact, I don't even know if he was...I mean, yeah, she was sneaking out to see him. I'd hear her say she was going to walk the dog. She said it to the dead guy. Before he was dead."

"I get it." I didn't need Ronnie tripping over his own syntax.

"Anyway, she'd say something like, 'I want to take Fatty for a long walk.'"

"Pudgy," I corrected him automatically and immediately regretted interrupting his chain of thought. "So she'd pretend she was only going for a walk," I prompted.

"Uh huh." He nodded vigorously. "And I couldn't follow. I mean, I have a job." Translation: Cheryl was either too quick or too slick for him to follow. "But twice I did see a guy. And once I heard them talking. Only, I couldn't really hear."

"It's a bit late to get cold feet." I pointed out the obvious.

"I think she called him her brother." His face kind of squished up on that last word. Even Ronnie had some limits.

"I'm sure she was talking metaphorically." He blinked, confused. "She didn't mean it," I translated. "Or maybe they were cooking up their alibi. Anyway, what did this guy look like?"

"I don't know." He shrugged. I waited. "He was a guy."

I waited, looking around the room from the crusty towel in the corner back to Ronnie. "Young, fancy haircut," he said finally.

Not Benazi, then. I hadn't thought this was likely, but it was good to know. "So not an older guy, with gray hair?"

"No," he shook his head. "Just kind of normal brown. I mean, he wasn't even that buff. Kind of skinny, if you know what I mean."

Coming from Ronnie that could have meant anything. He weighed in at well over two-fifty. But it did tend to rule out the beefy blond from the restaurant, even if I had seen him poking about before. "Did you ever see him come to the condo, like when Teddy Rhinecrest was out?" I was thinking of those phone lines, though why Cheryl's boy toy would do anything so obvious was beyond me.

"Nuh uh." Ronnie was shaking his head. "Never. Mr. Rhinecrest didn't even have any of his friends over."

I thought of Benazi then. "He had friends?"

"I guess." A shrug. "I mean a rich guy like that? It's not like there's a lot to do around here, except…uh…" He was blushing again. "Be alone with his girlfriend."

"I heard he liked to play cards." It was time for me to disengage. "But speaking of —you ever actually talk to Cheryl Ginger?"

"No, never." He looked disconsolate as he stared at the desk.

"But she called you." Something wasn't making sense. "Looking for me?"

"No." He shook his head, adamant. I was about to call him out. To break through this final lie, when he explained. "She wasn't the lady who was looking for you, Pru. This one came up from the city. I think she was the dead guy's wife."

Chapter Twenty

"So, can you do something about the rabbits?"

Ronnie's words made no sense. I blinked up at him. "What?"

"The rabbits," he repeated. "They're like everywhere. I'm supposed to get the grounds all nice for the open house next month but they're just going to eat everything."

I waited, not understanding.

"I thought, maybe…" He leaned in, his voice dropping. "… you had some traps?"

"No, Ronnie. I'm not going to kill rabbits for you." I put my hand up to keep him from moving in any closer. "And back up. You said Teddy Rhinecrest's wife—his widow—called for me?"

"Yeah, yesterday." He shrugged. "She said she wanted to talk to you. To the lady who found her husband. I've got her number here."

He crossed over to a desk that looked like it did double-duty as a dinner table, if the crumbs and greasy paper bag were any indication. Pushing aside a dirty plastic fork, he pulled out a pile of stained paper napkins. On one of them, I could make out a number.

"These?" I tried to read the name on top.

"Theresa," he said. "And that's a 212 number." City, then, rather than the suburbs.

"Of course." I folded it with the grease—and the number—on the inside and tucked it into my pocket. "Wait, did she ask for the lady who found her husband, or did she ask for me by name?"

"She knew your name." He blinked, but he must have seen something on my face because he followed up. "I think the cops must have told her," he said.

I wasn't about to reveal what Creighton had told me, so I nodded as I turned to go. This was a lot to digest.

"Hey, Pru?"

I didn't even bother turning around. "Forget the rabbits, Ronnie," I said. "I'm not going to do it, and neither are you. Try planting some rabbit-resistant plants, like irises. Or, hey, cat mint." Wallis would appreciate that, I thought.

"No, I mean—what you know?" I turned. He was blushing again, the flush highlighting the broken veins around his nose. "You won't tell your guy, right? I mean, he's a cop."

"That you spy on the pretty female guests?" He squirmed, and I thought of Wallis again. Wallis with a small rodent, pinned. I knew that Creighton was off the case, officially at least. Ronnie clearly didn't. "I won't if you stop doing it, Ronnie. Even pretty ladies are entitled to some privacy."

◇◇◇

I hadn't gotten much from Ronnie, and I doubted he'd change his behavior. His life was too dull without his illicit thrills, and his mental capacity was such that he wasn't likely to hold onto to a threat for very long. Still, I made a mental note to check the blinds and curtains in my own house as I got back into my car and drove back toward town. I had a few other appointments that day, but by now my curiosity was piqued. It seemed obvious that Teddy Rhinecrest's girl on the side had some extracurricular activity of her own. But now that the widow was in the picture, the motives for his demise were adding up.

On a whim, I called Creighton.

"Hey, Jim." I got his voice mail. "You around? I know you said you're off the case, but can you think of any reason why Teddy Rhinecrest's widow would want to talk to me?" I mulled over the possibilities before the line cut off. If Benazi hadn't surfaced, I'd have bet she'd be a prime suspect. If Creighton wasn't looking into her, I wanted to know why. And why she'd called me. "She can't think I'm the girlfriend, can she?"

I considered this as I drove. Cops are notorious for not sharing information. From all I knew, the Feds were worse. And yet somebody had told the widow that I had been the one to find her husband's body. Either somebody had slipped up, or Teddy Rhinecrest's widow had a lot of clout. Unless, I thought, my eyes searching the sky for that hawk again, someone wanted to set me up. Wanted me in the hot seat, answering questions.

"Oh, Gregor." I tried the name out as I drove. The sky above was empty at midday, but that was as ominous a sign as any. Spring is prime time for birds. Mating, nesting, bustling about to feed themselves and their young after the long winter. A sunny day like this, I should be seeing four or five species, easily, without any effort. Unless the cardinals and catbirds had a reason for staying low and under branches.

One way or another, I was going to have to deal with the old man. Not that I was going to give him any information. It wasn't simply that I didn't have any, but to pass along things I learned from my clients—or their pets—was, if not unethical, not quite kosher either, and I wasn't going to establish the precedent. He liked me, in his way. I knew that. But I needed him to respect me—respect more than my facility with animals.

And then it hit me. I'd been blinded by my fear, the mouse before the cobra. Benazi had caught me off guard by showing up unexpectedly, and not by accident. No, this was an old tactic, designed to counter my defenses. But I was a behaviorist. I had my own set of skills, tools I used to break down defenses and ingrained bad habits. And I had experience with killers who were cooler even than Benazi. Smaller, maybe, and covered in fur, but more blood-thirsty.

I thought of Wallis, of what she had taught me. And I knew I could do this. I could turn this around. Stop being the prey and regain some control over my own life.

If I was careful, if I was good, I could use my training—much like Benazi's own tricks—against him. I could get him to respond, as any wild beast would, to my cues and prompts. It wouldn't be easy, not like the simple routines I used on Tracy Horlick. He was smart enough to be aware of my techniques, and that meant he not only would resist, he would be on his guard.

I didn't see any other choice.

Chapter Twenty-one

I had lied to Cheryl Ginger when I'd said I was busy. Let clients think you're available at all hours, and they'll come to expect immediate service. Let them believe they have to make an appointment and wait, they'll respect you more. It's not a technique I use on animals. They can handle honesty—prefer it, actually—and I play my role straight with them whenever possible. People, though, they need manipulating. And so with everyone —everyone but Benazi, that is—I did this automatically, almost as a second nature, although Wallis would probably take credit for some of the attitude I gave off to unexpected requests.

As I drove, I found another reason to be grateful for the routine mind game. I'd been acting on instinct and habit—reacting, mostly—and I wanted time to step back. To consider what was going on. To prepare.

Cheryl Ginger, Benazi, and now Theresa Rhinecrest all wanted something from me, and that had put me in the middle of something I had no interest in. Yeah, a guy had been killed. But I didn't really know him, I didn't like him, and he wasn't even a client when he died. I had no dog in this fight, and even less interest now that he was dead.

But as long as the redhead was willing to pay, I couldn't simply stop taking her calls. And Benazi, well, I'd figure that out. In the meantime, I decided to enlist a little aid. Creighton might be off the case, but that didn't mean he would be out of the loop entirely. And if he was still pissed off at the Feds, so much the better.

Beauville's cop shop is in the new part of town. Built of red brick that's supposed to evoke our New England heritage, it's got a big glass foyer that's too cold in winter and a sweat box in summer, proof that architects don't pay attention beyond the basic look. It also shares an interior wall with the Beauville Shelter, a bare-bones office for animal control that also houses a few, usually empty cages in back. Albert's too lazy to collect nuisance animals, and anyone in the know—myself included—would rather bring any poor beast to County, our animal hospital, than here.

"Hey, Albert." I pushed open the glass door to the right, figuring I'd use my visit here as my excuse, in case anyone asked. "How's it hanging?"

"Hey, Pru." He started to rise from behind his desk, the crumbs falling off him like rain. "Been meaning to call you."

"Oh?" I leafed through the fliers on his desk. He probably hadn't, and I did like to keep abreast of the latest developments. "You see this about mosquito spraying?"

"What? No." He looked down, blinking, as I handed him the paper. "Oh." He nodded, and I had to wonder if he could read.

"You should post this." I pointed to the bulletin board. "Tell people to close their windows and keep their pets inside."

"Yeah, yeah." He lumbered over to the board, hiking up his pants with one hand as he walked. I averted my eyes, turning instead toward his desk.

"You bring Frank in today?" The little mustelid liked to lurk in Albert's desk drawers. Sometimes, I knew, that was because he'd find his person's forgotten edibles in there. Sometimes, I suspected, it was because he was embarrassed.

"No, not today." Albert lumbered back. He'd managed to tack the paper up—over a notice of the county's mandatory vaccinations. "He's still kind of frisky. Spring fever, I guess." He chortled and put his hand up over his mouth, though whether embarrassed by the sexual allusion or his poor dentition, I had no idea.

"You might think about taking him over to Doc Sharpe," I said. "Get him neutered." I don't begrudge anyone their sexuality. Pets, however, get along better when they're not hormone-crazed. Come to think of it, Albert would do a lot better with a few snips himself.

From the look of shock and horror that came over the animal control officer's face, I wondered momentarily if I had spoken my thoughts out loud. Then I realized that, no, Albert simply identified a bit too strongly with the ferret. That he did so, simply in terms of sexuality and gender and not intellectual curiosity, was not something I could explain.

"Never mind." I shook my head in apology. This wasn't a battle I wanted to fight. Not now, when I needed Albert's good-will. "Hey, Albert, I wanted to ask you about Ronnie."

He had sat behind his desk again and looked up, blinking. I took that for assent.

"Is he...?" I debated how to phrase this. "Can his perception be trusted?"

Albert's mouth opened a bit more as he parsed my question.

"I mean, when he says something, do you believe him?" It wasn't completely what I meant. I thought it likely Albert would believe almost anything anyone said to him, but it was a start.

"Do you —ah—like him, Pru?" Albert's eyes were wide with astonishment.

"It's just that I asked him about something." I paused, trying to find the simplest words. "And I'm not sure if I can believe his answer."

He shrugged. "He told you about the lady, right?"

"What about the lady?" If Albert asked me about the voyeurism, I was going to set him straight.

"The one who called for you. The wife?"

"The widow?" That woman was thorough.

He was nodding. "She called me, too. She really wants to talk to you. Said there'd be money in it."

I didn't have a good feeling about this, but I couldn't blame Albert for that. He knew I was usually looking for work. Hell, most of Beauville was usually on the lookout for a few quick bucks. Somehow, though, I didn't think this would be easy money.

"I gave her your number, Pru." I closed my eyes. There was no sense in taking this out on Albert. "So, maybe, you know, you might introduce me, too?"

My best intentions only go so far, and I left before my claws came out, letting the glass door slam behind me.

My phone rang while I was walking to my car. I'd meant to swing over to Creighton's office, but Albert had gotten me riled up, and I didn't want to be seen as running to my boyfriend all ruffled. Better I should pick up something for lunch, and then come back and interrupt his paperwork. Maybe I could satisfy another appetite with my beau.

"Hello?" The number wasn't one I recognized. From the area code, I had a good idea what to expect. "Mrs. Rhinecrest?"

"Why, no," said a male voice. "Were you expecting her?"

"I—" I hate being at a loss for words. "I'm sorry, I thought I recognized her number."

"Don't get too many calls from the city, do you?" The man chuckled, a deep rumble.

"May I help you?" I turned to look back at the cop shop. Two of Creighton's deputies walked back, deep in conversation. "I'm rather busy."

"Did I step on the country mouse's tail?" Another chuckle. I was ready to hang up. "Well, I'm sorry. But I am an associate of Theresa Rhinecrest's, and it's in that capacity that I'm reaching out to you."

"Yes?" He'd bought himself a minute more of my time with the use of her full name. No more.

"I'd like to talk to you about your acquaintance with the late Mr. Rhinecrest." He must have sensed my impatience, because he started talking more quickly. "About his time in Beauville."

"I'm sorry." I wasn't, and my tone made that clear. "I didn't know the man, and I'm busy."

"I'll make it worth your while." His voice had an edge of desperation now.

"I said, no. Now, Mister—" I paused.

"Parvis. Martin Parvis. I can meet you anywhere. Today, even. Please, Ms. Marlowe. I'm sorry if we got off on the wrong foot. I'm a private investigator, licensed and everything, but I get it—look, I'm just sorry. Okay? It's important. I can come to you. To your home."

"No." I didn't want this man in my town. There was no way I would let him in my house.

"Pick a place then." I thought of the dead man, of what his widow would want to know. I thought of my mother after my father left. I sighed, and he knew he had me. "A restaurant. A public place. I can be anywhere in Beauville by ten," he added. The way I drive, I could have gotten here from the city in three hours. Then again, most men don't drive like I do.

I paused to think. Happy's was the logical option. At ten, all the regulars would be there, and maybe I'd have a chance to figure out what Creighton had been doing at the dive bar the other night. It also meant I wouldn't be alone with this guy.

"There's a place called Happy's. It's on the main drag," I said at last. "I'll be at the bar."

"Ten, it is," he paused. I imagined him trying to enter Happy's in his GPS. "Thank you."

Well, he'd make it or he wouldn't. Beauville isn't that big, and Happy's worked for me, so with that, I hung up and leaned back on my car. This was getting complicated, and I didn't understand how I'd gotten involved. But I did know I would rather speak to a third party—a factotum—than a grieving widow. Besides, this Martin Parvis had pretty much said he'd pay me. And if he was willing to make the drive, it was no skin off my back.

It was curious, though, how interested everyone suddenly was in Beauville, our little know-nothing town. Enough so that I wondered if soon I might be bringing Creighton something more than lunch.

Chapter Twenty-two

Which, it turned out, would have to wait. I'd gone around the corner for sandwiches before bearding my particular lion in his den, only to find him gone.

"Sorry, Pru." His deputy looked up at me from his desk. "He's been out all morning."

Paperwork, indeed. I knew better than to ask. I didn't want the help to gossip about me getting needy, and instead retired to my car to eat my own provolone and soppressata. As I've said, Beauville is getting gentrified. That's not entirely a bad thing.

However, the size of the sandwich—not to mention the olive oil that had begun to drip down my hand—did make eating in the bucket seat a little awkward. Especially when my phone rang again.

"Jim…" I wiped one hand on the wad of napkins and reached for my cell. No—this wasn't local. In fact, the area code was once again 212. I hesitated a moment, and then clicked through.

"I said I'd meet you tonight at Happy's," I said, through a mouthful. If Martin Parvis wanted to cancel, that was fine by me. "And you can just tell your Mrs. Rhinecrest she can wait."

"Tell her yourself," said a throaty female voice. "I'm dying to hear more."

"Mrs. Rhinecrest?" I swallowed the last bit of salami, half chewed, and winced. "Hang on."

A swig from my soda—orange, imported, and fizzy—and another grab at those napkins and I was back. I hadn't wanted to talk to this woman at all. Now she had me at a distinct disadvantage.

"Sorry about that, Mrs. Rhinecrest." I sat up straight. Your posture affects how you sound on the phone, and I needed to regain some stature here. "And, please, accept my condolences. You see, I only just got off the phone with your…" I paused, unsure of what to call Martin Parvis. "Your employee."

She laughed at that, a low chuckle that had little of humor in it. Little of mourning, either. "I gather he made quite an impression."

"He was quite insistent." That was noncommittal. I didn't want to cost the guy his job, but there was something about this woman that set my teeth on edge. Maybe it was her accent—that touch of lockjaw that denotes a certain country club set. Maybe it was that she didn't trust the people she employed to do their jobs. "Which I assume is what you want," I finished the thought.

"Indeed, it is." There was a curious upward lilt—almost a question—in her voice. "And I'm glad to hear that Marty is heading your way. I've been beginning to think he had blown me off."

I didn't respond, but the picture was becoming clear. Theresa Rhinecrest was the kind of woman who expected people to jump. Parvis had probably waited all of fifteen minutes before calling me.

"Did he ask you about Teddy—about Teddy's friend?" I had to admire her resolve. Her voice barely changed on that last word.

"He said he wanted to speak with me," I repeated. "We're going to meet up here in Beauville, as I gather you figured out."

"Yes…" She drew the word out, which made me wonder. Now that she had called, and done me the service of confirming that, yes, Parvis was indeed working for her, I couldn't figure out what she wanted.

"What precisely did you hire Martin Parvis for, Mrs. Rhinecrest?" Sometimes a direct approach is best.

"I'm sure Mr. Parvis will make everything clear." She was done with me. But my curiosity had been piqued.

"I'm sure he will." I agreed to create a bond. The human equivalent of saying, "good boy!" and giving a treat. "But since you have me here, why don't you fill me in? After all, there may be something I can prepare."

I was fishing. I heard a sniff on the line. Tears or—could it be?—was the widow scoffing at the idea?

"No, no." She wasn't crying—that much I could tell. "I'm hoping to gain a little insight into my husband's stay in your quaint town. To find out if he made any excursions."

Not laughter, either. She was hesitating over her words, though, and I couldn't see why. Excursions? Clearly, this was about Cheryl Ginger. Excursions was about as nice a way to say "stepping out" as I could figure. But her husband was dead. If she was looking to catch him in flagrante, well, she was a little too late.

"I didn't know your husband." I needed to set her straight. "And I've only met Ms. Ginger since his death."

"That's not what I heard." I didn't think I could sit up straighter, but I did.

"Excuse me?" I could match her tone, icicle for icicle.

"Please, I'm sorry, I'm simply overwhelmed." A sniff for sure this time. "It's all been…so much."

I waited. I didn't care what the Feds thought—or my beau for that matter. When a cheating man is killed, there's an obvious suspect. I was talking to her.

"And I'm afraid dear Teddy wasn't always clear in his plans. And certain papers, well…I'm simply trying to sort everything out."

"Look, I don't know anything about your husband, and I don't know anything about Cheryl Ginger." That wasn't entirely true, but I wanted nothing to do with this woman. "I am sorry for your loss, but I think it may be best to leave the investigation to the authorities."

"The authorities." She huffed, the tears gone. "Please."

A quieter sort than her husband, with all his swagger: *"Don't you know who I am?"* A matched pair, nonetheless.

"Please, just meet with Mr. Parvis, won't you?" She tried to soften the note of command. It didn't work. "Maybe you'll remember something you weren't even aware you knew."

"Goodbye, Mrs. Rhinecrest," I said. "Again, I'm sorry for your loss. " I was curious, but not that much. As soon as we'd disconnected, I scrolled back through my calls to cancel the meeting with Parvis. He wasn't answering, and his voice mail was full. It didn't matter; when I didn't show, he'd get the message.

Chapter Twenty-three

My one afternoon appointment wasn't enough of a distraction to take my mind off the Rhinecrest widow. Changing the filter and cleaning the fish tank at our local Chinese restaurant were mindless chores. Gouramis are as boring as you'd think, and the google-eyed angel fish had been squabbling since they'd been paired up.

If I hadn't told Cheryl Ginger I'd come by, I'd have gone home. Wallis would be amused by the domestic drama, I had no doubt, and her insight into handling this Parvis—a scavenger if ever there was one—might be useful. But home was the other side of town, and as much as I wanted out of that particular storyline, I knew I could use Cheryl Ginger's fee. Besides, my brief conversation with Theresa Rhinecrest had given me some sympathy for the younger woman, if not for the man they had shared.

Lucky Dragon—we're not that gentrified—was in the older part of town. And as I pulled away, I realized I had another option. Despite her age, Marnie Lundquist was certainly capable of caring for her granddaughter's rabbit by herself. But she had been uneasy about the bunny the day before. I suspected that she was simply nervous about the responsibility, but it wouldn't do any harm to drop by. Besides, I liked the old lady, and I had some questions that the fluffy leporid might be able to answer.

"Thank you, Mrs. Lundquist." Twenty minutes later, I was on the floor with the rabbit. "Now, do you mind?" The old lady had been surprised to see me, but not unhappy. And when I explained myself—that I was in the neighborhood and that I had been aware that her concerns had not been entirely answered during my other visit—she had welcomed me in.

I wasn't speaking to her, of course. Sitting on the braided rug, which already looked a bit chewed, I was focusing on the rabbit, Henry. I wasn't looking at him. He was a prey animal, and I didn't want to scare him. But I did address my question toward him, reaching out as I've been learning to do with gentle thoughts of grass and sunshine.

He'd been in the room when I'd come in, nibbling on some hay in an open box. But although he'd frozen when we'd entered—those liquid eyes going even wider to take in possible escape routes—he'd calmed a bit, as I talked to his surrogate human. Now he hopped over, his reddish legs extending as he considered my presence.

"What's your story?" I slowly extended my hand for him to sniff. *"Are you at peace?"* I wasn't sure how to ask what I wanted. This, after all, was a creature of the wild, far different from the cats and dogs I usually communicated with. *"Are you happy?"*

I wasn't even sure what I wanted to ask. Partly, I did want to help Marnie Lundquist. She had reassured me that the bunny hadn't threatened her again—no more of that odd rabbit growling—but she had confirmed that "Henry didn't seem quite himself." Partly, I felt an obligation to the little beast. Pet or no, he had not been raised to live with humans. If he was miserable, or going slowly nuts, I would do what I could to set him free.

Partly, I'll confess, I was curious. Beyond a brief internship at a wildlife rehab center a few years ago, I'd had little chance to spend time with something truly wild. The few interactions I'd had recently—with a raccoon and with a wild cat—had been fascinating, their impressions more vivid than anything I would have imagined. Henry hadn't even let me hold him on my first visit. More than his soft fur, I wanted to touch his mind. To see what made the little bunny hop.

Marnie Lundquist seemed to sense this. Rather than respond to my query, she sat a few feet away, perched like a small bird on an ottoman, and watched as Henry and I sized each other up.

"Safe?" The thought was more an appraisal than a direct question, as the twitching nose sought out my scent.

"I'm a friend," I replied, softly. This animal was somewhat used to human companionship, and I hoped my low, calm tone would be reassuring. And, perhaps, familiar.

"Family?" The bunny took one step closer, sniffing. Once again, I was struck by the delicacy of the creature's face. From a distance, a rabbit can look like a puffball with legs. Up close, I could see those large eyes taking in everything: me, the room on either side. Even much of the area behind his muscular rump. Everything including Marnie Lundquist, I assumed.

"Friend," I repeated. I couldn't tell if Henry associated Marnie with her granddaughter, or how he regarded his relationship with these women. But I've found that honesty works best with animals. They know better than most of us that deceit can mean danger.

"He's quite taken with you." Marnie Lundquist's voice was equally low and soft. "He's treating you like a member of the family."

I started and caught myself. Made myself smile. Her words—echoing the rabbit's—were most likely coincidence. Although it was possible that she, too, had some kind of sensitivity, an ability to read the little animal's intent, if not hear his thoughts.

"I wonder if he'd let me pick him up," I said, as much to announce my intention to the small beast as to his person. "I'd like to examine him."

I'm not a vet, but I have been trained in animal emergency care. Although the rabbit seemed fine now, animals can be very skilled at masking injury or illness—especially in front of a stranger, like me. When hiding a vulnerability can mean the difference between life and death, a prey animal can go a long while in pain, and the odd behavior that Marnie Lundquist had told me about might have been the only sign that something was very wrong. Besides, there was something going on—another whisper, or whispers, just beyond my reach. Something I couldn't quite catch…

Not that I wanted to mention this to Marnie Lundquist. Between her soft voice and gentle manner, the old lady had more than a passing resemblance to the rabbit I now reached, ever so slowly, toward.

"Come here, little guy." The rabbit sat up, eyeing me with—I thought—suspicion. Those velvet ears twitched, and I wondered—was Henry hearing what I couldn't? Or was he simply picking up cues from the room? Waiting, perhaps, for Marnie Lundquist to respond?

"Be gentle," she said, though whether she was talking to me or asking her pet not to bite was an open question. I glanced sideways to see that she, too, had drawn her hands up to her breast, in anticipation or concern. Yes, the old lady genuinely was like her pet.

"Henry…." Was I like Wallis? The image of my tabby's face filled my mind—her wide white whiskers against the tiger-striped fur. That piercing green glare.

"Oh!" Marnie Lundquist might have been responding to Henry's response, as he turned and leaped away across the room. Or not. Cursing my undisciplined thoughts, I sat back on my heels and smiled ruefully as his white tail bounced away. It would take a while to make up for that error.

"I think maybe I rushed things." I said, to save face.

"You never can tell with Henry." She shook her head in disappointment, though with me or the bunny I didn't know. "You simply can't tell."

Chapter Twenty-four

I could almost hear Wallis' purr of contentment at that. She has a very definite attitude toward prey animals, and views my desire to communicate with them a character flaw.

"Really?" I could imagine the rumbling drawl in her voice. *"And those lovely roast birds you dine on?"*

As I've said, animals have little tolerance for deception. And Wallis has spent enough time with me to recognize hypocrisy as a version of the same. As for compassion—or the fact that I made my living dealing with animals of various sorts—well, she saw these as the weaknesses of my species.

"Wouldn't last a night out in the wild," she would mutter, as she stalked away. *"Wouldn't last a night."*

But Wallis wasn't around—either to argue with or to commiserate—as I apologized again to Marnie Lundquist. With a last fleeting glimpse of Henry— *"Go away!"*—I took off.

I did my best to banish the embarrassment of defeat—and the nagging feeling that I had missed something—as I made my way, finally, over to the Chateau. Stewie, the spaniel, was a fine, healthy dog, and I didn't foresee having any problems with him. His owner, though, was a different matter. Cheryl Ginger might be used to being the center of attention. Women who looked like her usually were. But there was too much going on around her for my comfort. At least, as long as I was tangentially involved.

If only I didn't need the money. The winter had been hard, though, and my house still needed work. Insurance had covered much of the rebuilding after a fire had destroyed the entrance hallway of my house. But the bare-bones package I had thought sufficient didn't include niceties like upgrading the insulation, or painting, for that matter. And if I wasn't going to be reduced to chewing on the forsythia myself, I needed to take every gig that came my way.

"Pru Marlowe for Cheryl Ginger." I gave my name at the front desk.

"Of course." The desk clerk was as well trained as that spaniel, and possibly more smitten with the curvy redhead. "Go right up," he said with a smile, a moment later. Although he clearly would have liked to follow me, the brief interaction on the house phone had clearly made his day.

"Pru! Thank you so much." The 100-watt version of Cheryl's own smile greeted me as she opened the door. "I'm so glad you could make it."

"My pleasure." I stepped into the room and looked around. Open suitcases and strewn clothes made the suite look smaller than it was. "Are you taking off?"

"God, I hope so." She sighed audibly. "It's just been…"

"Of course." Whatever I thought of this woman, her boyfriend had been killed. "I'm sorry."

"No, it's—" Another shake of the head. "The investigation. It's just terrible."

"I can imagine." This close, I could see the strain. Her complexion was still perfect—a ski-slope tan giving her a golden glow—but there were shadows below those gold-green eyes and the faintest of lines around her mouth. The woman had undoubtedly been involved in something shady. But I'm no moralist, and, besides, I knew firsthand how hard it can be to live alone in the city. "So the Feds have been questioning you?"

She shivered. "Yes. They wanted to know about Teddy's message."

Enough's enough. I remembered. "What did they make of that?" I watched her. It could mean a lot of things. Her expensive tastes. Her other boyfriend. Or simply that he was sick of playing cards while she schussed down the slopes.

"I don't know." Her voice faded to nothing. Clearly, she had some thoughts on the matter, too. But she wasn't going to share them. "That's why I'm so glad you can take care of Pudgy." Her voice bounced back to its normal perky volume as she turned from me and pulled a leash from inside a fluffy white fur jacket.

"Take care of Pudgy?" I looked around for the dog. "What's wrong with him?"

"Oh, he's fine." She opened the door to the bathroom and the little dog came bounding out. "But I can't give him the attention he needs right now. So if I can hire you to walk him twice a day, until we can get out of here, that would be wonderful."

"Wait." I put my hand up, but not to take the leash. "Don't get me wrong. I'm happy to walk your—Pudgy. But surely, the investigators wouldn't begrudge you a stroll twice a day, would they?" Even as I said it, I looked around. If this was lockdown, it was the most luxurious version I could imagine.

"No, I'm sure—they've been perfect gentlemen." I didn't respond to that. I had a little idea what Cheryl Ginger was used to, and I have a different idea of what constitutes respect. "But I'm a little timid about going out alone."

She smiled, which only made those fine lines more obvious. It was a nervous smile, as fake as I hoped that fur to be. Submissive. Which seemed quite unlike the woman I was beginning to know. Something had shaken the redhead up.

"You're afraid of going into the woods?" I knew what wildlife was out there. She didn't. "You can always walk along the road, you know."

"Yes, but…" That smile again. Forced and sad. "After all, we don't know who did this yet. I mean, Teddy…"

Benazi. I nodded. I didn't know what Cheryl Ginger was up to, but at least she was finally taking my warning seriously.

"Fair enough," I said, naming my fee. "I can walk Pudgy here once a day for as long as you're in town. I'll give him a good long walk and use the time to go over the fundamentals of training."

Not that he needed it, but I prefer to earn my money the honest way. "You'll have to let him out in the evening, though."

She nodded her assent and went back to packing. That's when I it occurred to me I should tell her about the widow.

"You should probably know, I got a call from Theresa Rhinecrest." She looked over at me but didn't say anything. "Teddy's widow." I said, just to make it clear. "She heard that I was the person who found him, and she has some questions for me."

"About what happened?" She was fighting to keep her voice calm. Guilty conscience, I figured.

"Not exactly." It registered then—the grieving widow hadn't asked me anything about her husband. "She seemed to think that I knew him, or that you and I were acquainted."

"We are." She turned. Her big eyes blinked at me.

"Yes, but before." I was having difficulty explaining. "And she seems to want something. She was asking me about his stay here. About his belongings."

Cheryl nodded and stared off, looking lost in thought. "Yeah, she would."

"Excuse me?" That wasn't the reaction I had expected.

"I think she was planning on divorcing Teddy." She went back to packing. "I told Teddy, but I think he knew it, too. I think he was probably trying to hide his assets. You know, so she couldn't claim her share?" As she said this, she folded a blouse. Her face, in profile, looked tired but unruffled, as if none of this mattered anymore. Maybe it didn't.

"You know she hired someone to look into him? To look into his affairs." It wasn't nice, but I thought Cheryl should know. She had, after all, just provided a motive for the widow: Why divorce your cheating husband when you can make a cleaner break? And if I saw it, I was pretty sure the Feds would, too. Still, the widow had sounded like she could defend herself. A flash of something—call it sisterly concern—prompted me to add. "She's looking into you too, probably."

"I'm not surprised." She turned toward me, and I saw that my words had gotten to her. The fatigue was now matched by sadness that she only emphasized as she forced a smile. "Hey, a woman does what she's got to, right?"

I wanted to ask more. To see if she'd heard anything about the widow—about the Rhinecrests' relationship, about what the Feds knew, or were asking. But she was handing me the leash, and I let her show us to the door.

"Is he here? Is he coming to meet us?" The spaniel was too well trained to bark, but as we took the service elevator down to the back entrance, I got the query behind that intent tail wagging loud and clear.

"Sorry, Pudg—" I caught myself. I would have to tell him about Rhinecrest, though I suspected that wasn't who he was missing. "Sorry, Stewie."

"Huh, been a while." I was going to try to explain when the door opened. We were on the far side of the lobby, behind the artificial waterfall and its hothouse ferns, and I scooped the spaniel into my arms. I still didn't know what Cheryl Ginger's arrangement with the management was— and if it would carry over to the help. All in all, speed and discretion seemed to be called for.

"Ms. Ginger?" The name rang out across the fancy lobby, clear above the burble of water, and I ducked. Ahead of me to the right, a nondescript hallway led to the service entrance, and I made for it, the dog in my arms. "Cheryl Ginger?" With my dark hair, I didn't look anything like the sun-kissed redhead I'd left upstairs, but for all I knew the desk clerk was colorblind.

"Why, yes, she has been receiving visitors." Discreet, he wasn't, but I relaxed and stood a little straighter as I entered that hall. "Shall I ring her room?"

"No, no, don't." I stopped. Something about the voice—male, young—had caught my attention. With the dog still in my arms, I turned. From here, the ferns screened the lobby. I could see the desk clerk's arm, if not his eager face. But even as I peered over and around the fronds, I couldn't make out who had come calling. Only that he was big and, I thought, light-haired, and then he was gone.

I slipped out the back, but found myself regretting the missed opportunity. "Let's go around the front, shall we, Stewie?" The spaniel had begun to squirm, and so I put him down. Once he'd emptied his bladder, I led him around the outside of the building, hoping to catch a glimpse of the man who'd been asking about his mistress without making ourselves too obvious. "Maybe you want to, too?"

I looked down to meet those dark eyes. *"Meeting?"*

It wasn't a response I could read. I'd wondered, in the brief pause while he'd watered the foundation planting, if the visitor could be Cheryl's boyfriend. The other man who she met in the woods. But the dog's response was too vague for me to tell if he'd recognized the stranger. It certainly wasn't the eager yearning I'd been hearing from the dog since we'd met.

Rather than wait and question the animal, though, I'd try to catch up with the man. But when I reached down to pick up the little dog again, he stepped away.

"Sorry." I should have known the dog would want to proceed under his own power. Spaniels are work dogs, energetic, smart, and proud. Because of their size, however, they are too often seen as house pets, and I suspected that despite her own athleticism, Cheryl Ginger did not properly respect her canine companion.

I did, and despite the growing fear that the visitor would be long gone by the time we circled the kitchen wing, I let Stewie lead the way. To his credit, he didn't stop, although I knew from the images passing through my own mind that the grounds were rich with the scents of spring.

Not that it mattered. As we circled the cedar fencing that camouflaged a dumpster, I could see that the drive was empty. Although the man who had come to the front desk might have parked in the adjacent lot and might still be lurking around, waiting for the redhead to come out, I thought it more likely that he had left his car in the waiting area out front—and that he had already driven back down the curving drive toward the road.

"You think he's waiting around here somewhere?" The question was more for myself than for the spaniel. As soon as I formed it, however, I was made aware of the little dog's interest. I was asking him to track someone, more or less, and that was what he did.

"Follow?" The question came to me as the eager black nose sniffed the air. *"Meeting?"*

"Maybe." I didn't want to mislead the spaniel, and so I tried to empty my mind of my own suspicions. Instead, I tried to replay the query I had heard at the desk. The sound of the visitor's voice and the impression of a large, light-haired man, seen from the back as he went out through the door. As far as I could tell, there were several possibilities as to who was asking about Cheryl Ginger—and about anyone who might have been visiting her. The fact that he had left rather than talk to the redhead, and that I would be pretty easy to identify as one of those visitors, didn't make dismissing these thoughts easy.

"Who is he?" I unclipped the lead from the dog's collar. That's against protocol for a dog walker, which was what Cheryl Ginger had just hired me to do. And it wasn't the smartest move to take with an energetic young animal who had recently disappeared into the woods. "Who?" I said the word out loud to give it extra emphasis.

While I waited, I let the possibilities drift through my mind. The man could be a Fed, following up on Ronnie's information that the redhead had a love interest besides the dead man. I had no doubt that despite his pleas for discretion, Ronnie would have given up everything he had when questioned. If Teddy's last message meant he was breaking off with the pretty ski bunny, the lovers might have tried to pressure the sugar daddy into one last payment—or to blackmail him.

It was just as likely that he was the boyfriend. I still remembered the blond man at the bar that first night at Hardware—I wouldn't swear that the stranger at the front desk was the same man, but it was possible. What I did remember was the way he'd stared at Cheryl. That intensity might have indicated fury at how Teddy Rhinecrest was treating her. Or murderous jealousy at the fact that she had left with the older man.

Or, and this was the possibility that made the hair on the back of my neck stand up, he could be an associate of Gregor Benazi. Associate being the most polite term I could muster for the kind of younger, bigger colleague who might be sent to do the dirty work that the dapper gangster would prefer to avoid.

I had wondered at her reticence to leave the hotel. Now it made sense. I wasn't sure the suit at the front desk would offer much protection. Still, better for her to be indoors than out in the woods. Where, it hit me, she was sending me, daily. That realization sent another chill up my spine, and for a moment I longed for the simpler days of the brutal winter we had just survived.

No, I was being silly. A dog-walking gig was just that. Besides, I wasn't going to downplay myself, but no red-blooded man alive was going to confuse me and Cheryl Ginger.

I had another out. If the blond guy did indeed work for Benazi, I was off the hook. The man himself had asked me to get information. He knew I was meeting with Cheryl Ginger. Knew before I did, in fact. Still, as we stood on the walkway, to the side of the Chateau's main entrance, I couldn't help but wish that I hadn't come here. The redhead was trouble, and I had enough of my own.

"Follow?" The dog had gone ahead of me. Now, although his small, muscular body was on point, his nose into the wind, I heard his request. He wanted me with him, and he was too well-mannered to go off on his own.

"Sure." I said. Maybe Stewie would have something for me.

"Here." He was heading toward the lot. Following, I gathered, the scent of the big stranger.

"Good boy." I followed him down the slight slope. On the far side sat three cars. One late model Honda and two older imports, all silver. If I had to guess, I'd say Cheryl's was the newest, though I couldn't remember precisely what she'd driven up in. Otherwise, all those cars look alike. My baby blue GTO was the only distinctive set of wheels here, and I'd left her up by the lot entrance. With a car like mine, you want to avoid any chance of accidental dings, and besides, I'd been running late when I'd pulled in.

At the entrance to the lot, the spaniel paused. The stranger had indeed left, and a wave of relaxation washed over me. As much as I wanted to know who he was, I was content to let the problem be academic. This wasn't my fight. But then the little dog set off again. And as I stood there, watching, he walked around my car, sniffing, slowly, as if tracing the path of a man who had been examining my vehicle only moments before. Looking for any trace of who I was, or where I might have gone.

Chapter Twenty-five

That spaniel got a workout. By the time I digested what had happened, my fear had turned to anger and I was looking for a way to fight back.

"Find!" I gave the little dog the command, and with one glance up at me, he began, dipping his head to the ground to take the scent. I knew that I would have to groom him before we went back inside: his long locks were already picking up twigs, and I could see leaf detritus hanging from his ears. But he had a good nose and was thrilled to use it: leading me first to the corner of the lot where, I assume, Blondie had parked, and then back to the hotel entrance. While the spaniel seemed a tad disappointed that I wouldn't let him follow the trail back inside, I could tell he was enjoying this. Spaniels aren't scent hounds—he wouldn't be able to find a fugitive who had trampled through the woods, say, or over water. But centuries of breeding have endowed them with hunting skills that haven't been totally eliminated, even in a so-called toy like this Stewie. He could smell and identify prey, and would point out the subject before I was likely to notice him, which would be useful if, in fact, we ever ran into Blondie again. Plus, he was a gun dog. If I needed someone near me who could keep a cool head in a fight, I'd chose this brown and white fellow. Despite his fancy collar, he was a serious worker.

"He went out..." Even as he tracked, the spaniel was piecing together the man's activity. *"He paused, he walked..."*

I got glimpses of what he saw. The big man standing—his feet had made a slightly deeper impression here, in the leaf mold by the parking area. Starting in one direction and then shifting to walk back over to where I had parked.

The man was gone, that much was clear. But Stewie's actions confirmed my suspicions. Before Blondie had asked for Cheryl Ginger, he'd scoped out the hotel, doing his best to figure out who was visiting. Cheryl was lucky, I thought, that her room was on one of the upper floors. Lucky or smart.

When the spaniel led me to the far side of the lot, I hesitated. Once before, I'd heard a car, starting, beyond a stretch of trees. Despite the scenic setting, we were still in a pretty well-settled area, and it would be entirely possible to park down on the main road—or even beyond a bend of the Chateau's driveway—and climb back up, through the woods. I knew the little dog's nerves would hold; I wasn't sure I wanted to test my own.

"Follow!" For a small animal, he had a strong sense of leadership. Probably the toy breeding, I figured, as I gave in and let him set the pace. With his size and good looks, he probably had the same sense of entitlement as a small child.

For a moment, I imagined the spaniel in Cheryl Ginger's arms, cuddled like a baby. I saw his tail wagging as she cooed and rocked him, a vision of more warmth than I had yet seen between the two, and for a moment I lost my focus.

"Bunny!" Stewie brought me back. We were about five yards down the path, still within sight of the lot. He had frozen in place, one paw up in the classic pose, and his long snout held still.

"Rabbit?" I asked under my breath, the thought more disturbing than I'd have liked. A good-sized hare could probably fight off the spaniel, and the breed was used more commonly for game birds. Still, with that nose, that pose…a hunt is a hunt, and I bet Stewie would hold his own with any beagle if the appropriate prey surfaced nearby. It would be more than a sport to him, and I had no business being sentimental. But when I thought of Marnie Lundquist and little Henry, I confess, I felt a twinge of…let's just call it discomfort.

"Bunny," he repeated, as I looked around, confused. Then I remembered what Wallis had told me. Although I "hear" what animals are thinking, usually a stream of consciousness consisting of their observations along with fears and desires, what I am really getting is something much more basic. Their take on the world, their basic thoughts—only my paltry human brain translates these impulses into language. My language. And since my exposure to Henry, I'd been thinking of rabbits as "bunnies." Stewie had no more said *"bunny"* than he had commanded me to *"follow."* He was simply receiving impressions. I was the one who labeled those impressions with words.

Fifteen seconds, then thirty, and we still hadn't moved. Somewhere out there was a scared animal. It was early for a rabbit—still an hour or so till dusk—but the winter had been hard, and it made sense that one or more were out foraging.

"Family." The word came to me like an echo of my earlier fancy. Only this time it was accompanied by an impression of a nest, of small creatures cushioned by leaves and fur, that grounded it in the wild—in the forest around us. I wasn't sure what Stewie was getting, but I trusted that it was real. A hungry mother, perhaps, had emerged from her warren, looking for food. Or maybe the nest was right nearby, its occupants holding so still that my eyes couldn't make them out on the variegated forest floor.

"There you are." The human voice startled me, and I turned with a gasp. It was only Cheryl Ginger, picking her way carefully along the trail. She had traded in her heels for boots, I noticed. Leather lace-ups that probably wouldn't have been out of place in Milan. "I was worried that something had happened," she said, ignoring the wet leaf mold that was darkening one capped toe.

"Why?" I don't like being frightened. I also don't like being set up.

"Oh, I didn't think you'd be out here so long." Something about her voice told me she was lying, as clearly as Stewie's nose told him there was prey nearby.

"I thought you were afraid to come out here?"

She pasted on that smile as her eyes darted back and forth between the trees. "Alone, yeah." Even Stewie turned to look up at her, her voice high-pitched and tense. "But I saw you from the doorway." She pointed back to the hotel. "And when you left the lot to go into the woods, I wanted to make sure you were okay."

"Wait." I held up a hand to stop her. "You were worried about us, but you saw us?"

"I was worried when I was up in my room, and so I came down." That smile again. She made it seem natural. "Then I saw you, but you went into the woods and I thought, this is my chance to go for a walk and not be alone."

"Did you talk to the desk clerk?"

Stewie whined. He heard the suspicion in my voice. Dogs don't like dissent, and he could tell that the woman holding his lead was at odds with his owner.

"No." She shook her head, a little too hard. "I didn't. Why?"

"Someone came looking for you." I was watching her face. "A big guy. Young. He asked for you at the desk." I didn't tell her he'd asked about any visitors. I wanted to draw her out, not give away the game.

"Oh, I know who that was." She laughed. It almost sounded natural. "I'll have to call him later. So, are we exploring this trail?"

"Bunny!" The spaniel barked once, assenting to the question in her tone. And so I handed over the lead and stepped back behind the pair as they began to walk. I had been hired to train the dog, to exercise him, but Cheryl Ginger was clearly the one giving the commands.

Chapter Twenty-six

I got to Happy's early. After that encounter with the redhead, I was glad that I hadn't cancelled, after all. Marty Parvis might be the one who had called with questions, but I wanted some answers too.

My timing was partly strategy. I figured I'd scope out the bar before this Parvis arrived, make sure he didn't have any backup sitting in the shadows by the booths. Part of it was simpler: I wanted to drink. I wasn't a fool. There was no way I would let my guard down with Theresa Rhinecrest's investigator. But I didn't have to get wasted to enjoy the simple pleasure of bourbon and a beer back.

When most people say they know how to handle their liquor, it's a sign they don't. I don't brag about it, but I've drunk enough so that I can gauge its effect. Maybe that's my father's legacy—or the discipline my mother tried to instill. At any rate, with Wallis making herself scarce, my house felt as homey as a doctor's waiting room. Better to come to Happy's and set the stage as I liked it.

I chose my seat with care. Happy's is a small place, long and dark as a shoebox. The bar up front might once have been classy, deep wood with a mirrored back. The years have darkened the finish beyond ebony, though, and decades of forgotten cigarettes have left the rounded rail nicked and burned. Still, this was my post of choice, offering a better vantage point than the booths in back, with their cracked leatherette banquettes and perpetual haze. Sure, smoking in bars is illegal now. I don't know who would enforce that at Happy's.

Not Happy, for sure. The barkeep—the second of that name that I knew—was as smoked-stained as the fixtures, yellowed and weathered. His scowl made a mockery of the moniker, dragging down his bristled cheeks like some kind of short-muzzled dog.

"Thanks." Happy brought over my drink of choice, a lowball glass of liquid gold, without asking. When he saw me sipping, he hesitated with the follow-up, but I nodded and the beer followed. Better not to do back-to-back bourbons until I had some answers.

"Anybody been asking for me?" I wouldn't normally talk to Happy. He's good at what he does, but he doesn't seem to like people much. Still, the only other customer was slumped so low over his shot glass, I doubted he knew that I'd walked in.

"For you?" Happy's eyes shot up, making the resemblance to a pug even clearer. "No."

He walked away before I could ask about Creighton, and continued wiping down the bar. Since cleanliness is not high on Happy's priorities—and my sole fellow drinker was only a few stools away—I figured his barkeep's radar was working. The sour old coot wasn't thrilled to be asked about anyone.

"Pru." The drinker roused and turned toward me, bleary-eyed and blinking. "As I live and breathe."

"Hey, Vince." I turned away. It doesn't pay to engage with drinkers as far gone as Vince was. Then again, it also doesn't pay to antagonize them, either.

"What you up to, Pru?" Happy's isn't big, but Vince is, and his voice carried. "You and that cop still hanging out?"

"What's it to you?" I turned to face him. We'd gone to school together, back in the day. Vince hadn't done much else since. But if he wasn't going to shut up, I would at least make use of him. "You and he been catching up?"

He laughed. "Your old man's got a better poker face than you do, sweetheart."

I nodded. "So he was with you the other night?"

"If that's his story, I won't argue." He pointed to my empty, his cold laugh ending in a belch. "You want? I'm buying."

"No, thanks." I looked over. The barkeep was ahead of me, moving in with his rag.

"Go home, Vince." Happy reached for his glass.

"I got money." Vince whined, pulling it back. Happy stood there, waiting.

"Hang on." Vince made a show of lifting the empty tumbler, shaking out the last few drops onto his outstretched tongue. Only then did he slide off his stool, wobbling a bit as he turned back toward the bar.

"Don't try to rip me off," he said, raising a finger in warning. Happy ignored him. "No fun here tonight, anyway," he grumbled as he waddled away. "I'm going home."

"It is kind of quiet." I looked around, once the heavy front door had swung shut again.

"Yup." As I've mentioned, Happy is a taciturn fellow.

"Thanks." I accepted a refill. I would've expected Albert and maybe Ronnie to be here by now. Vince had probably scared them off. He has that effect on people. My ex, Mack, didn't hang here anymore. He'd been on the wagon for a few months, but I figured even coming into a bar would be pushing it. Still, tonight I would've welcomed the company.

"Happy, is there something else going on tonight?" It didn't seem likely. Then again, I didn't understand why Albert and his crew weren't here. "Something I should know about?"

"Card game, I heard." Happy is better with a direct question. "Someone staked a game at the VFW. Food, too."

"You know who?" Happy only shrugged. "I guess that's where Vince was heading, huh?"

"Maybe." Vince liked to play. That was no secret. And if he did have money, I doubted that the bar had been his final stop.

Another bourbon and another beer later, I was ready to call it quits. I'd already tried this Parvis' number. I'd wanted to leave a message—traffic on the thruway can be tricky—but the voice mail box was still full. No matter, over an hour and it's not late, it's rude. Or, I thought as I slid off the stool and made my way toward the ladies', it's a ploy. If I'd been a little steadier, I'd have kicked myself. Someone wants to look into me, they say they'll meet me and…then what? Would I get home to find my house had been broken into?

"I'm out of here." I called to Happy on my return, reaching for my wallet as I did.

"No need." He shook his head as he came to take my glass.

"Come on." I wasn't getting this. "I don't need charity. Or sympathy."

"Already paid," he shrugged as he walked away.

"What? When?" I went after him, catching him halfway down the bar. "Why didn't you say anything?"

He looked up at me then, his eyes cold. I didn't blink.

"Happy." I felt as sober as a judge. "Somebody buys my drinks, I have a right to know who." His eyes were as cold as a lizard's.

"Shit." I'd been set up. I was angry. "Happy, who was it? You want me to call the cops—or the department of health?"

That stopped him. Not because he was worried, I think, but because he could tell how desperate I was. He's known me long enough to know I'm not the kind to alert the authorities.

"Look," he said. "I know you can take care of yourself, Pru. I seen enough to know that. But this guy? I don't know. He came in, smooth as silk. Said you'd be by. Said you shouldn't have to pay for anything. Like it was your birthday, or something."

He reached into the register and lifted the cash drawer. From underneath, he pulled out a crisp Benjamin, and I whistled. At Happy's prices, I could have been drinking all night. "Said he wanted you to have a good time, and stay out of trouble. All right?"

"All right," I said. Smooth as silk, with bucks to boot. It had to be Benazi. "But next time—if there is a next time—tell me up front, okay?"

The barkeep shrugged, his eyebrows eloquent in their silence as he went back to wiping down the bar, and I shrugged on my coat to face the night.

I'm not a fool. I had my phone in my hand before I hit the door. Parvis, or whoever he was working with, must have wanted to set me up, must have figured that the generous bar tab would keep me at Happy's. Keep me out of the way. Maybe this card game—if it even existed—was for the same reason.

Something was going down. I didn't know how Benazi fit into it—or even if I'd been correct in putting together a smooth guy and a C-note to come up with the gangster. But if I was wrong, or if something had changed with the old gent, the motive could be darker. Someone—again, Parvis came to mind—could have wanted me incapacitated. Tipsy, if not drunk, and leaving alone, late at night. I thought of Albert and his cronies, lured off by hot dogs and a chance at a fifty-dollar pot. Neither the animal officer nor his pals were the chivalrous type. I was a better fighter than most of them, even if they had the weight and the reach. But bystanders make for complications, I knew that.

I'm no coward, and Beauville isn't the city. Not by a long shot, and in my years here I'd come through iffier situations without a scratch. Maybe I was getting old. Past thirty, a girl stops believing in her immortality. Maybe it was the body I had stumbled over, just days before.

Maybe it was just the constant morass of lies and play-acting, I didn't know anymore. Something was wrong, and I was sick of it. But I wasn't going to be its next victim. As difficult as it was for me to admit to any vulnerability, I made myself dial Creighton as I pushed open the door. Hey, at the very least, maybe the sound of me talking to someone—talking specifically to our town's top cop—would give pause to whoever might be waiting for me out back.

"Jim?" It was his voice mail, but as I stepped out the bar's back door, I decided to pretend otherwise. "Yup, I'm just leaving Happy's now. Parked in the back, like always."

I was going to pay for this. Not that Creighton would be mad. He'd love it, in fact. Say I was being sensible, when in truth he'd be thinking that I'd come to rely on him. Times like this made me wish I had other friends in town. Friends of the two-legged variety, that is. But when your main confidante is an eleven-year-old tabby, your options for a possible late-night rescue are limited.

"I've got to tell you about this new client of mine." I kept talking, even as the machine cut me off. There was something odd going on. Beauville isn't the city, as I've said, but the parking area behind the row of storefronts seemed even darker than usual. Clouds, maybe, over the moon. Or a case of our spare streetlight going out.

"She's a hoot, this Marnie Lundquist." I'd parked off to the side, my usual m.o., even more important when I was heading to a drinking establishment. My baby blue baby was not going to get dinged or scratched just because someone else couldn't hold his booze. "And she's got this bunny."

I paused. Maybe it was the thought of Henry. Creighton isn't involved with the fish and wildlife commission, but he is law enforcement. The last thing I wanted to do was out the old lady and her illicit pet. But, no, there was something else. Some shadow over by my car.

"Hang on, Jim." I switched the phone to my left hand. With my right I pulled out my knife. A drunk, maybe, keeled over before he could get to his own vehicle. Albert, or some other regular, hoping for a lift home. Then again, if someone was waiting for me, crouched down by my car, I was not going easy. "Who's there?" I called. "Show yourself."

Nothing. The shadow didn't move. I made myself breathe and approached, my knife at the ready.

But it was the phone I would use. "Creighton, it's Pru." I wasn't feeling conversational this time. "You've got to meet me behind Happy's—as soon as possible. I've found another body."

Chapter Twenty-seven

"I don't know, Pru." Creighton handed me a coffee, shaking his head. "You've got to stop doing this."

"Finding bodies?" I cradled the Styrofoam cup. Its warmth made me realize I was shivering. "It was never my intent, Jim."

"Maybe not the bodies part, but the people you work with—you associate with." He was standing, probably looking down at me. But with the floodlights up, all I could see was his outline, tall and lean in the frosty night. And so as I huddled over my coffee, staring instead into its steaming depths. "You know, just because we're not city out here…"

"I know, Jim." I took a sip. Whoever had prepared it had made it milky and sweet. Utterly wrong, but exactly what I wanted at the moment. "I did call you."

"I know." He'd shown up in record time, that first long message redirecting him as he drove home from "a late meeting." With whom, I didn't ask, not even when I overheard him discussing the vagaries of five-card stud. "It's just…"

I looked up to see him running one hand over his face. It was late. Now that the adrenaline was wearing off, I was exhausted, and he didn't look much better.

"Pru," he started again. "It's one thing when it's people you know. Beauville people. I get that. But to get involved with this Cheryl Ginger just because you felt bad for her—"

"Jim, that's not it." I didn't have the energy for this, I really didn't. "I'm not 'involved.' I found her dog and now she's having me walk it." I hadn't told him about Benazi. There was too much he knew—or suspected—about me that I didn't want to share. Besides, I thought the old gangster would consider it a breach of etiquette.

"Uh huh." Then again, Creighton had his sources, too. I turned away, looking for an answer in my sweet, hot drink.

I hadn't known who it was at first. Even as I'd called, my hand starting to shake, I'd told myself it was one of the regulars, too drunk to even make the door. Or that Vince had forgotten where he'd parked—that he'd come around the back and gotten into a fight. But when Creighton had roared up, his headlights had shown me the mop of light hair. Or what had been light. In the artificial glare, the white-blond was splotched with something dark. I was grateful, then, that the bulky body was slumped forward, and that I couldn't see his face.

Creighton had taken over, ushering me away and calling in his crew. The body was now out of sight, if not already on its way to the county morgue. And I'd told Creighton what I knew. The light-haired man had been following Cheryl Ginger. I'd seen him at the restaurant and at the hotel. And while Ronnie hadn't ID'd him as the redhead's other man, I thought it likely that he was involved with her—and maybe involved with what had happened to Teddy Rhinecrest.

He'd let me talk—partly, to calm me down. And then he'd disappeared, handing me off to an EMT who wrapped me in a blanket and sat me here, on a low wall behind the bar. Now that he was back, I was ready to start over—to dredge up any details I'd forgotten. Anything except Benazi. I wasn't going to fool around with murder.

"What happened to him?" I didn't want to know, not really. The question just came out.

"To your friend?" Creighton's face was still shadowed.

"He's not—honest, Jim. I don't know who he is."

"He knows who you are, Pru." He sat down next to me. I could see his face, now, tired and sad. "He's got pictures of you in his cell phone. Out on your walks. Driving. And don't say you didn't know him. I've seen your number in missed calls."

"Calls?" The coffee had gone cold.

"You kept trying to reach him." Jim's voice was flat. "Tonight. While you were at Happy's."

"Wait, that's Martin Parvis?" Clearly, we'd crossed signals.

"So you do know him."

"I—no, he called and asked to meet. I thought he was driving up from New York." I explained the situation to Creighton, ending with my theories about Theresa Rhinecrest. "I gather Teddy Rhinecrest was hiding assets, or his wife thought he was. But why she'd bother investigating him now, I don't understand. I mean, it will all come to her anyway. Unless he made a will?"

That was all I had. Creighton, however, wasn't giving me anything back. "Okay, I believe you," he said. "But others might not. And in case you've forgotten, I'm not working the Rhinecrest case. So Pru? Go home. Go to bed. And don't do anything foolish."

I was dismissed, and I knew it. But while I hadn't learned anything, the brief exchange had given the shock a chance to wear off. I was steady on my feet as I walked over to my car. And although I was grateful that the area around it was now empty, I knew better than to look for any scratches or stains over by the rear tire well, where Parvis had slumped. Time enough for that in the morning.

"Someone's had quite an evening." Wallis brushed up against me as soon as I was in the house. To an outsider, her move might look like a greeting. I knew she was reading the smells of everyone I'd encountered and probably the pheromones prompted by shock and fear.

"As if I had to smell your sweat for that." She huffed and sat back, waiting. I needed something to eat, too, and broke a half dozen eggs into a pan.

"I feel like a fool, Wallis." It was easier to talk to Wallis than to Creighton, in part because I was staring into a pan. "I mean, I was sitting in there, drinking, while he was right outside."

"And why was that, do you think?" She twined around my ankles, letting me know that she'd prefer the scramble sooner rather than later.

"Hang on." One more shake of the pan, and it was done. Stepping out of her circuit, I fetched two plates. "Well, I just thought he was late. But he must have been ambushed as he came to talk to me."

"Mmmm…" The purr that rose as she began to lap up our midnight snack almost obscured her words. *"Maybe,"* she said. *"Maybe you're right."*

I dug into my own plate, too hungry to bother with my usual dash of Tabasco. "Yeah, he was coming into the bar and someone must have grabbed him." I paused. "So did someone know he was meeting me? Or was he being followed?"

"Coming into a bar he didn't know, using the back entrance?" Wallis could have been talking to herself, I wasn't sure. *"Or was he waiting for you to give up and leave? For you to be out there, alone, in the dark?"*

Chapter Twenty-eight

I didn't sleep well. I'm tough, sure, but stumbling onto two dead bodies in one week is a lot, even for me. Wallis didn't help, with that last comment about the parking lot. Of course, it could have been a ploy. I ended up scraping most of my eggs into her plate, which she was licking clean as I went up to bed.

"Should've used the Tabasco," I muttered as I left. I was in a mood.

Images of bloody bunnies hopped through my dreams, chased by small, intent dogs. I looked for Wallis when I woke, thinking she'd used my bed as a launching pad for the first moth of the season or some other nighttime escapade. But she was nowhere to be seen. And so I lay there as the ceiling gradually lightened, the wan sun promising more warmth than it could provide, and I could go about my day.

My first thought, as I drove to Tracy Horlick's house, was to confront Theresa Rhinecrest. She'd set me up with Parvis, and I had a sneaking feeling she knew more than she had shared. It probably had to do with money—it usually does—though I did wonder if perhaps payback to the other woman might have a part as well. Whatever the widow was up to, I wanted no part of it. I was happy to let the Feds carry out their investigation in peace.

But—and this was where Creighton had my number—I was curious. An explanation, and then out. She'd dragged me into this, setting Parvis onto me, and I felt I was owed that much.

And so despite the hour—I suspected that the widow wasn't an early riser—I dialed as I drove.

"Pru Marlowe." I growled to her voice mail when it picked up. "You have my number. Call me."

My next thought was Cheryl Ginger, but I'd be there soon enough. First, though, I had to face Tracy Horlick.

"Heard you had some excitement last night." She had the door open as I walked up the path. "Over at Happy's."

One day I would find out how she got her information so fast. One day I'd quit drinking, too.

"Good morning." I willed myself not to engage. This was a dominance ploy on her part, and I couldn't submit. "How's Bitsy this morning?"

"Better than that friend of yours, what's his name?" She tossed her ash into the shrubs. They were used to it. I was not. I stood my ground, silent, while she fussed with her cigarette. Finally, she had to look me in the eye. "It was that ski bunny again, wasn't it?"

"I'm afraid I don't know what you're talking about, Mrs. Horlick." I kept my voice even, as a thought hit me. She had the basic, but no specifics. "You know, listening to a police scanner can give a person nightmares."

"Huh." She grunted, but she retreated, leaving me to wonder if I'd finally uncovered her secret.

"Hey, Bitsy!" The little dog came running out, tail wagging despite the grayness of the day. That early sun had disappeared behind a solid bank of clouds. A month ago, I'd be looking for snow. Now, I couldn't tell. Rain or just a dismal outlook, matching my mood as we walked.

"Bitsy, my ass…" The way he'd come trotting had been misleading, I saw now. He'd been desperate to get out, but his state of mind was no brighter than this day. Or than mine, for that matter. *"Give something a cutesy name and you expect it to respond…"*

"I'm sorry, Growler," I said as soon as we were out of earshot.

"You were trying to placate her." He watered a tree and moved on. *"All your talk of training and dominance…"*

He was right, of course. All I could do was admit it. "It was her asking about last night," I tried to explain. I assumed that he'd be privy to all the information Horlick had, as well as most of what I was thinking. Animals do pick up a lot more than we know, as Wallis had explained. "And that ski bunny crack."

"That's another one." He was pulling me ahead, behavior that I wouldn't usually tolerate in a client animal. Action designed to show me who was boss. I let him. *"Bunny, indeed. A cute name, but you don't know what those animals can get up to. You don't know what they'll do."*

Chapter Twenty-nine

The widow hadn't called me back by the time I relinquished Growler, disgruntled but a little more relaxed, to his sour-faced person.

"Took you long enough." She paused to pick a scrap of tobacco from her tongue. "I was beginning to worry."

"A little rain wouldn't have hurt either of us." I was referring to myself and the bichon, but she only scowled more. "I think it's too late for snow."

"There are worse things than weather." She squinted for emphasis—or because of the smoke. I smiled and bent to pet poor Growler. There were no words for what he had to endure.

I had words for the widow, though, as I drove away. Slowing below my usual cruising speed, I checked my messages once more, and thought about calling Mrs. Rhinecrest again. Only my next destination made me hesitate. I doubted I'd get anything from Cheryl Ginger. She was cagier than she looked. And I certainly didn't consider myself to be on the widow's payroll—I'd never promised anything to Martin Parvis, and now he was dead. But if she was looking for information, and I had some, it might give me some leverage to understand just what the hell was going on.

"There you are." Cheryl Ginger was at the front desk as I walked in. And any qualms I'd had about the hotel accepting the presence of her spaniel evaporated: she was not only openly holding the dog's leash, she appeared to be pressing it into the desk clerk's hand. "I was hoping you'd get here soon."

"I'm on time." I could hear myself growing defensive. Not that I cared. My work is one of the few things I'm proud of. "Maybe you were unclear about our agreement."

"No, no, it's all fine." She was all smiles as she came over, handing me the leash as she buttoned her white fur jacket. Behind her, the desk clerk scuttled for safety. "Only I have to run an errand, and I didn't want to leave Pudgy alone."

"I gather." I took the braided leather and got an immediate hit of anxiety. The dog was uneasy about something. I looked down into anxious brown eyes. Something was different, something wrong. "Let me take him out of here."

"Thank you." With a nod, she dismissed me, but I had more pressing concerns. I was dying to know the arrangement she'd made with the desk clerk, who'd acted almost as uncomfortable as the spaniel. But I'm not paid to look into human problems, no matter how tempting. I had an animal in distress, and I was pretty sure what was causing it.

"Come on, Stewie." I used the little spaniel's real name as an offering of respect and recognition as I led him off toward the door. Away from the front desk, I knelt and quickly checked for a physical source for his discomfort. A little dog with a coat like his can pick up burrs, ticks…what have you. But Stewie was clean. So much so that I suspected he hadn't been out since my last visit. And his collar—I was glad to see that Cheryl had replaced the gaudy jeweled one with plain leather—held no twigs or mats, either.

That left emotion. Not because Stewie was a toy spaniel, though the smaller breeds do tend to be higher strung if not more anxiety prone. No, dogs in general are rule-followers. We've bred them for it, and it's why they retain primacy among man's best friends, no matter how many of us would opt for the more idiosyncratic affection of a cat. This is just how they are, and if I was going to understand what made the little dog tremble, why his tail hung down like that, I had to think as he did. Kneeling made it easy. I looked around at our surroundings—seeing them at dog-level, so to speak—and between the fake waterfall with its glistening rocks and a floor so polished claws slid off it, I identified a probable source of Stewie's unease.

Cheryl Ginger's privilege be damned. The rules were in place for a reason: this was no place for a pet. An animal as well trained as this one would experience profound discomfort knowing he was someplace he shouldn't be. Standing around in this lobby, with all its polished, pet-unfriendly surfaces must have been as upsetting for him as eating off the dinner table or soiling a rug. If I wanted him to feel good about who he was—about his training—I had to get him out of here as soon as it was possible. I got to my feet and led the little fellow to the door.

"Let's run," I whispered, letting him feel my thoughts.

Exercise is therapeutic, and the toy breeds tend not to get enough. Besides, after Tracy Horlick and now Cheryl Ginger, with her sense of entitlement, I could use some fresh air myself.

But Stewie was having none of it. In fact, the farther we got from the entrance, the higher his anxiety level ratcheted. Although he was too well disciplined to disobey my lead, he grew increasingly unhappy as I led him through the parking lot and down the trail. By the time we had passed into the trees, he was audibly whining and pulling at the leash.

"What is it, boy?" I knelt and put my hand on his back. Direct contact can aid communication, and I tried to clear my head as I stroked his silky curls.

"Can't leave her." His body was trembling. *"Don't."*

I was floored, and asked again, doing my best to leave my question—and my mind—open. "Why are you scared?"

"Must go to her." He was straining to see through the sparse foliage, through the shadows and bare trunks behind us to the hotel.

"Okay, then." He couldn't be more clear than that, and I let him lead the way back up the path. We emerged into the parking lot in time to see her duck into a late model car—a silver Honda—and drive away. This only increased the dog's agitation.

"No! Must go to her!" His whining was pitiful.

"We don't know where she's going, Stewie." I wasn't sure if I could reason with the little beast. "But I'm sure she'll be back." Even as I said it, I realized I wasn't. People around Cheryl Ginger were facing bad ends, and I hadn't heard from Benazi in a while.

"Do you know where she's going, Stewie?" In this light, the little dog's concern seemed reasonable. But even before I got an answer, I was fishing my keys out of my pocket and striding toward my own vehicle. Cheryl Ginger had a head start, but I knew these roads. That bunny could run, but I would catch her.

Chapter Thirty

Cheryl Ginger drove like she must have skied. She was nearly down the hill before I caught up with her, her silver sedan taking the curves almost as well as my GTO. Stewie had grown silent in the pursuit, his latent hunting instincts kicking in and focusing him forward. He sat in my passenger seat like a statue, holding his point even as we rounded the hill's biggest curve.

"There she is," I said as much to myself as to him. The spaniel was clearly aware of who we were pursuing.

He did glance up at me as we turned onto the highway, however. I'd fallen back, letting her get almost out of sight before accelerating. "I don't want her to see me," I said out loud, unsure of how much would translate. "There aren't any other cars on the road, and this car is kind of obvious.

"By the way," I added. "Is there anything else you can tell me?" I didn't think he'd be able to give me more than he already had, but I figured I'd check. Besides, it wouldn't hurt to distract him. His focus was intense enough to be almost painful. "What is she going to do? Who is she going to see?"

"*To see him.*" The answer surprised me; it came so clear and fast. "*But she won't, won't, won't…*" The thought translated into baying, and I reached over to soothe the poor beast. Fondling his silky ears calmed him—and saved mine—quieting him before he could give me more. It didn't matter. I knew where we were headed now. Murmuring reassurances to the distraught pup, I turned off the highway and onto the county road. Cheryl Ginger might drive like a slalom racer, but I'd grown up on these roads. A few more turns—and a whispered promise to the spaniel—and we were closing in on The Pines.

◇◇◇

I didn't have much of a lead. That girl drove fast. What I had was enough time to park, down by the end of the development, where even my classic ride wouldn't be obvious. With Stewie's leash tight, I crept up toward the condo, still easily identifiable by the yellow crime-scene tape. Although the plant life here was still winter-bare, I found a holly to hide behind, only a few doors away. Four-season foundation planting has its uses.

"Shh, boy." I probably didn't need to put my hand on his muzzle—this dog had more self control than most humans would ever know—but I wanted to be sure nothing would eke out that might alert the woman who was walking up the drive. She, too, had chosen not to park near her destination, which only confirmed my suspicion that something wasn't on the up and up. Besides, the contact had other benefits. Once again, I got the deep sense of concern—this dog was worried about the redhead. My own animal mind told me that, odds were, she was here because of a man.

"Where's she going, Stewie?" The question wasn't an idle one. As we crouched, waiting, I watched the pretty redhead approach. She was back in heels, not that I'd thought she'd driven out here for the hiking. And that left me wondering which condo she'd duck into, or whose car would be coming for her.

To my surprise, she stopped by the side of the road, not far from where I had seen her the day I found Stewie. Even from my vantage point, I could see how uneasy she looked. Her perpetual smile was gone, replaced with a tightness that aged her around the eyes. Even that pretty mouth looked tight, as if she were on the edge of pain. She might have been, the way she was dressed. Those pumps couldn't have been warm enough on this brisk day, and if the rain that threatened came, the buff leather would soon be ruined. But despite her apparent discomfort, she showed no signs of moving on. Almost, I expected her to call, and I put my hand on the spaniel's back, ready to restrain him if she did.

"*She's waiting for him.*" That came right away, still with an undercurrent of anxiety. Did the little dog know something about what had happened? Was he trying to tell me that the redhead had conspired to kill Teddy Rhinecrest?

My line of thought was broken as she turned and walked toward the condo. She moved slowly, which could have been the heels—or perhaps reluctance to cross the yellow tape that was hanging lower over the door. I saw her reach for the knob, and then catch herself. Reluctant to leave a trace of herself, or to see where her lover had died, she quickly turned again and with a fresh energy started off into the woods.

She wasn't dressed for it. At least once I saw her reach out to balance herself, as her stilettos sank deep into the soft earth and leaf mold, and she moved slowly, deeper into the woods. Her pace made my decision easier. Despite Stewie's whine, I bundled him off, back to my car, locking him in with the window open a crack.

"Be good," I said, emphasizing the idea of quiet. "I'll be back soon."

It might not have been my smartest move, but it was easy to follow her into the woods.

Chapter Thirty-one

What was less easy was to avoid stumbling over her. In my boots, worn as soft as slippers, I can maneuver over rotten branches and sudden dips with no trouble. But despite her head start, Cheryl Ginger hadn't gone far at all. Maybe fifty yards from the road, I nearly ran into her, crouched by a giant and overgrown stump with her back toward me.

Catching myself as quietly as I could—two grackles offered their own commentary on my progress—I stepped carefully back. Out here, most of the trees are new growth—thinner than I was and springing straight up toward the light. That stump, however, must have predated this generation by a good hundred years. As wide around as my car, with roots that extended out as long as a man's leg, it was a fragment of the past. Trees like that don't grow around here anymore. We don't let them, but even in decay, I could tell this remnant was a part of the living forest. As the redhead crouched in front of it, I could hear the worried thrum of rodents, quieting their young and waiting for the interloper to leave. Above us, out of my sight but not my hearing, a small raptor waited. She knew about the nests here, but her hope was different. If human interference prompted anyone to flee, she'd be waiting.

I waited too, my curiosity growing. The way she was crouched was suspicious, and though I couldn't see the her squatting in the woods like—well, like Stewie—I couldn't rule out such a basic explanation. From where I was, I only saw the fur of her jacket. When she rose and turned, I saw she hadn't undressed, and the mystery deepened. Whatever Cheryl Ginger had gone into the woods to bury, it wasn't something natural.

I had little doubt this had been her mission. Even as she stood there, looking around, she visibly relaxed, her shoulders settling down and the tight lines disappearing from her face. I was lucky, in fact, that her mood had lightened. Whereas on her way into the woods, she had been wary—moving slowly and carefully on those ridiculous heels—now she picked her way—slowly, but without that frantic urgency—back toward the road. Right by where I had flattened myself, breath held, behind a yew barely wide enough to hide my hips.

"She's gone!" The squeak of relief as a chipmunk head popped out served as my all-clear. Daring to move once more, I saw the white of her jacket moving into a patch of shadows, and I took my chance. Running, half-bent toward that giant stump, I marked where the exposed wood shone wet and red. Yes, the leaf mold here had been disturbed, the darker under layer inexpertly spread as cover. It struck me then, how odd it had been, to see the coiffed beauty crouching here, digging in the dirty forest bed with what must have been manicured hands.

I had no such restrictions. My nails are utilitarian—although Wallis would disagree—and dirt is part of my job. I moved carefully to brush away the leaf cover, however, unsure of what I would find. When I did, I still didn't understand. Two inches below the leaf cover, under an oak leaf made lacy by its own acid, I found it: Stewie's fancy collar, with all its jewels intact.

I picked it up and turned it over. No, I saw, the pretty, foolish thing wasn't entirely intact. One of the decorations had come loose and hung from its setting. The stone was red—a garnet, perhaps. Certainly not a ruby. And with a touch it snapped back into place. Surely, this couldn't be why Cheryl Ginger had discarded it, and even if it was, why go to the bother of taking it out here into the woods?

I was pondering this, turning the gaudy thing over in my hand when voices interrupted my reverie. Whispered voices but elevated by anger. I dropped to my knees and peered around the young tree.

"Where have you been?" A man, for sure. I could make him out, by the edge of the woods. He was tall—taller than Cheryl, whom he held by the arm—and while his face was in shadow, I could see short dark hair. "I've been waiting."

"I can't do this anymore." Cheryl, her newfound calm dispelled. "They're watching me!"

He pulled her close at this, and I waited for the kiss. He was too angry, though, and only whispered in her ear. Whatever it was, it had its effect, as she slumped in his grasp. I confess, I felt disappointed too. The redhead hadn't seemed that different from me, not at heart. And I hadn't wanted to think that a woman, alone, had been so predictable. The older boyfriend, the handsome lover. A plot, a pact, and now the revelation.

Only it seemed this soap opera had another tawdry act to run.

"So you see, you can't back out now." I could hear him, now that her head had dropped in grief or shame. "The stakes are too high."

"I don't care." She was shaking her head, backing away, and I liked her for it. "I can't do it," she said. "He'll just have to fend for himself."

Chapter Thirty-two

The dog gave me away.

I waited till the dark-haired man had taken off, making his way into the depths of the woods with more grace than his female counterpart had been able to summon simply getting to their rendezvous. She watched him, too, though I didn't think she was admiring his stride. Then I knew I had to act. What I'd heard sounded like the aftermath of a conspiracy. And while I'm no rat—Wallis would not stand for that—I knew this was worth bringing to Creighton's attention. He could take it to the Feds, or not. Hey, maybe it would win him some points. I had no problem with helping my guy out.

But even though I managed to sidle through the woods, working my way around Cheryl Ginger and back to the drive more quickly than she could manage, I'd forgotten about Stewie. The twenty minutes locked up must have been maddening for him, and as soon as I popped open the door, he slipped out, barking like a watchdog at a free-for-all.

"*No! No! No!*" I dived for the spaniel, even as he headed toward the woods. "*Beware! Beware!*"

"Stewie, no!" I missed, slipping on a damp patch and landing hard on my outstretched palms. "Quiet!"

"*I'm here! I'm here!*" The little dog called. "*Come back!*"

"Stewie!" I climbed to one knee. It hurt. So did my hand. But what stopped me cold wasn't the scraped raw skin, or even the embarrassed awareness I felt at having been outrun by a toy breed. It was the sight of Cheryl Ginger standing there, all five-eight of her in the skin-tight jeans and those stupid shoes, holding the longhaired spaniel in her arms.

"Pru Marlowe." She sounded shocked rather than frightened. Then again, I was the one who'd been sprawled on the road. "What are you doing here?"

"Your dog…" I gasped as I stood up. My knee was not happy. Did I exaggerate the pain to buy myself time? Maybe. "He was anxious." It was the truth, and as I paused for a moment, rubbing my knee, I wondered if she'd heard me use his real name.

"Anxious?" she asked. I looked up to see her glancing from me to the silky pup in her arms. "Pudgy?"

"Severe separation anxiety." I brushed off my palms, relieved to have something I could explain. "He started whining as soon as I took him out. I was going to take him back, but we saw you leave…" I left it at that. Explaining that I'd tailed her without her knowing—and then second-guessed her destination—would sound a little sinister, even if it was the truth.

"Oh." She nodded. This was too easy, and it hit me. She wasn't thinking about me or the dog. Her mind was still back in the woods, with the dark-haired man and the plans she no longer wanted to be part of.

"I couldn't help but overhear your conversation," I said. Sure, it had taken place beyond earshot of the road. I wasn't going to get into that. "You and your *friend.*"

"You heard?" From the way her eyes darted to the woods and back again, I thought I'd gone too far. She was going to call me on my claims—both that I had accidentally overheard anything and that I'd been following her for the dog's sake. "It's not what you think," she said instead.

I had her attention now.

"You know what I think, don't you?" I took a step closer to her. More to intimidate—and, okay, to retrieve some of the dignity I'd left in the gravel—than because I thought she could make a run for it in those shoes. "You want to hear me spell it out?"

Those wide eyes took on a deer-in-the-headlights look. Her mouth opened slightly, but when no protest emerged, I proceeded.

"You killed Teddy Rhinecrest," I said. "Really, you helped your *friend* do it. You both made sure you had an alibi. Made sure people saw you skiing, all day, miles away. But there's no reason for a real skier to come out here. You came for the privacy, and because it's close enough to the city so that your *friend* could come and go easily. Maybe establish his own alibi back in town."

"No." She was shaking her head. Stewie squirmed, and she let him go. "No," she repeated as he jumped to the ground. "No, that's not true."

"You knew Rhinecrest was getting tired of you. Maybe you even egged him on, in case you needed an excuse—self-defense. A battered wife, only he had a real wife who was clamping down. Your days with this particular sugar daddy were numbered."

"No," she kept saying. The dog at her feet looked from one of us to the other. Waiting, I thought. Watching. "I never meant him any harm."

That stopped me. Something about the phrasing: never meant him any harm? It wasn't simply that the words were cold. They were too damned polite.

"But, wait a minute." She was looking at me now. Truly seeing me, I thought, for the first time. "Why did *you* come here? Who are you, honestly?"

"Uh, me?" I stumbled as I fished for my own name, stuttering as I tried to answer, my mouth suddenly bone-dry. This was what I'd long feared: the confrontation I couldn't explain. So much for Cheryl Ginger being a vapid airhead. So much for my exposing her web of lies. The redhead had caught me out—my taking my cue from her dog. My *talking* to her dog, using a name other than the one she'd given him.

"Ms. Marlowe is who she says she is." I whirled around as a familiar figure stepped out from the shadows by the condo. Gregor Benazi, looking courtly in a trench coat and shoes too well-buffed for this weather. "One of the finest animal behaviorists I've had the pleasure of meeting. A real animal communicator, if you will, rather than a simple trainer."

I blinked, unsure whether to be grateful or afraid. Benazi had once again taken me by surprise, using words for me that were a little too close to the truth for comfort. Communicator, indeed. I had been planning to use my expertise on this man. To manipulate him with the tricks of voice and gesture that I use on the pampered pets of Beauville. What I hadn't considered was that he would see through me and call me out, hinting at something dangerously close to my secret. If that was in fact what he was doing. With Benazi, I couldn't be sure. What was certain, I realized now, was that I couldn't try to "train" him to do anything.

Holding my breath, I waited, sure that he would make the next move. I felt paralyzed. Unable to react. But whatever I did or didn't do was apparently beside the point. Benazi had turned from me to approach Cheryl Ginger. If I had been unclear on who was the alpha, I knew now.

"Ms. Ginger." He smiled as he held out his hand. As dangerous as she was to me, I wanted to shout a warning. To pull her back from taking that hand. I didn't. "I've been hoping that we would have a chance to speak again."

"Mr. Benazi." She licked her lips. Her mouth must have gone as dry as mine. "I'm sorry I haven't been in touch," she said. "What with everything going on." She waved her free hand, a gesture that encompassed the condo, the woods, and everything around us. The old man kept hold of her other hand, limiting her range of expression. His smile didn't waver. Instead he stood there, smiling. Waiting.

"I don't have it." Her words came out as a whisper, rasping between those dry lips.

Benazi placed his other hand over the one that held hers. In any other setting, the gesture would look affectionate. Grandfatherly. I recognized it for what it was: dominance. Possession. I shivered.

"But if you did…" he said finally. "If you find you do, then you would do the right thing, I have no doubt." His voice was nearly as soft as hers but smooth as the silk of his tie. "You would do the smart thing. Wouldn't you? I don't believe in the tactics some of my colleagues use, Ms. Ginger."

He released her hand and continued talking as if she had replied. "It's so much better for everyone if we keep our dealings civil. Don't you agree?"

"I don't..." she stammered, a denial neither of us believed as she cradled her right hand—the one he had been holding—against her breast as if it had been burned. "I never found it."

Without responding, he bent to pet the spaniel, hiking his pants legs up at the knee as he crouched by the little dog's side. Clearly, his supposition had been just that—he hadn't been asking the redhead what she would do. She wasn't arguing anymore, but it wasn't her I watched with a new curiosity. It was Stewie. The spaniel wasn't growling. He wasn't even whimpering. Instead, I got a sense of questioning—of waiting, as if for the answer to a question.

"Good dog," said Benazi. "What a fine fellow you are, and what a careful dog, too."

He stood and brushed an imaginary fleck of mud from his trousers and then turned to me with a wink. I couldn't be sure—maybe I never would be sure—but this seemed like confirmation of what I had feared. Gregor Benazi hadn't simply eavesdropped on us, catching my roadside interrogation of the redhead. He'd picked up on why I was there—the how of it, perhaps—or he had known all along. I was no more training him than I could train, well, any wild beast out in these woods. Which led me to wonder in what role he had cast me in this drama, and whether he had followed us—followed me—out here, or if he had known we'd be here all along.

"Good dog," he repeated, as he turned to go. But before he'd taken two steps, he turned back again, as if struck by a sudden thought. "You would do well to listen to him, Ms. ...Ginger." The pause was obvious. Pointed. "And to Ms. Marlowe, too."

Chapter Thirty-three

Even before we heard the muted roar of Benazi's sportster, I was trying to digest what had just happened. That Cheryl Ginger was involved with something crooked was pretty clear. That she was trying to buck the elegant gangster was something else again. The woman had spunk, and I felt a grudging admiration for her.

Not enough to get in Benazi's way if he felt the need to take off the velvet gloves. But enough to try to warn her, once again. Maybe even help her out of a jam.

"Sister, you're in big trouble." I took a step closer to her. I didn't think she'd try to run—not in those shoes—but I didn't want to risk it. I also didn't want Ronnie eavesdropping if he was anywhere on the premises. "If you know what's good for you, you'll talk to me."

"Sister?" She shook her head in disbelief, and again I felt a pang. I was just talking, but I got it. A woman who looked like this didn't get a lot of fellow feeling from her own gender. Especially not one who'd made a living off those looks. "You don't know."

I stopped her there, before she could start the whole litany of denial one more time.

"Don't," I said, putting my hands on my hips. As I did, I felt an unfamiliar lump in my pocket. That fancy collar. "I saw you. I heard you," I said, and pulling the gaudy strip of leather out of my pocket, I waved it in her face. "I saw you getting rid of this."

She gasped, and I waited. I didn't want to misstep here. Didn't want to give her an out. "Pudgy's collar," she choked out the words, as she reached to take it from me.

"Not so fast." I drew it back, running my thumb across the colorful stones. The red one came loose again at my touch, and I felt the rough setting with the ball of my thumb. It left a cavity like a missing molar, but a touch of glue could have set the garish thing right. "Tell me about this pretty thing."

"What's to tell?" Her voice was growing breathy. "It's a collar. A silly, trashy collar. Pudgy deserves better."

I didn't disagree, but I also didn't see her disposing of it in the woods. "Was it a gift?"

Another gasp. I was onto something. "From Teddy?" I looked at the bright colors. Could they be gemstones? It didn't seem likely. "You said he would give you silly gifts sometimes."

"Yes, yes, he would." She was nodding. This was too easy. "The teddy bear. The ice cream scoop. All sorts of things."

"No." That gap. The man who came to meet her. "He didn't. That man did, the one you were talking with in the woods." I looked at the red stone, the way it came loose, as if it were hinged. "You passed messages with this, didn't you? Set up assignations, maybe?"

She looked like she was going to cry.

"Maybe planned when to kill your rich boyfriend?" My sympathy only went so far.

"It wasn't like that. That man, he's not..." She had her hands out to me, imploring. I wasn't going to give her the collar, though. I wouldn't give her the time of day. But even as she pleaded, an odd thought came to me. Stewie—the spaniel who had brought me to these woods one more time—was quiet. No whining, no growling. Although his sensitive snout was turned up to look at Cheryl as she begged, he wasn't acting like he was concerned about her or worried about me. No, he was observing.

"*What is it?*" I looked down at that silky curls, willing the dog to turn those large, liquid eyes on me. "*Why are you so calm?*"

"He's gone." The reply came back immediately, silent and calm. *"We are safe,"* his canine composure said, as I caught the wave of peaceful observation washing over him.

He's gone. I thought for a moment of the man Cheryl had met in the woods. He'd been insistent. But even as I pictured him, the dog didn't change. Barely moved, as he looked up at the woman in his care. That left one option.

"Maybe this is what Benazi was looking for," I said, turning the collar over in my hand. "Maybe it's that simple, after all."

"Please." The dog didn't respond, but Cheryl Ginger did. Our brief détente was shattered as she stepped toward me, hands outstretched. I stepped back, wary of a ploy to disarm me—or to grab the canine bauble. Creighton had said what a great skier Cheryl Ginger was, and that takes muscles. But while she might be an athlete, I bet I knew more about fighting. Besides, she was wearing those shoes. "You can't—that man. He would kill me, if he knew."

If he knew. "So this isn't what Benazi and his cronies are looking for?" I held it up. The clouds had broken up, and the sun highlighted the colors. Green for the trees that would soon be in leaf. Red for blood.

"No." She slumped, shaking her head. "No, it's not," she said. I was looking for the move. Waiting for the trick, but the way her shoulders hung, I thought she might really be defeated. What I didn't know was why.

"Why?" Sometimes it pays to ask. "What's going on here, Cheryl? Why is this thing so important? So dangerous?"

She turned and began to walk away, Stewie staying perfectly at heel. I didn't know whether to grab her or follow, like her little dog.

"Cheryl?" She wobbled a little. Those shoes. Fatigue. "What does this mean?"

She muttered something, her voice lost in the growing distance.

"Cheryl?" I called.

And then she turned, her face supremely sad. "Ask your boyfriend," she said.

◇◇◇

I let her go. I wasn't sure what other option I had. I stood and watched as she walked down to her car and beeped it open. Stewie jumped right in as if this was the most natural outing in the world, and as Cheryl did a slow k-turn and started down the drive, I tried to make sense of what had happened.

"Jim?" I'm not stupid. I called Creighton as soon as she'd driven off. "I've got to talk to you as soon as possible. Call me back, please?"

I'd gone back to my own car by then and, after a moment's hesitation, slipped the garish collar into my glove compartment. There was no way I was putting it back in the woods, but I didn't think I wanted to be found with it on me. Gregor Benazi had an uncanny way of showing up without warning, but I thought that he'd consider breaking into my car impolite, for lack of a better word.

I started back to my house. There was no point in following Cheryl. Unless I missed my guess, she'd accomplished her one errand. She'd take the spaniel back to her fancy hotel and hole up there, until Benazi or the Feds or some unknown third party to be named later came for her. I wasn't sure if I cared.

As I drove, I mulled over what I'd tell my guy. Driving relaxes me, especially now that I've got my ride in top condition. It's not that I zone out, although the roads around Beauville at this season were empty and any black ice had melted. No, as I shifted gears and felt the reassuring roar, it was that driving required more than thought. To master a car like mine, especially as I liked to drive it, meant concentration and physical coordination. My baby blue baby took what I could give, with neither of us holding back. In that way, it was a better relationship than I could ever have with Creighton.

My phone buzzed, jumping from its vibration. "Speak of the devil." I reached for it, only easing my foot off the gas slightly. "Jim?"

"No." A woman. For a moment I didn't recognize her. "It's Marnie," she said, sensing my hesitation. "Marnie Lundquist.

Can you come over?" It was her voice that had confused me: tighter and higher than I had ever heard it. "Please, Ms. Marlowe. Henry is…he's gone."

Chapter Thirty-four

Marnie Lundquist hung up too quickly for me to ask what had happened. But she had sounded so distraught, I feared the worst. I turned off at the next intersection and headed toward her house. I'm not naturally empathetic—not with humans, anyway—and my years in the city had trained me to question any urge to sympathize with the average sob story. But I liked the old lady, and I heard the pain in her voice.

I also felt culpable. My first instinct had been right· wild animals aren't pets, and Henry was probably doomed from the start. If we'd gotten him to a wildlife rehab center, he might have had a chance. At least Marnie Lundquist would have thought he did, rather than being burdened with a small carcass going cold and stiff. If I couldn't convince her to relinquish the bunny—he was her granddaughter's pet, after all—I should have pushed for a visit to the vet. Should have insisted. Old Doc Sharpe might have been persuaded to see the little leporid without reporting her.

There was another reason I blamed myself—one that I was loath to admit—and that was that I personally had failed, somehow. As I sped toward the poor woman's house, I went over what I had gotten from the rabbit. What I had missed. Wild animals are good at hiding the symptoms of injury or illness; their survival can depend on their seeming strong. But with my sensitivity, I should have gotten some clue. What had I heard? Stray thoughts about family, about safety.

"Watch out!" A voice shrieked in my ear, and I slammed on the brakes. Bad idea. The snow might be gone, but the road was wet from the day's shower and I felt myself spinning out, my car spinning sideways—a nearly two-ton pinball whipped between inertia and friction. I eased off the brakes and felt the skid begin to even out, my tires catching the road.

I was shaking as I drove off. The smell of burning rubber and the prone body of the opossum leaving me trembling. Not that the sight of that shaggy body meant anything, I reminded myself. The ugly little animal had yelled a warning, but I had felt no impact, neither through the car nor mentally. The opossum and I had both had a good scare, and his response was to keel over temporarily. We were both lucky he had made it to the side of the road before the odd reaction had kicked in, and I found myself taking deep breaths to steady my hands and heartbeat as I went on my way.

The interaction did give me a glimmer of hope. "Henry is gone," his caretaker had said. Only, maybe he wasn't. And maybe there was something I could do to help.

Driving with more care—and more optimism—I rounded the corner of Marnie Lundquist's block. She was there to greet me, running down from the front door even before I had pocketed my keys.

"Ms. Marlowe!" She clasped her own hands tight to her breast, as if evoking the bunny. "Please help me."

"Of course." I followed her into the house, wondering what I'd find. "You said Henry was gone?"

"Yes, yes." She turned back and saw the confusion on my face. "Oh, no! I Not that, I hope. I only meant, well, Henry has gone missing."

"Ah." I nodded. "Well, that's better."

I regretted those words as soon as they were out of my mouth, Marnie Lundquist looked so distressed. "It's my fault," she said. "We have to find him."

"Of course." I led her into the living room, where we had begun our last visit, and sat. She didn't, the look of distress knitting her face. "Please," I motioned to the sofa beside me. "I need to hear what happened."

"All right." She perched on the edge of the seat, as if afraid the bunny might hop by at any moment. Or, I realized, that he might be—might have been—under the cushions. I shifted to the edge, too.

"What are Henry's usual hiding places?" I asked, not wanting to suggest a possible tragedy if I could help it. "I assume you've checked those?"

"Yes, yes." That verbal tic was getting annoying. She had lost her granddaughter's pet, I reminded myself. "Under the stereo, next to the refrigerator, and in the cat bed—excuse me, bunny bed—that he always sleeps in."

I nodded. The first two made sense—electronics are warm—and the bed probably smelled familiar. "Why don't we check them again?" I suggested.

The old lady looked up at me, eyes wide.

"Animals have a way of disappearing and then reappearing," I said, with what I intended as a hopeful inflection. It was true, but I also needed a moment to consider. Domestic animals aren't that hard to track down. House cats who get lost, for example, almost always hide someplace close by. Their people see them hightail it out the door and they go blocks, calling and putting up notices. Most of the time, Fluffy stopped running right around the garbage bin, and a close inspection of the immediate environs—the basement window wells, the trash area—will result in relief, both for the freaked-out house pet and for the frightened owner. I didn't know rabbit behavior that well, though. I didn't know a behaviorist who did. Then again, I had skills that most lacked.

I followed her quick nervous steps into the kitchen, getting down on hands and knees to peer into the crevice by her fridge. Nothing, not even dust bunnies—Marnie Lundquist kept her house as neat as her hair. Same when I looked under the stereo. When she took me to see his bed—a quilted, covered basket in the corner of her small sitting room—I could feel her begin to panic.

"Please, wait." I left her at the door and got down on my knees. Watching her fret, kneading those long, white fingers, was distracting, as well as distressing, and I wanted to focus. *"Henry?"* I tried to reach out, calling the only name I had for the little brown bunny. *"Are you there?"*

I reached into the bed. Despite Marnie Lundquist's house-cleaning habits, there was bunny fur on the pillow. Although the rabbit was nowhere in sight, the fur felt warm under my hand. Silky, and as soft as the lining of a nest. A strange idea began to form in the back of my mind.

"Mrs. Lundquist?" I didn't want to accuse the kind old lady of lying to me, but I was beginning to think she had not exactly shared the whole truth. "Has Henry gotten out before?"

Her face crumpled, and for a moment I feared she would start to cry. "Yes," she said, just once. "He did." I waited, my silence and her guilt over obscuring the truth having the same effect as the forces that had nearly wrecked my car on the way over.

"That's why I was so worried the first time I called you," she said, after another moment of handwringing. "It was a few weeks ago, now. My granddaughter had told me I should give him some time on the grass, if possible. And it's been such a horrible winter. I thought, with the first thaw…"

More hand-wringing. She was blinking back tears. "I'm not as young as I once was, and he's rather fast," she said. "I must have looked away for a moment, and he was gone. I was in a panic. It was all my fault. But then I found him, under the rho-dodendron, nibbling at something as if everything was perfectly normal. He was only gone a few minutes but, my stars, I thought I was going to faint after that."

She wiped at her eyes, but I thought her color looked better, now that she'd confessed. "When he started acting strange, I thought he may have picked up some disease or, perhaps, been bitten…" She paused, looking at me, the unspoken question in her eyes.

"You're wondering about rabies," I said.

She swallowed and blinked several times in rapid succession.

"It's very unlikely." I reviewed everything I knew before proceeding. The last thing I wanted to do was give this kind woman false hope. "Like any warm-blooded animal, rabbits can get rabies. But the disease is transmitted by bites from an infected animal." I'd had my own run-in with rabies, and I couldn't make light of the threat. "And we do have reports of infected animals in the county. Have you seen an infected animal—a raccoon acting strangely, or anything like that?"

She shook her head.

"I think he's fine then," I said. "That's the only way Henry could get a disease like rabies. And, to be honest, I think you'd have noticed if he'd been bitten. He hadn't, right?"

"No, no," she was beginning to sound relieved. "I'm sure I would have been aware if he had."

I was, too. Rabies is not common in rabbits because rabbits don't usually survive the initial attack. "Then I think you're good. And Henry is probably just making himself scarce somewhere in the house."

She nodded, more in relief than agreement. Now that I'd identified her real concern, Marnie Lundquist would be fine. There was something else, though. Something I'd almost gotten from Henry's bed.

"I'm wondering," I said. "Could I see where you feed Henry?"

"Of course." She led me back to the kitchen, which had an old-fashioned pantry. There, under the lowest shelf, I saw an improvised hay rack: a wire magazine rack, it looked like, half full of the sweet grasses I had seen the rabbit nibbling the other day. I knelt again and leaned in. The hay smelled fresh and sweet. Tender, almost, like something one could burrow into, although of course the rack was much too thin to hide a bunny Henry's size, the stalks too sparse…I reached to touch it.

"How strange." The voice behind me startled me.

"Excuse me?" I sat back and looked up at her, my train of thought broken.

"It's just…" Her brow knit in confusion. "I filled that this morning."

"Well, that's a good sign." I sat back on the floor. "I can't imagine anyone else eating Henry's hay."

"No, but it's a bit confusing." Whatever she had been intending to say next was interrupted by a loud ringing sound, like of an old-fashioned phone.

"I'm sorry." I reached for my pocket. "I may have to take this."

Sure enough, it was Creighton. I looked up at the white-haired woman. "I am sorry," I repeated.

"Please." She backed off into the kitchen to give me privacy.

"Jim." I felt a bit silly, crouched in the pantry, but this was not a conversation I wanted overheard. "Thanks for calling me back."

"What's up?" He cut right to the chase. "You said it was urgent."

"It is." I looked around. Marnie Lundquist had turned the sink on. She was making a great show of washing a dish that I could have sworn was clean. "Look, I'm with a client right now, but I need to talk to you." I dropped my voice even lower. "About Cheryl Ginger."

"Ah, so it's not life or limb." I could almost hear him exhale. Creighton does worry about me at times. What I didn't hear was any surprise. "It's you poking your nose into things again."

"No, Jim." I paused. "Not—look, she hired me to take care of her dog, all right? But something came up, and I have to talk to you. Give me five minutes, and I'll call you back." I started getting to my feet. "Even better, I'll come down to the station."

"No, I don't think you should do that." His quick reply surprised me. "How about an early lunch? Maybe Hardware again?"

I wasn't sure what was going on. I did know that I'd kept Marnie Lundquist waiting long enough. "I'm sorry, Mrs. Lundquist," I said as I emerged from her pantry. "That was an urgent matter. Usually I turn my phone off—"

"No, please." She was smiling. "You came over on a moment's notice when I called. I can't expect you to drop everything for one old lady."

"You're a client." I smiled back. It was hard not to. She was a nice woman, and her obvious relief was infectious. "And besides, I want the best for Henry."

"That's just it." She turned back toward the fodder and nodded, that white bun bobbing up and down like a cottontail. "Don't you see? Henry must be somewhere right around here. All that lovely hay didn't eat itself!"

Chapter Thirty-five

It didn't feel right leaving then. I hadn't helped solve Marnie Lundquist's problem. Henry was still missing. And he didn't have to be. I had a strong feeling that I'd picked up clues to his whereabouts. Hints from his bed, from his hay rack. Even from the kind old lady who so clearly doted on her granddaughter's pet. Clues I couldn't quite decipher.

What I hadn't done was hear from the brown bunny directly. It was almost as if the little beast was hiding his thoughts. But when I'd visited before, he'd seemed quite comfortable with domesticity. Had I somehow put the creature off?

This hadn't been a day for confidences. But I was going to have to tell Creighton something, that I knew. As I drove to the center of town, I thought about what Cheryl Ginger had said. "Ask your boyfriend." Right.

The dead man's girlfriend couldn't help being beautiful. She'd gone out of her way to be provocative, though, bringing up Creighton like that. She'd been tired. Scared, I figured, and I'd been so close to breaking her down. So she'd shot back, and I'd let her go. Partly because the spaniel Stewie was being so quiet. He'd seemed quite fine with the redhead, once she and I were alone. Once Benazi was gone. Though, come to think of it, the long-haired spaniel had calmed down as soon as the man in the woods had taken off. Could that dark-haired man have been the cause of the spaniel's anxiety? Was it the collar? This was not how I had wanted to spend my day.

◇◇◇

"Ma'am?" The skinny man in the tight suit addressing me couldn't have been more than five years my junior. Still, I bit my tongue, only nodding in response. The lunch crowd at Hardware was a sight more downscale than for dinner, but even by Beauville standards, my work clothes—denim, not too clean—were pushing it. There was no question I was going to be seated. I could see Creighton already raiding the breadbasket. Besides, this was the same youthful maitre d' who had been on duty during my previous visit, so he knew I could do better. I'd let him have his little victory, this little man with his stylish little suit. "Follow me, please."

As the host made a grand gesture of pulling out my chair, I realized that Creighton was at the same table we'd had the other night. I could tell from his smile that he'd gotten the gist of what had just happened, probably from the way I was walking, head high enough for a queen.

"That's right, you were working," he said, as I sat. The maitre d' handed me a menu and left.

"You know that." I eyed him. "You wanted to meet me someplace public, where I'd be off guard." Where I'd be reminded of Cheryl Ginger and Teddy Rhinecrest, I thought. Why, I didn't know.

"You're right about the first part of that." He handed me a breadstick. "But you should order."

"In a minute." I leaned across the table. "Jim, this is serious. Cheryl Ginger is hiding something. I mean, specifically. I was walking her dog, and I saw her hiding his old collar in the woods."

"Hang on." He put his hands up, as if I were a speeding car. "Just a moment, Pru."

"No." I pulled his hand down, beside the breadbasket. I didn't need more people staring at us. "There's more, Jim. She was meeting with this guy—"

"Pru!" Creighton has a command voice, too—not loud, but forceful—and he used it now. Between that one word and the way he took my hands in his, I shut up.

For a moment, anyway. "Yes, Jim?" He had to give me something.

He saw that. He sighed. He wasn't getting away. "You know I'm off the case, Pru."

I didn't believe that. Not anymore. Not entirely.

"I have been brought in to consult," he said when my silence grew too uncomfortable. The waiter was hovering behind him, but I warned him off with a quick glare. "As a courtesy," Creighton continued.

"Then as a courtesy, you need to know—"

"No, Pru," he said. "I don't. And neither do you." He emphasized those last words, but before I could ask why, he went on. "Cheryl Ginger is not someone you can interrogate. Not someone I can, either."

"I already have." The waiter was gathering his nerve up to approach us again. I had to talk fast. "She's hiding something. Literally, I think the collar had a secret compartment—"

"Be *quiet!*" He clamped down on my hands, leaning in as he hissed the words. Which did, in fact, shock me into silence. "Pru," he said in a more usual tone. "Please, there are some things I can't share with you, as much as I'd like to. But, please, Pru? Leave this be. This is a matter for the Feds, and not something either of us wants to be messing with. Waiter?"

The poor guy had seen it all, but he came over anyway.

"I'm having the burger. And you?" Jim turned back to me. I nodded. "Rare," I added. I wasn't going to get anything else.

Chapter Thirty-six

An hour later, I had a good idea why Creighton had taken me to lunch. Not to remind me of Teddy Rhinecrest's fate—or not only. But because someone wanted to look through my house, without the benefit of a search warrant. I was furious, and I hadn't been fooled. One advantage of being able to talk to your cat? She's better than a watchdog.

"A man was here." Wallis sauntered into the kitchen as I was putting my leftovers away. After that scene in the restaurant, my appetite had dwindled. Now I felt what I had eaten congeal into something cold and hard in the pit of my stomach. *"He came inside."*

"What?" I whipped around to face my tabby. "Are you sure?"

She ignored my questions as unworthy of her notice, jumping off the table and proceeding to sniff at the bag. *"Is that... mmm...beef?"*

I left it on the counter as I ran into the living room to see for myself. I thought of Creighton as such a boy scout, but he was a cop, first and foremost. And he knew I'd hid things from him before. I cursed him as I pulled pillows off the sofa, looking for damage. Looking for...anything. Up in my bedroom, I started tossing clothes around, fury blinding me.

I can't trust him, I thought. *I can't trust any of them. Men!* And that thought stopped me as cold as if I'd seen a ghost. In a way, I had. I was sounding like my mother. She never did get over my father. And I?

Well, I knew I had inherited some of his bad habits. The empty bottles in the kitchen were proof of that. But hers, too? I looked around at the house that I had so recently restored. In my own way, I was as practical as she was. Maybe I even worked as hard. But that bitterness? That lack of trust? I had my own reasons to be wary, but they were rooted in my life. My reality. And I liked to think I could make my own judgments about people. I also liked to think I would have noticed that someone had been in my house had Wallis not said anything. I couldn't be sure.

I also couldn't be certain that Creighton had been involved. Despite that initial hot surge of certainty—and, I'll admit it, rage—this didn't seem like him. He knew I didn't tell him everything. Sure, but he wasn't the type to cross the line. Not this line. One day, I'd come home to find cruisers out front, I had no doubt. But this? The timing could have been coincidence. Or…well, I couldn't be sure.

One thing I knew: the search had been professional. Despite my own whirlwind inspection, nothing was really out of place. In fact, before I'd rushed in, the mess was roughly at the same level as it had been when I'd left that morning. And nothing appeared to have been taken. My old turntable was still hooked up to the stereo. My mother's pearls were still in their velvet-lined box, untouched since long before she'd died.

I descended the stairs with heavy steps. Wallis blinked in acknowledgment—she could read my apology in my thoughts and probably on my face as well. Then she turned toward that bag, and its foil-wrapped contents.

"And?" Out loud, I heard a rumbling mew that sounded more like a query than a command.

"Of course." I wasn't hungry anyway. I peeled the bun off the burger and scraped off the last of the onion. "Here." Putting the bare patty on a plate, I slid it over to her. The rumble became a purr.

"He was quiet, but he knew you weren't home," said Wallis, between bites. *"He took his time."*

"He knew..." I started to doubt myself again. To doubt Creighton. The delay in calling me back. The lunch downtown. "Was it cops? Or Feds?"

Wallis looked up at me, her ears going slightly flat as they did when she concentrated—or when she was annoyed. "You know, official?" I visualized uniforms. Jim.

"Perhaps." She went back to eating. I didn't press her. Wallis doesn't like it when she doesn't know something. I'd say it's a cat thing, but I know the feeling myself.

"Creighton, hell..." My fury had burned down to simmering resentment. That was better than being frightened, but even as I grumbled, I told myself that I might be jumping to conclusions. After all, I'd originally thought that Creighton had taken me out to keep me from causing a scene. Wallis might react badly when her blind spots are exposed, but she's nothing as bad as I am when I'm being told to lay off a line of questioning. There was also the possibility that he'd wanted a nice lunch, and thought to take me along. Or even, I let the thought surface, that he'd wanted to treat me. We'd been getting more serious, and I'd heard that people do such things.

Besides, he wasn't the only one who would know that I'd not be home. Cheryl Ginger had seen me at The Pines, a good thirty minutes away. It was quite possible that she'd called someone as soon as she'd left to tell him that I was out—or even that she'd followed me to Marnie Lundquist's. I'd been so distracted, I might not have noticed.

And anything I thought the redhead capable of was certainly true of Gregor Benazi. I like to think I'd have noticed his red sports car. We gearheads tend to be aware of each other. But I also suspected that the elegant gangster was the type to delegate. What else he might choose to offload to someone younger and perhaps less scrupulous wasn't something I wanted to dwell on. What had he been saying to Cheryl Ginger? Something about the methods of his colleagues?

A loud bell sounded behind me and I jumped. My phone—I'd

never turned the ringer back down, and I grabbed at it with irritation as Wallis looked on, bemused.

"Yeah?" I was ready to bite someone's head off.

"Ms. Marlowe?" The voice was familiar. Female, but I must have been more flustered than I knew, and paused too long. "Theresa Rhinecrest here. I'm looking for Martin Parvis."

"Parvis?" It had been more than twelve hours since I'd found his body. Then again, she wasn't next of kin. I shook my head to clear it and took a breath. "You haven't heard?"

"Heard what? Has that little sneak run off?"

"Not exactly." I leaned back on the counter. I wasn't looking forward to breaking the news. Wallis gave up all pretense of eating and watched me, tail flicking with interest. "I'm sorry nobody called you, Mrs. Rhinecrest, but, you see, there's been an…incident." I'd almost said "accident," as if the private investigator had tripped and fallen on someone's blade. "He's dead."

"Oh, that greedy fool." Her response was immediate, and not what I expected. "That stupid fool."

"Mrs. Rhinecrest?" Most people, you tell them of the death of an employee—even an acquaintance—they express shock. Horror. Sympathy. Then they ask how it happened. Teddy Rhinecrest's widow had skipped a step or three.

"Look," she kept talking, "I had nothing to do with this. He was under strict orders to look for bank accounts—for financial assets only," she said.

"You knew he was murdered?" I was only stating the obvious.

She sighed, and I could hear her as if she were in the next room. "I knew he wasn't working only for me, no matter what he said. And that he was a greedy idiot. I didn't think…" She paused just when I would have wanted her to continue. When she did, she seemed to have switched a gear.

"So, did he find anything?" Her voice was tighter. Anxious. "Were you able to give him any leads?"

"I never got to talk to him in person." I was suddenly deeply tired. "I went to meet him. He never made it."

"So he *was* planning on meeting with you." She said it like she still doubted me. "Does that mean you found something?"

I should have denied it, but I was so tired that I hesitated a moment too long.

"You did, didn't you?" Her voice took on an edge I didn't like. "No, don't tell me," she said, before I could respond. "I don't want to know. I don't want to end up like Parvis, and you should be careful that you don't either."

Chapter Thirty-seven

It was the collar. It had to be the collar. Only there was something I wasn't getting. As soon as Theresa Rhinecrest had hung up, I'd gone out to my car. The gaudy thing was still in my glove compartment, and I kept it low in my lap as I examined it once again, looking for some reason this bit of froufrou should cause so much fuss.

Using my knife, I pried the remaining colored "jewels" off the leather. I'm no expert, but it seemed pretty obvious they were glass. Real topaz wouldn't chip like that, and real emeralds probably wouldn't have been glued in place. Still I tucked them in my pocket, wondering if I held the key to financial security as I did so.

They'd come out easily. Only the red one—the one I still thought of as the ruby—had anything like a hinge holding it on, and the tiny space between its concave back and the soft leather was empty. I poked at it with the point of my handy blade, and then rubbed the surface with my thumbnail to make sure, turning up nothing. Only a small cavity, big enough for a rolled-up bit of paper or—who knew?—some kind of small chip.

Whatever it was supposed to hold, it was gone now. Leaving me with only the conviction that the collar was more than a bit of doggie decoration. But why it should matter so much was beyond me. Even if the two lovers had used it to pass messages—maybe plan a murder—there was nothing incriminating here.

In fact, I was the only one who could tie it to Cheryl Ginger or the dark-haired man at all.

That was not a comfortable thought. I recalled what I'd read and heard about the late Teddy Rhinecrest. He might never have been convicted, but he'd kept the kind of company that made his complete innocence of any crime highly unlikely. The kind of company that wouldn't need a clear burden of proof before deciding on a death penalty. Then again, those kinds of people didn't need evidence at all. If they knew the redhead and her outside man were responsible for the death of one of their own, the ski bunny and her beau would be gone by now. Not being questioned by the likes of Gregor Benazi.

As I sat there and looked at the collar in my hands. I was tempted to toss it. Drive out of town and fling it into the woods. Cheryl Ginger had tried her version of that, and I'd seen her. I'd be more careful, of course. And I knew these woods and these roads.

Only Benazi had come to me first. He knew I'd be talking to Cheryl Ginger, and he expected me to find something. And everyone seemed to know that I'd been the one to nearly stumble over Teddy Rhinecrest's body, entering his apartment that morning.

The apartment. I looked down at the collar again, this time really seeing it. This wasn't the key, or if it was, I didn't know what secret it unlocked. No, there had to be something else going on—maybe connected to the tacky collar. Maybe not. I pocketed the thin strip of leather then, sliding my knife into my boot where it was almost as handy but wouldn't make quite as obvious a bulge.

I'm not a possum. It's not my nature to hide or play dead, and besides, I would rather be angry than scared. And since everybody from Theresa Rhinecrest to Gregor Benazi seemed to think I knew what was going on, it only made sense that I should find out.

Chapter Thirty-eight

This was one of those times when driving settled me. When the motions verged on automatic and focused my churning mind. The shadows had lengthened as I raced through Beauville, and I liked the dappling of the road for the cover it appeared to give. Dusk was approaching, the hour of the hunter, and my GTO soared like a hawk as I passed the outskirts of town.

I didn't need the worried robin to remind me that I was acting precipitously. Even as she chirruped her concern, I knew of the predators in the area. Knew, too, that Creighton had done his best to warn me off, smoothing the message with a nice meal downtown. But he hadn't even let me tell him what had happened, and by shutting me up, he'd relinquished any authority he had.

I'd been careful to lock up my house before I'd taken off. Wallis knew enough to keep herself safe—and to be on guard. But she and I were more alike than Creighton would ever know. We might not be the biggest predators in the woods out here, but we were hunters too. And I was sick of being played for a fool.

◇◇◇

Someone had already searched the condo. Although I was ready to pick the lock, the door opened with a gentle push, and I ducked under the yellow crime-scene tape with no compunction. I hadn't wanted to get involved in this, after all. I just wanted a way out.

I did find myself holding my breath, however, as I stepped into the unit and closed the door quietly behind me. The memory of Teddy Rhinecrest lying there, bloody and still, would keep popping into my mind. To deal, I made myself stare at the floor, which now held nothing but a dirty doormat. Dark footprints left by large men suggested that whoever had been here before me hadn't cared about covering their tracks. Creighton's men, the Feds who'd taken over, or some thuggish acquaintances of Benazi's, I didn't know. I'm not some kind of bloodhound who can figure out a man's profession from his shoe size. All I knew is they—he?—had not worried about leaving traces of their presence.

I gave my eyes a moment to adjust. The condo didn't get a lot of natural light, and at this time of day it was in shadow. Still, I hesitated before reaching for the switch. Whoever had been here had come and gone—the mud from last night's rain had dried outside. But I remembered Benazi, appearing out of nowhere. I didn't know if the building was being watched.

Once I had my bearings, I looked around. That wainscoting panel—the one that had been so badly repaired—had been torn loose. Ronnie hadn't even used good nails, and I found the one he had bent and hammered into place, lying by that mat.

The rest of the condo had gotten as thorough a going-over as the entranceway. Boxes of fancy teas had been emptied onto the kitchen counter, and both the protein powder and Metamucil had been dumped into the sink. I needn't have worried about the lights. The fuse box, by the back door, was open; the floor littered with the wires that had been pulled from it. Whatever was being searched for must be small if it could've been hidden there. I thought about the collar, about the multicolored stones I'd so casually pocketed. About the empty compartment. None of this was making any sense.

I'd followed the muddy footprints up the stairs with a growing sense of dread. Cops didn't act like this. I'd expected the closets to be emptied—at least partially. Cheryl Ginger didn't look like a woman who traveled light, and I knew that whoever was investigating had let her pack, even if they watched. But I didn't think it likely that she'd been the one to pull out the drawers and toss them on the floor when she was done. Nor had she upset the mattress that lay tipped at an angle, suggesting it, and the box spring sprawled beside it, had been turned and inspected.

I was sorry then that I didn't have Stewie with me. His nose would have been invaluable, not only to tell me about who had done this but also, perhaps, whether they had found it.

I hoped they had. I didn't care what *it* was. This thorough a search was disturbing. It meant somebody was not going to stop.

"Eat up! Eat up!" The trill of a robin, in the condo's eave, broke into my reverie. He'd found a fat earthworm and was thrilled to bring it home to his mate, who was putting the finishing touches on an early nest. Spring was coming, despite it all, and the recent rain had softened the earth and driven that juicy worm up to the surface.

For a moment, I enjoyed the domestic scene. Then I froze. The rain—it had stopped earlier today. That mud that I had noticed? This condo had been searched before my house. And that meant that whatever was being sought had not been found.

I took a deep breath as I considered the implications. For Cheryl Ginger. For Creighton. For me. The leggy redhead's urge to dump the collar was beginning to make sense. If both the Feds and Benazi wanted it, the gaudy thing was too hot to handle. What I didn't know was why, and it struck me again that I had more questions for the spaniel. He might not understand the value humans would place on something, but I bet he could tell me something about who had been interested in it and when it had come into his life.

I was so busy thinking about the spaniel that I almost missed it. The low squeal of a door opening on the floor below. It was the footstep that alerted me, the heavy tread of a large man stepping past that dirty mat and onto the stone tile floor where Teddy Rhinecrest had lain only days before. I had just stepped from the bathroom back into the upstairs hall, and I racked my brain, trying to remember the location of the nearest large window and whether the building had any kind of fire escape.

"Hello?" The voice—deep, male—sent shivers up my spine, until it came to me: I knew that voice. That tread.

"Ronnie?" I stepped to the head of the stairs. If he wasn't alone, I'd bolt for the bedroom: it had a picture window that I could smash with the vanity chair if it didn't open quickly.

"Pru! What are you doing here?" His round face stared up at me. Alone, as far as I could see.

"Me? What am I doing here?" Fear turned to anger. "You scared the hell out of me, Ronnie. Someone got killed here, you know."

"I know." He blinked up at me, his voice petulant. "When I saw the door was open, I thought…I don't know, a ghost or something. Albert says I'm crazy, but Vince swears someone's been following him. He says he's laying low."

"Vince drinks too much. You know that." I was pissed, and having to agree with Albert wasn't helping. I was also, I realized, missing something. "Ronnie, the door wasn't open," I said and began to walk down the stairs.

"It was." He blinked up at me. "I was doing my rounds, and I saw it move."

For a moment, I froze. It was possible someone had come in after me. Was now on the first floor as I descended. Possible, I decided, but unlikely.

"No you didn't." I grabbed his arm and marched him out. No harm in being careful. "What are you doing here, Ronnie?"

"That's what I asked you." He let me lead him down to the road, but there he stopped. "You're not supposed to be in there."

"I'm taking care of Cheryl Ginger's dog." It was true, if unrelated. Before he could question me further, I moved onto offense. "And since you've been keeping an eye on the place, you can tell me who else has been in."

"I haven't…" He stumbled over his own words, and that's when it hit me.

"You come and go pretty freely, don't you, Ronnie?"

He blushed. "I let the cops in. They needed to get in."

"The cops?" I was missing something.

He nodded. "Not, you know, the local guys. But they were cops."

That could mean anybody. The Feds, Benazi's men. Somehow I doubted Ronnie's ability to discern legitimate inquiries from any other kind. "You go in there, too." I wasn't sure what I was going for, but it seemed worth pursuing. "You know they're looking for something, right? Something valuable."

He was shaking his head. "I don't know anything about that. I wouldn't ever..." He stopped, and I stared at him.

"Ronnie, what did you take from Cheryl Ginger's condo?"

Chapter Thirty-nine

"I'm not a thief." A half hour later and Ronnie was getting sulky. "I don't care how many times you ask me, Pru. I would never take anything, like you think."

"As if you know what I'm thinking." We were in his office again. I was in the desk chair; he was on the sofa this time. It was the closest I could come to grilling him.

"Ronnie, I know about the poker game at the VFW." It was time to try a different tack. "Have you been losing? I know Vince can get pretty mean."

"No way." He shook his head. "And Vince didn't even show."

That was odd. Even that drunk, I'd have thought Vince would be able to make it the three blocks to the hall. "Who was playing then?"

"Some out-of-towners. But, Pru, it was all aboveboard. Your guy was even there."

I nodded. That fit with what I'd heard.

"Look, Pru, I wasn't stealing." A whine crept into his voice. "I really did just think someone was in there."

I didn't try to hide my suspicion. For starters, I didn't see Ronnie as the kind of man who would volunteer to interrupt a break-in. "Someone?" I asked.

"I thought, maybe, Cheryl…" he said, after a moment's pause. "I thought maybe she'd come back."

That had the ring of truth to it. While Ronnie was not the kind of man to investigate a possible break-in, he was exactly the kind to surprise a pretty tenant.

"You like her, huh?" I looked at the desk in front of me. The valentine I'd remembered was still there, leaning on the teddy bear.

He nodded, blushing, and I decided to try another tack.

"You know she's in trouble, right?" He didn't look up. "Not just with the cops, Ronnie, but with some very bad men. They think she has something."

"I know he was pressuring her." His voice was so soft, I had to lean forward to hear him. "He kept telling her she had to get it."

"Get what, Ronnie?"

He shook his head. "Some kind of picture, I think."

I sat back. A picture could be a lot of things. A photo used in blackmail, which would explain the widow's involvement. Or…

"Did he say anything else about the picture, Ronnie?" I leaned forward, emphasizing each word. "Anything at all? If she's in danger, and you can help her…" I let him imagine the possibilities.

"All I heard was that they want it back," he said. "And if she helped them, he said he'd help her."

It was crazy. I knew that. Still, I needed to find out. Ronnie's desktop computer was barely serviceable, bogged down by a truly impressive amount of high-definition porn. But once I got out of the "hot teen action," I was able to search for Teddy Rhinecrest, looking for the article I'd read only a few days before.

It took a while. Ronnie's browser was slow and my memory woefully sketchy. My first search—Theodore Rhinecrest—produced a phone book, and when I added "picture" to the mix, I ended up following a wedding photographer of the same name. In between, I had to keep batting down pop-ups. Ronnie, I gathered, preferred large-busted women of Eastern European origin.

"Hey, Ronnie," I said. I could sense him shifting uncomfortably on the couch. "You want me to respond to one of these girls for you? I bet I could get you married in a month."

"Oh come on, Pru." From the hurt in his voice, I wondered if he'd considered it. "They're not, you know, real women."

I snorted. "Could've fooled me." Outside the bird noises had settled down for the night. I switched on a dented desk lamp, almost upsetting the white plush teddy bear that leaned against it. "You must have had a sweetheart at some point," I said as I righted the little bear, tucking the red felt heart emblazoned with "One and Only," back into its little arms. "What happened?"

"It—ah—she didn't..." Ronnie squirmed so much the sofa squeaked. I looked up in alarm.

"You okay, Ronnie?" He had turned an unhealthy red. "I'm only teasing."

"I know, it's just..." He kicked at something on the carpet. A pizza crust, I thought, and was grateful that nothing scampered out.

"Look, why don't you take off? Go find a card game or head down to Happy's?" My motives weren't purely altruistic. It was hard to work with his fidgeting. "I'll lock up when I'm done."

The name of the bar had the desired effect. His color was still high, but he was breathing more easily as he stood before me.

"Go," I said, with a smile. He looked so uncertain that I was beginning to wonder what else was on this computer. "I'll lock up. I promise."

"Okay," he said as he fished the big ring of keys off of his belt loop. "And Pru?" He shifted from foot to foot. "If you can..."

"Don't worry," I said, turning back to the keyboard. "I'm not interested in your personal life, Ronnie."

It was easier with him gone. Even the porn wave seemed to subside, and as the dusk outside deepened I found what I was looking for. The key had been adding the word "indicted," and there it was: Teodros —not Theodore—Rhinecrest, aka "Teddy," cleared of charges. I clicked through and figured out why it had sounded familiar. The art heist had been big news, even out here. Three Old Masters had been stolen from a famous museum overnight while the museum was closed. Originally, suspicion had fallen on the guards, but the ongoing investigation had revealed that the security for the old institution had been so out-of-date as to be practically worthless.

"It was no wonder that the museum had been burgled," the chief of detectives had been quoted as saying. "What was a surprise was that nobody had done it sooner."

Once the guards were cleared, the investigation had turned instead to recovery. Two of the paintings were quickly retrieved, jettisoned apparently during the escape. But after that, the search had ground to a halt. "We're stymied," that same chief of D's said only three months later, in an article that some clever wag had titled "Billion-Dollar Bunny Goes to Ground."

"*Berkshire Forest*," said the chief, giving the missing masterpiece its official title, "has disappeared."

It wasn't that the investigators didn't have leads. The basic assumption was that organized crime had been involved—the poor driver they'd caught had confirmed as much with his refusal to speak about who had hired him or where he was supposed to go—but beyond that, nothing.

"Guys like these, they're not looking for something pretty to hang on the walls," the lead investigator had said. "This is about money. That bunny will surface for sale at some point."

That had been three months ago

I stared at the screen for so long it went dark, and as I tapped the keyboard to wake it, I heard a door opening. "Hey, Ronnie," I called out. I wasn't in the mood to be interrupted. Not while I thought about the possibility of one Hudson River masterpiece and two dead men. "You didn't have to come back. I said I'd lock up."

"You should have thought of that before," said a man. Not Ronnie. I whirled around in my seat.

"You!" Even in the darkened room, I recognized the dark-haired man from the forest. He stepped toward me and I pushed the chair back, away from the desk lamp. I didn't want him to see as I reached into my pocket.

"I'm not going to hurt you." He came closer. My hand closed around leather—and I remembered the collar. I'd slipped my knife into my boot when I'd pocketed the discarded froufrou.

Now, instead of the familiar handle of my blade, I felt only the soft band and the empty, ridged settings sharp against my fingers. "I was in Rhinecrest's condo with you earlier." The man kept talking. "And I left you alone."

The door. The one Ronnie had said was open. "What do you want, then?" I slid my chair back, calculating how quickly I could get my blade out of my boot.

"Same thing you do." He reached for me—and I braced for an attack. But he only rolled my chair back and, leaning in, reached for the computer keyboard. He began pulling up the history of my recent searches. "I want to see what the fat man here has been looking at."

"Leave him out of this." I never thought I'd defend Ronnie, but he was a simple creature. A woodland animal of the burrowing kind, and here I had ousted him. Exposed him to this alpha predator. "He's done nothing."

A bark like a wolf. The man was laughing. It was a joyless sound. "Maybe, but he keeps showing up where he shouldn't, and that's not safe."

I gripped the collar tighter, feeling those empty settings sharp against my palm. The jewels. I was at least partly responsible for Ronnie's safety. "Here." I dug around, fishing the colored stones from my pocket. "I don't know what these mean and neither does Ronnie. Just take them, and don't hurt him."

"Hurt him." He was smiling. "I'm trying to save his fat ass. But thank you." He reached to take the collar, leaving the gaudy stones in my hand. "This will make everyone a lot safer."

"Why?" I looked at him and down at the stones in my hand, the desk lamp making the colors glow. "What does this mean?"

"You don't want to know," he said. A few more clicks and he was back to the original story. "Your boyfriend says you're smart, Pru Marlowe. Prove it."

He had both hands on the keyboard by then, and I realized I was in a perfect position. He wasn't looking at me. I could grab my knife easily. I could attack, or I could run. He wouldn't be able to stop me, not without getting hurt. But the words he'd

just uttered were bouncing around my head. My boyfriend?
What was Creighton involved in?

I looked again at the "gems" in my hand. At the red one that
had concealed a space just big enough for a message or a signal.
And it hit me.

This man wasn't a gangster. He was a Fed. Cheryl Ginger was
working with the Feds.

Chapter Forty

"You can't think that Ronnie has anything to do with any of this." I'd watched the dark-haired man erase my search history and move onto Ronnie's e-mail. "He's clueless."

"We know." He had stepped back from the computer and was wiping down the keyboard by then. "We've been watching."

"Then why?" I didn't even have the words for what had just happened. The surveillance, the search of the condo.

"He's too nosy for his own good, and we're trying to keep civilians out of this." He stopped to stare at me. "We're not the only ones watching."

With that he had left, and I found my heart rate returning to normal. The dark-haired man might be a Fed—I'd asked, he'd only glared in response—but he wasn't a good guy. I didn't think he cared about civilians, for starters, innocent or not. After all, he'd left me there, alone, in the dark. No, whatever kind of lawman he was, he was very different from Creighton. This man's main concern was keeping anyone from interfering with whatever trap he had set. Hunting, we both knew, is incrementally more difficult if your prey has been alerted.

Was that what had happened to Marty Parvis? I found myself thinking of the dead PI as I pushed myself out of that chair. I'd only been sitting there for an hour—the entire interlude with the dark-haired man had taken maybe fifteen minutes—but I was shaking as I rose to my feet. Had the chubby blond man drawn

the attention of Teddy Rhinecrest's associates? Or had he inter-
fered too much in the Feds' investigation? I didn't know what
the dark-haired man was capable of, only that I didn't like him.

I also didn't know what hold he had over Cheryl Ginger. And
warning or no, she'd gotten me involved in this—she was going
to give me some answers.

I wanted to approach her. To drive straight to the Chateau
and confront her and the spaniel, too. But something else the
dark-haired man had said stayed with me: "We're not the only
ones." I thought of Benazi, appearing out of nowhere, and I
knew he was right. Besides, on the off chance that I was wrong
about the stranger, about him being a Fed, I needed to be extra
careful. At times, I might be paranoid. Then again, I'm still alive.

For the same reason, I didn't want to go home. No, I wanted
a place where there'd be people around me. People who wouldn't
bother me too much while I thought things through. It wasn't
much of a decision. I headed to Happy's.

It was early, even for me. But daylight was long gone by the
time I reached the center of town, and it took an effort of will
to drive around to my usual spot in back. Happy's is sort of
centrally located, holding down a decrepit row of shops that
once marked the edge of downtown—and traffic is never that
bad here. But my life savings have gone into my GTO, at least
once over, and I wasn't going to leave her out front. Besides, I
needed to reclaim my dignity.

I knew what Wallis would say about that, and could imagine
the way she'd sway as she'd saunter out of the room, using her
tail for emphasis. Wallis considers herself the alpha predator of
our household and finds any pretensions I may have risible. But
for all her attitude, she'd been a house cat now for years. I wasn't,
and if I was going to function in this town, I needed to feel like
myself again. In her terms, I needed to mark my territory.

I wasn't going to spray. The crepuscular creatures who scur-
ried as I stepped from my car might have picked up my intent,
but what I was battling was in my head. Careful to move my
knife back up to my pocket, within easy reach, I walked around

the small lot—from the dumpster to the back curb and back again. Two rats watched as I paced off the space, curious but not alarmed. The raccoon who'd been hoping to get into the dumpster was a little more concerned. He'd seen firsthand what odd behavior could mean when one of his own littermates had gotten sick. Their mother had driven the rabid cub from the den before he could infect any others, but the image had stayed with the young male, even now that he was out on his own.

My pulse was still elevated when I finally opened the bar's back door, but I felt better than I'd thought I would. Maybe it was that I'd already faced down one threatening stranger today. Maybe it was knowing I was going to get a drink.

"Pru." Happy came over with a lowball glass and a bottle, filling it without me having to say a word. I drank it off before he could return to his post and he refilled it just as silently, without so much as a raised eyebrow. Happy is a pro. He knows why people come to his bar. He also knows that I'm one of the few regulars who can pay the tab at the end of the night, even without a mysterious benefactor.

That first drink took the edge off, and I lingered with the second, enjoying the warmth that spread its own golden glow. My usual stool is on the short end of the bar, by that back entrance. I can see everyone who comes in the front, this way, and I'm out of the spotlight, such as it is, where any randy male—the ones who don't know better—might mistake me for available. Tonight, I felt a bit vulnerable there. The door at my back looming even as the bourbon made itself felt.

"Happy?" I didn't have to say more. He topped me off with a nod, and I took my drink to the back of the room.

"Hey, Pru." I had no desire to sit with Albert. He and Ronnie were sharing one of the back booths, a greasy bag of fries spilling out between them.

"Al." I nodded and turned toward one of the two other booths, eager to drink alone, with the wall at my back. Then I stopped. Ronnie had probably told me all he knew, but I had something to share with him now. A warning, at the very least. "May I?"

I slid next to Albert before either could respond, glad of the bourbon's dulling effect on my senses.

"Have some." Ronnie pushed the bag toward me. I shook my head, but I felt myself smiling. He wasn't an attractive animal, but he wasn't malicious, either. I was glad I'd decided to warn him.

"No, thanks." I slid the grease-spotted sack back. "I just wanted to come by. Thank you for letting me use your computer today." Albert who had been staring at me whipped his head around at that to stare at his friend. "You really helped me out."

"Thanks, Pru." Ronnie blushed. "I'm sorry about the...you know."

"No big deal." I dismissed his concerns. If he wanted to lust after surgically altered Russians, he was free to. "I wanted to talk to you about something, though. Something else."

I looked sideways at Albert. He stared back at me, wide-eyed. These two were as much a pair as me and Wallis. I plunged ahead.

"You remember what I said about privacy?" Albert might be Ronnie's sidekick. That didn't mean I had to help spread the word. Ronnie must have felt something similar because he turned to look at his friend and then nodded. "About getting into trouble, if you're not careful?"

"You didn't, Pru!" A note of panic crept into his voice. "I promised I wouldn't."

"Don't sweat it." I made myself smile. We didn't need a scene here. "Only, you see, sometimes people have friends, and they might take things the wrong way."

"You mean, like you and Detective Creighton?" Albert piped up. "Like when you and Mack were still—?"

"No." I cut him off. "I mean, if Ronnie here is taking an interest in someone and her friends find out, he could get in trouble. Big trouble."

I stared at Ronnie. He had to understand this. There was a limit to how much I could do to protect him. A limit Wallis would say I had already passed.

"You don't think that I…" He looked around, as if Happy might jump over the bar and rush him. "That what I did had anything to do with what happened to Mr. Rhinecrest, do you?"

"More likely that guy they found in the parking lot." Albert was into this now. "You found him, too. Didn't you, Pru?"

"I did." I kept my eyes on Ronnie. "Look, I don't think you had anything to do with that. This is just for your own good. I want you to be careful, Ronnie."

"Yeah, okay." The big man was nodding spasmodically. "Yeah, you're right, Pru. I will be. From now on."

I didn't have anything more to add. Besides, I had almost finished my drink. Three should be it. I was fine to drive, but I didn't know what else I'd run into tonight. I wanted to keep my edge. I drained my glass and started to slide out of the seat.

Before I could shove off, though, Ronnie started fidgeting. "'Scuse me," he said, pulling his bulk out of the booth. As he lumbered toward the bathroom, Albert grabbed my arm.

"Hey, Pru," he said. This close, the combination of beer, fried food, and negligent dental care was enough to knock my head back. "Hang on."

I shifted away from him, but he kept his paw on my arm. Even my cold stare—usually enough to make him coil into a ball—didn't deter him.

"Albert." I put enough growl in my voice to warn him.

"Wait." He leaned over me and for one horrible moment, I thought he was going to kiss me. But as he craned his head around, I realized he was checking out the room—or making sure that his friend had in fact retreated to the restroom. "Pru, he's not telling you everything."

"Oh?" I shouldn't have been shocked, only I hadn't thought Ronnie was smart enough to dissemble. "You mean he hasn't stopped spying on pretty ladies?"

"No, it's not that." His grip on my forearm tightened. Albert was scared. "It's what you said about friends. That's why he got so freaked out."

He paused and knit his brow. But if he had any second thoughts about talking to me, the need to unburden himself was stronger. "I thought, you know, when I brought up that guy…"

He stopped again, but I couldn't wait. Ronnie would be back any moment, and Albert was losing his nerve as it was. Besides, I wanted to get him off me, and get myself on the road.

"He didn't have anything to do with the rich guy. I'm pretty sure," he said at last. "But Pru? Ronnie was talking to the other guy—the one who was asking all the questions about the girl. Ronnie was with him, here, that afternoon when you called him to set up the meeting. And then that night he was dead."

I wanted to corner Ronnie then. To grab him and make him confess. Albert would have a fit. He was growing more nervous by the moment, nearly pushing me out of the booth when I refused to move. Finally, I had enough.

"This is serious, Albert." I stood and brushed off the crumbs he'd shed on me. "We're talking about murder."

The room was basically empty, and the two old-timers at the bar didn't even turn as I strode toward the men's room. Happy looked up as I kicked the door open, but he had the sense to quickly look away. It didn't matter. Ronnie wasn't there. The big man had snuck out.

Chapter Forty-one

My first instinct was to go after him. It's an urge I share with many predators—the unthinking desire to chase anything that's running away. That's why baby bunnies instinctively freeze when confronted by danger. But even though I didn't actively want to tear Ronnie's throat out, I had a good reason to want to track him down. Simply put, I'd thought I'd saved his fat butt by interceding with the dark-haired man. I'd done it I because I thought Ronnie was essentially innocent, or at least guilty of no more than the usual adolescent lewdness. The fact that he'd slipped out? That and Albert's revelation meant something more was at stake than I had originally figured. I'm not in the habit of extending myself for almost anybody. I certainly don't appreciate it when I'm made a fool of for my efforts.

But the advantage most predators have was denied me. I neither had the running prey in my sights or the scent of him. Cursing volubly, I stamped out the back door. Too late, I recalled my earlier misgivings, but it was fine. Nobody was waiting out back, either alive or dead. In fact, the whole area was strangely silent as I strode over to my car.

"What's going on?" I was talking out loud. I didn't care. "Or should I say, *who?*" I startled the small barn owl whose presence was the real reason for the unnatural stillness. Tiny as he was, he was used to being the alpha. My question—along with the fact that I didn't scurry into hiding—made him blink and turn away.

Maybe that was all I was dealing with here. Ronnie was mouse-like in all but his bulk. My questioning him about anything may have made him run. Still, I couldn't help but feel that I'd let him get away without telling me something. And as inconsequential as his secrets probably were, I didn't feel like I could take a chance. I pulled out of the back lot still cursing. I had no interest in ending my night by tracking the man down.

I needn't have bothered. I'd been hoping to see Ronnie's truck on Main Street and had already begun strategizing how to get him to pull over without risking my own car. When I didn't see him there, I circled the block. Beauville doesn't have many late night options beyond Happy's, and I'd been hoping he would head back once he figured the coast was clear. But Beauville doesn't have much traffic, either. As far as I could tell, I was the only driver out on the streets. With more grumbling, I decided to beard this particular bear in his den. I turned toward The Pines.

What makes a pleasant drive on an early spring afternoon is less so at night, especially after a few drinks. As I've said, I was fine to drive. The reason I was fine was that I'm aware of how alcohol affects me, and I counter it—giving myself extra time to respond and taking a little more care on the curves. Creighton wouldn't like it, I knew, but I'd been driving these hills since long before it was legal. Besides, I wasn't crazy about some of the things he'd been up to lately, and I was pretty sure I was safe. Only the extra effort—and the awareness that just maybe I was fooling myself—didn't help my mood.

A drive I'd done in twenty minutes took me forty, and I was white-knuckling it by the time I pulled up to the condo development. It wasn't just the bourbon. The day had been too much for me. I needed to sleep. But as I drove I only became more convinced of the need to confront Ronnie. I'd known something was off with that man, and I was kicking myself for not following up when I had the chance.

It didn't look like I would now, either. I'd had time to think about how to approach him and decided that I'd treat him like I would any poorly trained beast. I rolled up to his office quietly, hoping not to alert him. But even when I flipped my lights on, I saw no sign of his truck, and a quick walk around the periphery—I'd neglected to use the bathroom at Happy's before I left—showed no signs of the man or his vehicle. No signs of anyone else, either. Ronnie was going to be out of a job if business didn't pick up with the weather.

I got back in my car to wait, but soon enough I was shivering. Turning the engine on was the logical response, but when my eyes started to close, I jolted myself awake and cracked the window. Booze, sure. Fatigue, maybe. But I couldn't discount the thought that despite the best care I could afford, my exhaust system might be leaking—and what I interpreted as fatigue might be carbon monoxide poisoning.

Besides, I liked hearing the night noises. Even this early in the season, I could make out the rustling of a hungry raccoon. He paused to sniff the air, and I got a flash of coyotes—and of other, larger males—but the night was relatively calm, and soon his thoughts turned to something soft and wriggling beneath a rotting log. The brown bats had begun to stir as well, their hibernation broken by the recent thaw. It would be a few weeks before they could eat their fill of insects, however, and they knew it—one sniff of the air giving them all the information they needed. Within a few minutes, the entire colony was back asleep, dreaming of true spring. Warm nights, and…

I sat up with a start, my heart racing, and looked around. It wasn't any noise that had woken me. In fact, the woods had grown quiet—too quiet for the natural world as I experience it. Moving slowly, as if I were being observed, I reached for the key and turned the engine off. Nothing. I rolled the window down a bit more, acutely aware of every squeak and rustle.

That I didn't see anything didn't surprise me. If Ronnie had driven up, I would have woken, and I didn't expect any other vehicle at this hour. That I didn't hear anything, however—that was bad. Leaning out of the car, I strained to catch whatever I could. I even tried opening my mouth, as Wallis would, to let the scents and the taste of the night aid my perception. But although I may have sensitivities that other humans lack, I don't have a cat's flehmen response either. The only thing I tasted was the bourbon I'd drunk, that and my own breath going stale.

No, what spooked me was the silence. Utter and complete, even as I listened for the wind around an owl's wings, for the imperceptible pad of paw on the moist forest floor. I wasn't trying to catch the sound—those night hunters wouldn't be heard until it was too late—but for the movement. The intent. The *hunger*. I should have gotten something. I remembered the little owl from less than an hour before.

I didn't. And that's when it struck me: this is what the night felt like to a vole or a rabbit. A prickling of the skin the only sign that something was amiss. I wasn't used to waiting.

I wasn't used to being prey.

The thought hit me like a slap in the face, and just as from a slap, I recoiled, pulling my head in the window and reaching once more for the key. I keep my engine tuned up for pleasure more than purpose, but right then I was grateful as my baby blue baby jumped ahead, my boot on the accelerator. Kicking out gravel, the tires grabbed the asphalt as I spun around the development. I wasn't going to slow down to turn and instead took the road around the building. My heart rate began to level off as I realized there was nobody parked here, no one on either side. Still, I had no trouble staying awake as I hit the highway full-throttle and raced the shadows back home.

Chapter Forty-two

I didn't sleep. I didn't expect to, after that, and even Wallis' gentle scorn couldn't rid me of my fears.

"Afraid of the night?" She'd joined me in the kitchen, where I'd poured myself another bourbon, my hands shaking. *"So we're just now comprehending we're not the meanest creature in the woods, are we?"*

"It wasn't that, Wallis." I raised the glass—and put it back down. I wanted to be alert while I thought this through. "I had the feeling that something—someone—was watching me. Had been watching me while I slept."

"Huh." Wallis sniffed at the glass and recoiled, her ears back. *"Don't you know we always are? You move like a...like a..."*

"Dog?" I'd had some interactions with canines recently. Wallis thought them beneath her.

"A rabbit," she corrected me. *"Jerking all over the place, as if it makes any difference."*

"What do you mean?" I poured the whiskey in the sink and started a pot of coffee. "Are you saying me, personally, or people in general?"

"People, huh." She'd picked up on my use of the word. *"As if humans were the only species that..."* Her thought trailed off as she licked her paw. *"I thought you would know better."*

"Help me." I put down my mug and looked at her, before lowering my eyes in supplication. "Please, Wallis, I don't know what's going on."

"No, you don't." She jumped off the table and strode over to me. *"Hunters seek prey and prey seeks shelter, the same as it's always been. And you don't know what's going on."* She rubbed against my shins, which was some comfort. But then she left me, alone, in the dark.

◇◇◇

By morning, I was more angry than frightened. Above all, I wanted an explanation. But as tempted as I was to race over to the Chateau and corner Cheryl—if not her dog—I had other responsibilities. And so, after putting out some food for Wallis, I made my way to Tracy Horlick's house.

"You're up early." The harridan who met me at the door might not have taken off last night's lipstick, but the cigarette in her hand was nearly all ash. I hadn't woken her. I was in no mood to argue, though, a fact I tried to convey with a glower.

"Rough night, huh?" Her lipstick cracked with the smile, but she turned without waiting for an answer. As my clients have taught me, nonverbal communication can be the strongest.

"You needn't be afraid of her." Growler took one sniff and turned to stare at me quizzically, his little tail uncharacteristically still. *"She's just trying to get by."*

"I'm not afraid of her," I barked back. "What made you think? No, never mind. Let's just walk."

With ears pricked—the canine equivalent of raised brows— he turned and led me down the street. I'd been worse than a brute, and I knew it. I'd been a human: tired, pissed-off, and snappish. And while I did my best to convey this silently— *"I'm sorry, Growler. I sincerely am."*—it seemed the best amends I could make would be to let him have his time with the scents and sounds of the outer world, to catch up with creatures who, unlike me, were sociable and kind.

I managed to escape without any additional unpleasantries, not even when Growler's person mumbled something about "the wrong side of the bed" on our return. It took an effort, but one I was willing to make. Growler I felt an allegiance to. He was a sensitive and intelligent creature who was making the most of a rough life. Tracy Horlick, however, paid my bills.

From there, it was over to the Chateau. Cheryl Ginger owed me some answers. And maybe, I conceded, I owed her a warning. If what I'd felt out there was real, she might have reason to fear, too—and it was quite possible that my actions had made her situation worse.

I breezed past the reception desk before the young clerk could stop me, so intent was I on getting to the redhead. He must have recognized me and called up, however, because she opened the door even before I knocked. Like old Horlick, she was in a robe, only hers was silk, emerald green to match her eyes. Those eyes had the faintest smudge of shadows underneath. That didn't do much to detract from her looks, but it did remind me that no matter how cool she might appear, Cheryl Ginger had reasons to be afraid.

"Pru." She did her best to summon a smile as she pulled her robe closer. "You're early."

"I wanted to talk to you." I leaned on the door, pushing it open. "I'll take Pudgy for his walk after."

"But…" She tried to block me, and for a moment I hesitated. If she had someone with her, it was none of my business.

"If you want, we can talk in the hall," I said, and she backed off. She knew what I was going to talk about, and she wanted witnesses no more than I did. Still, I took a look around as I stepped into the suite. I didn't want to be surprised, either. She stood, arms crossed, waiting. Meanwhile, Stewie had come to stand by her, curious but not alarmed.

I want everyone to be safe. I looked down into those liquid dark eyes. He needed to know I wasn't a threat. He sat and wagged his tail twice, thumping it against the floor, which I took as encouragement to continue.

"I had a surprise visit last night." I was watching Cheryl carefully, waiting for some sign that I'd hit a nerve. "I was doing some online research, and your friend dropped by. Uninvited, I might add."

She turned away with a sigh. I wanted to grab her, to make her look at me, but I held back. Whatever she did on her own would be more revealing than anything I could force out of her.

"He wanted to know what I was looking for," I went on. "He seemed very concerned with other people finding it."

She'd gone over to the desk and opened a drawer. For a moment, I tensed. If she pulled a gun on me, I had little recourse. When she pulled out a pack of cigarettes, I was nearly as stunned.

"Do you mind?" She didn't wait for an answer, lighting one by inhaling with rapid puffs.

"You smoke?" It was an idiotic comment. "I thought you were an athlete," I explained.

"I was," she said. The nicotine seemed to be calming her, her shoulders lowering as she exhaled. "I was also an ex-smoker until…" She gestured with the glowing butt. "All this."

"I don't want to make things worse," I said. It was true. "But I've been dragged into this. Or, I should say, people I know have been—*are* involved." I never thought I'd come to Ronnie's defense, but I had to admit, I was worried about the big guy. "So I need some answers."

Twin plumes of smoke from her nostrils and she took another drag. "I know," was all she said. "I mean, I'm trying to get to the bottom of this, too. I told him, I'm doing the best I can."

That might have been true in part. It wasn't the whole truth, though. It was time to put some pressure on.

"I've figured some of this out, Cheryl," I said. "I know what you're hiding."

She took another drag. The smoke wasn't only calming, it was cover. Holding the cigarette, inhaling—it gave her something to do with her hands, a reason to modulate her breathing. But Stewie—he knew something was wrong. The spaniel was still seated. His training, as I'd noted before, was good. His long, soft ears were at attention, however. His sensitive nose attuned to more than the smoke.

It was time.

"Cheryl, I know about Teddy Rhinecrest," I said. I'd been leaning against the wall. Now I stood and took a step toward her. "And I know you're working with the Feds."

"I don't know what you're talking about." She spit the words out as she marched by me, over to the dresser, where an ashtray already held several butts. "That's the craziest thing I've ever heard. If you know anything about this, then you know, that's not—" She stopped. I waited, but she'd clammed up, her pretty mouth set in a tight line.

"Cheryl?" She was so close to giving me something, but she only shook her head. "You can talk to me. I…" I paused, unsure of how much I wanted to give her. "I hear things. I know things I shouldn't, and I know about keeping secrets."

"So I gather." Her voice was cold. "You've been vouched for."

"Cheryl." This was getting nowhere. "Look, I just want out, okay? And I want my friends to not be part of this anymore."

A humorless laugh as she stubbed out the cigarette, not even half smoked.

"Cheryl, I gave him the collar."

She turned, eyes wide. "You what?"

"You heard me. He recognized it right away. Thanked me, too. What is it?"

She might have been a better actor than I'd thought, but I didn't think she was faking the way she stumbled back and sat down on the bed.

"I said—I told you…" She was shaking her head. "Don't you see what you've done? You've killed me. You've killed us both."

"What are you talking about? He recognized it. You got it from him, didn't you?"

"From Benazi? No." She had gone so pale, the dark shadows beneath her eyes stood out like bruises. "Even you…"

"Wait, I didn't give it to Benazi." She blinked up at me, and I realized we'd been talking at odds. "I gave it to your friend. I said that. The dark-haired man. The one you're working with."

"You think I'm…?" Her voice was unnaturally high. She was faking it, or trying to. Doing a decent job, considering the shock she'd had, but I wasn't buying it. It helped that Stewie was whining softly—not out of concern for his mistress, it came to me, but because I had pictured the man from the woods in my mind.

"Look, I know you're working with him. I know he's a Fed." I was watching her as I spoke, and so I saw when she started slightly. "I think you were passing messages to him about Teddy Rhinecrest," I said, my theory confirmed. "I think they're looking for whatever got him killed."

The pieces were falling into place. "And, yeah, I get it. Benazi's looking for the same thing." Now was the time to ask her something I didn't know. "It wouldn't have anything to do with that art heist, would it?"

Two pink spots appeared in her cheeks as she blinked up at me.

"Wow, you're in the middle of this, aren't you?" I sat back on the chaise, shaking my head. "Come on, Cheryl. I think it's time for you to tell me everything."

"There's nothing to tell." She slumped back. The fatigue was catching up with her.

"Come on." I wasn't buying it. I was, however, looking at Stewie. The spaniel had jumped up on the bed beside her and was wagging his tail. *"She's good,"* he was saying to himself and to me. *"We're both good. We do our job."* I was beginning to wonder about the little dog's intelligence. Then again, it was also possible that the spaniel didn't understand the extent of Cheryl's subterfuge. "Were you and Theresa working this together?"

"What? No." Cheryl shook her head. "I was supposed to find out what I could about Teddy's…activities. But I couldn't, and then he was killed. That's all."

"So Teddy was involved with the museum heist?"

She shrugged. "So they say. I never saw any proof."

"Then why…?" A memory was tickling my brain. Something about the one person who had been convicted—and the fact that I'd not been able to find any trace of Cheryl Ginger online. Something overheard—and misunderstood—by Ronnie. Something about family. "Ginger's not your real last name, is it?"

She shrugged again.

"It's—what?—Gittelson? Paul Gittelson is your brother. He was the driver, right?"

Stewie began to whimper, and I realized Cheryl was crying.

"He was just a kid," she said, swiping at the tears. It did no good; they were coming fast. "Just a stupid kid. I've taken care of him ever since our parents died. I knew he was hanging out with a bad crowd, but I didn't think he'd be so..." She sniffed and reached for a tissue. "So stupid."

"You made a deal to get him off."

She shook her head. "He's not getting off, but if I can provide some info, he might get parole. Might have," she corrected herself. "I don't have an in anymore, now that Teddy's dead."

"So you had no reason to kill him." One theory shot.

Another demurral. "Maybe it's just as well," she said, once she'd wiped her face. "I couldn't—I wanted out. Teddy never trusted me. He never trusted anybody. Maybe he didn't know anything."

I doubted that. "So what was his wife after?"

She shrugged again. "Teddy didn't like to talk about her. But they'd been married forever. I don't think she'd work with the Feds."

"No, of course not." I leaned back on the chaise, remembering how she'd responded. How she'd thought Parvis had abandoned her. "I think the PI was working on his own. He must have heard something, or suspected something, and thought he could cash in."

"He was a pig." She spit the word out, and I turned to her.

"He talked to you?" We'd both sat up straight.

"Threatened me, more like." She glanced up at me, anger sparking in her eyes.

"Did he know?"

"No," she said. "Not about me. But he'd put two and two together about Teddy, and he thought, 'cause he was working for his wife, it gave him leverage."

"With you?" Something wasn't adding up.

"No, with Teddy and then—with his friends." She shook her head in disbelief. "He was telling everyone that it was up to him what the wife got—what her lawyers knew about. He was threatening everybody."

"That was stupid," I said. What I didn't say was that it had probably gotten him killed. She nodded. She'd reached the same conclusion. "So what are you going to do?"

"I don't know," she said. "Brian—he's the guy who gave me the collar—he thinks I'm missing something."

"But surely…?" I looked around. The suite was luxurious. It wasn't that big, though. "They've been through the condo, right? And all your stuff."

"Brian and Teddy's friends, too. Each side thinks I'm holding out, and if Teddy's friends find out I was working with the Feds…" She didn't have to finish.

"I wonder if Parvis found anything?" I saw the answer on her face. "No, they'd have gotten it—the 'friends' who killed him—and they'd be leaving you alone now." I also saw how miserable she was. "Look, let me talk to Creighton—"

"No, you can't. Not now." She jumped up. "Please. I know I said that about your boyfriend. I was upset, and I thought he was working with Brian…" She paused. "It's all just gotten too complicated."

"You need some allies here, and I'm not enough." I stood, reluctantly, and looked at Stewie, who was also standing now, his ears perked.

"She has me. I'm here." His declaration was clear, his entire body alert. *"I'm on it. And I'm good at sniffing things out."*

Chapter Forty-three

I promised Cheryl I wouldn't talk to Creighton. I wasn't sure if I was going to keep that promise, but it was the only way I could keep her calm. After that, I took Stewie for his walk. Cheryl was nervous, even about that, but the way Stewie looked at her, along with his soft, plaintive whine, prompted her to give me the okay.

"We won't go far," I said, clipping the spaniel's lead on. "And remember, I'm working for you. It would look strange if I came by and *didn't* walk your dog."

Once we were outside, Stewie led the way through the parking lot and onto the trail we had started down the day before.

"Hang on, Stewie," I said out loud. "Cheryl doesn't want us going too far."

"We have to meet him. My master. He's here." The little dog was too well trained to pull on the leash, but he took all the slack I gave him and looked back, eager for more.

"He's here?" I dropped my voice, unsure of who besides the spaniel was listening.

"Up ahead! Up ahead!" The little dog barked, his tail wagging.

I was torn. I had no desire to run into the dark-haired man—Brian—again, but I knew more now and thought I could demand some answers. Besides, the spaniel was quite excited, and the exercise would do him good. Toy dogs may look like they're made to sit around all day, but they can get into trouble if they get bored. That was what I was getting paid for, after all.

"Okay, boy." I let him—and my rationalization—lead me farther into the woods. All the while, I was thinking about this man, Brian. I didn't like him. I didn't like how he had pressured Cheryl into helping him, into helping the Feds. It didn't seem kosher. Then again, I didn't know what heat he was under. Creighton might be a boy scout at heart, but I'm not so naïve as to imagine that law enforcement always plays fair.

"No!" Somewhere nearby a thrush surprised a blue jay, chasing the interloper out of his nest. *"Get away!"*

Right here, right here…yes!" A mole following his nose had found a nest of worms.

Stewie, however, was having none of it. Instead, he was positively quivering with excitement as he hurried me along at a pace that was giving me second thoughts. The little dog would not do anything to endanger Cheryl, and by extension, he would be protective of me. One thing about animals, unlike humans, they don't dissemble. That didn't mean their judgment was always good.

"Stewie, heel." I stood still as the dog turned to look back at me.

"Must I?" I didn't need my special sensitivity to read the plea in his eyes.

"Heel, Stewie," I repeated, for myself as much as for him. "We've gone far enough now."

"Indeed you have, Ms. Marlowe." The figure who stepped out from the shadows wasn't dressed for a walk in the woods. Not unless you consider a grey sharkskin suit proper attire for trekking.

"Benazi." I felt like I'd been punched in the gut.

"Gregor, please." He stepped forward with a smile and bent to pet the spaniel's head. "And how are you today, my friend?"

"I'm a little confused." I looked from one to the other, but all I saw was an old man petting a dog. That dog was wagging his tail.

"You were expecting someone else?" Benazi straightened up and turned his hawklike gaze on me.

I didn't answer. I suspected he knew who I thought was going to be there. I also suspected I didn't want to know what had happened to the dark-haired agent.

"Dear Ms. Marlowe, you needn't be concerned." His smile broadened as he read my face. "Sometimes it is necessary to employ intermediaries, simply to keep things uncomplicated."

"Wait." I looked from Benazi to the spaniel and back up again. Stewie was wagging his tail, happy as a lark. "Are you saying that Brian...?" I didn't like the man. That didn't mean I was going to name him as a Fed. "That he works for you?"

"He sidelines." Benazi dipped his head as he corrected me. "He does, in truth, work for a certain agency. But as you well know, all creatures are susceptible to both pressures and incentives. I believe you would refer to this as the basis for behavioral training. Am I correct?"

He paused, as if waiting for me to respond. All I could think of then was my plan to use my training on him. My farcical, suicidal plan.

I don't know what he saw in my face. I don't know if I wanted him to, but he began to speak again. "For various reasons, this one creature has become open to, shall we say, sharing certain forms of information?"

"Sharing information with..." I stopped myself in time. Gregor Benazi had an old-school charm about him, an air that made me think that calling him out as a gangster would be unwise. At the very least, he might consider it rude.

"He believes me to be working with a certain insurance agency." The silver-haired man answered my unspoken question. "He knows of my interest in retrieving various objects, and he doesn't believe that passing along information is against his interest."

"Then why did you threaten Cheryl Ginger?"

"Did I?" The smile grew broader. "Or did I simply warn her to be careful? As you may have overheard, Ms. Marlowe, I am more concerned about certain of my colleagues than I am about any government agency. Some of my associates are less forgiving of lapses in judgment."

Lapses in judgment. "You've got that girl coming and going." I was getting angry.

"Not I." He arched one white brow, a look that accentuated the hawkishness of his features. "Brian Dalehy's people roped her into this preposterous masquerade. My involvement has given certain of my colleagues cause to restrain themselves. Only they are not patient people, Ms. Marlowe. Not at all."

"Martin Parvis?"

He shook his head. "That was regrettable, but he was not a patient man, either. His search was becoming too public and too loud."

"And Teddy Rhinecrest?"

"Also regrettable." Another sad, slow shake.

"So much for honor among thieves." I was missing a piece. "Was he holding out? Was he making his own deal?"

"Are these questions you want to be asking, Ms. Marlowe?" That eyebrow again. "I met you here today simply to reassure you that Cheryl Ginger is in no immediate danger. I know you have come to feel responsible for her, and in my own way, so have I."

"Thanks." I couldn't put any warmth into the word, but he nodded anyway. And with another quick pet of Stewie's head, he turned to walk off. "But wait," I called. He paused and turned back. "You didn't arrange this—I mean, the dog…?"

He smiled and turned away again. I watched as he disappeared into the woods.

Chapter Forty-four

I stood there, staring, long after his suit—silver-gray like his hair—had disappeared into the shadows. Only when I heard the roar of an engine—a defiant growl, a statement—did the spell break, and I turned and tore back toward the hotel, Stewie running alongside me.

I didn't care what I'd told Cheryl. Just then, I didn't care what shortcuts my beau might have taken—or what stories he'd told me in the process. I needed to talk to Creighton. More important, I needed to warn Ronnie. The fat man had poked his way into a hornets' nest with this one, and no matter how distasteful I found him, I didn't want him to be hurt.

First, of course, I had to maneuver Cheryl. And that thought caught me up short right by the Chateau's front door.

"Stewie." I looked down at the little dog. He sat and stared up at me, good dog that he was, waiting for a command. "I need you to tell me everything you know." A quizzical tilt made one ear flop. "Come on, now, boy. You know you can."

"Tell?" I sighed at his simple question. That translation problem.

"Benazi, Brian…" I did my best to picture them in my mind. "Tell me about them."

"Trust the master." That tail started thumping on the ground again. To the spaniel, this was a no-brainer.

The master? Okay, I'd deal with that later. But, no, Stewie wasn't done. With one paw in the air, in a begging motion, he got my attention, and I crouched beside him, the better to hear.

"Trust the master." Those dark eyes were full of soul, willing me to believe. *"He trusts you."*

I didn't have much to say to that, and besides, I needed to get going. Although the hotel clerk averted his eyes as we walked in, it was clear he'd been watching us through the glass door. He'd broken the rules for Cheryl Ginger, but I thought he might be regretting that now—at least as far as I was concerned.

With a smile and a nod, I marched right past him, Stewie neatly keeping pace. Into the elevator and up—as I mulled over what to tell Cheryl. We'd hadn't been out more than fifteen minutes, but I didn't think her nerves would be improved by the wait.

What I didn't expect was to find her packed and dressed when she answered the door. All business as she thanked me and took Stewie's lead. Nor did I anticipate the envelope she handed to me, my name written on the front.

"This is for you," she said, and giving me the kind of smile I knew men paid for she began to close the door.

"Hang on a minute." I blocked it with my foot as I tore open the envelope. Another reason to wear boots.

"Isn't that enough?" I looked up from the crisp twenties to see that the smile had given way to a wide-eyed confusion. "You said, twenty a day."

"And you're paying me in advance?" I was offering her an out.

"No." She didn't take it. "I'm leaving. I think it best if I just take off. But you've been so…helpful."

"You were going to leave this for me." I held up the envelope, so neatly addressed. "You were hoping to get out of here before I came back—before *we* came back. That's why the extra money."

Her silence was my answer. I looked past her to the spaniel, who stared back with those big soulful eyes. *"I'm sorry,"* I said silently, hoping he would understand. *"I can't take you… Wallis wouldn't accept you."*

Turning back to Cheryl, I was more blunt. "You don't deserve a dog."

Chapter Forty-five

I hated leaving him there with her, but I didn't see any options. At worst, she'd abandon him in the hotel, where he'd be found by housekeeping. But I didn't think Cheryl Ginger would risk it. Leaving the dog behind would provoke at least a cursory search for her, and she might be acting tough, but she was going on the run. No way the Feds would have approved her taking off like that, and if she was being taken into protective custody—or witness protection—she'd have had some company. Besides, from all I'd gathered, it wasn't her testimony they wanted. No, the Feds— and whoever else was behind them—wanted what Teddy Rhinecrest had. A treasure that didn't wear heels.

As I drove, I thought about the envelope in my pocket. I'd taken it, sure. She had it, I needed it, and I wasn't going to start splitting hairs about how much she actually owed. But if the pretty redhead thought she'd bought my silence, she was wrong. If Stewie showed up in the county shelter, I'd use some of that dosh to re-home him. If not, Wallis and I would eat shrimp.

I kept that happy thought in mind as I headed back toward The Pines. I didn't know what I would do if Ronnie was there. Warn him, maybe. Make him let me back into Teddy's condo. I doubted I could find a missing masterpiece that nobody else had, but I figured I had to try. I was sorry, then, that I hadn't taken Stewie with me. The spaniel might have mixed allegiances, but he certainly had a better nose than anyone else on this hunt.

I could have used the company, too. I was pretty sure nobody had followed me as I turned off the highway and onto the winding drive up to the development. The roads are empty enough this time of year that I'd have noticed anyone, or so I told myself as I slowed to take the curves. What I couldn't explain was the creeping sensation I had as I made my way up to the condos, a feeling that something more than the forest creatures were watching me. Were waiting for me to make a wrong move.

Wallis would have had a field day with that, seeing me act more like a prey animal than an alpha predator. But she'd have to respect my instincts, as dull as they were. As it was, I didn't even park once I got up to the cedar-shingled buildings. Just drove slowly around, navigating the circumference road like some kind of security watch. Nothing was stirring, nothing seemed out of place. More to the point, nobody was parked there. I didn't know what had happened to Ronnie. All I knew was he wasn't here.

I didn't want to be either. It was time to give this all up—or at least dump it in the lap of someone who was paid to handle this kind of thing.

I began breathing easier the moment I was back on the highway. I was headed for Creighton's office, hightailing it just like one of those rabbits I'd watched all winter long.

I have a thing about secrets. I know that. Some of it is because of my parents. Not just my father sneaking out. His endless lies and evasions, but my mother's masquerade of normalcy—covering up for his drinking and womanizing until the day he finally disappeared with some barfly he'd met at Happy's. She never gave it up, entirely, insisting on me acting like the prim little lady she wanted me to be. It wasn't until recently that I've found myself wondering what other masks she'd donned. If her perpetual scorn hid something else, a debilitating grief that only her tightly wound propriety kept in check.

Of course, these days I have a real secret. One that would do more damage to my relationships than any amount of Maker's Mark could. Granted, the only time I'd actually spent in a locked

ward had been voluntary—those first few days of my sensitivity, when nothing made sense and I couldn't shut out even the
most inane pigeon warbling. But I'm a pragmatist—I get that
from my mother—and I knew how it would look, if I ever let
on why I was so good with animals.

It wasn't a chance I would take. But maybe I didn't have
to. Although Creighton had warned me away from Cheryl, he
couldn't stop me from working—and I thought I could tell him
about her deal without involving the spaniel as anything more
than a dumb animal, whatever he might truly be. I'd give him
Brian, Cheryl's dark-haired man too, if need be, though not
Benazi. I'm not a dumb animal, either.

But when I pulled into the lot besides our town cop shop and
didn't see Jim's car, I realized I needed to re-think my strategy. I
hadn't called because this was something I wanted to talk about
in person, on my terms. Even leaving a message at the precinct
house would have limited my options.

No, I decided, I'd wait him out. And in the meantime, I'd
check in with Beauville's other reliably intelligent male.

"Hey, Albert." The beard bounced up at my greeting. Formal
business hours are rough when you drink every night. "How's
Frank?"

"Hi, Pru." He sat up and looked around, a little lost until he
located his coffee mug and a grease-marked bag. "You okay? I
mean, last night…"

"Did Ronnie come back?" I had to talk to the fat man. From
what I'd learned this morning, the situation was more dangerous
than I'd thought. "Have you seen him today?"

"Not yet." Albert dug into the bag, the twin of last night's,
only this time he pulled out a broken cruller. "Want some?"

"No, thanks." I sank into the chair opposite to think. "Here
you go." I looked up, but Albert wasn't talking to me. Frank had
poked his head out of Albert's down vest and was reaching for
the donut with two agile paws.

"Whoa, not all of it." Albert pulled back, breaking the frosted
fragment and startling the ferret, who dived down into an open

desk drawer. "Look at him." Albert chuckled as he put the rest of the treat into his own mouth. "Isn't that what they call 'ferreting' something away?"

"Not quite, Albert." I answered automatically, my mind on the nimble little creature who was, as we spoke, nibbling the glaze off the doughnut. "That's finding something out."

"Finding out where the treats are hidden?" The thought reached me from the desk drawer, along with the taste of sugar. *"We're good at hiding things,"* he said, as he worked his way into the yeast dough. *"Better than you."*

"But Albert, I need to get in touch with Ronnie. I told you he let me use his office computer." I kept talking. Frank's words sounded like a warning in my head. Was I exposing myself? Had my focus on animals endangered my secret? "I should thank him."

"Creighton won't like that." I snapped to attention.

"Why not?" My mind raced. Did Jim already know about my search—or about my visit?

"It's obvious." Albert popped the rest of the doughnut in his mouth, washing it down with a swig of milky coffee. Most of it made it into his mouth. "He's that kind of guy. A cop." He wiped his beard, blending the mess in. "And it's pretty clear that he's getting serious about you."

"Great," I muttered. From inside the desk, I heard Frank talking to himself. *"Hiding things,"* it went. *"Better than you."*

"Thanks, Albert." I made myself look at the man before me. "But you really don't have to worry about my personal life." I tried to keep the growl out of my voice. "So where would I find Ronnie?"

"He—ah—spends a lot of time at his job."

So I was right. The man didn't have an apartment.

"I know he usually sleeps there, Albert." I wasn't going to let on that I'd already swung by The Pines. Twice. "But does he have anyplace else?"

A shrug. "Sometimes he just crashes in his truck." I did my best to keep a poker face, but even Albert heard how that sounded. "I mean, he sleeps in it sometimes. Like, if he has too many at Happy's."

"He drink anyplace else?" I would have recognized his truck if it had been parked behind the bar.

"Only if someone is buying." Albert made it sound like a pipe dream. I wasn't so sure. Both Benazi and his puppet Brian wanted access. Neither of them would blink at taking advantage of the fat man, whether or not he had anything to share.

"If you see him, tell him to call me." I got up, too anxious to wait any longer. I paused at the doorway, though, unsure of what to do. But the entrance to both offices is glass, and I knew my hesitation would be as much grist for the gossip mill as any message I could leave. Besides, it occurred to me as I pushed open the door to the cop shop, I had a legitimate concern.

"Hi, Pru." Sal, Creighton's deputy, looked up and nodded. "He's not in."

"I figured," I said. What was the point in pretending? "But I'd like to leave a message."

Sal's eyebrows went up at that, but Creighton runs a tight ship. No way was she going to ask why she had to be the intermediary. Instead, she typed a few keystrokes and, with a blank face, looked up at me. "Shoot."

"Tell him I'm looking for Ronnie, the manager at The Pines." I kept my voice as straight as her face. "Tell him he should be, too."

Chapter Forty-six

I like driving. Driving can be its own purpose, a meditative take on space and time. What I don't like is driving restlessly, without pleasure or hope of resolution, but there I was. Once Sal had shot the message off—"he'll get it as soon as he checks in"—I had no reason to hang around. What I didn't have was a place to go.

Being a semi-pro behaviorist isn't what you'd call a full-time job. Even if I had my certification, I'd probably be reaching to fill my schedule out here in the sticks. As it was, old Doc Sharpe, the County vet, threw me as much work as he could. He called it "training," when he was pitching me to clients, and that made my lack of credentials irrelevant. Sometimes I thought he saw something else in me—suspected something about the connection that made me such a hit with the perplexed pet owners who came in to see him. But he was an old Yankee, way too reserved to ever say anything, and I counted on that to keep me safe even as he directed every odd job he could my way.

A lot of it was simple dog-walking, the kind of gig I had with Growler and Tracy Horlick and, ever so briefly, with Cheryl Ginger and Stewie. Between that and the odd wildlife jobs Albert didn't want to handle himself, which is to say all of them, I got by. In a month or two, things would even pick up. Now, though, I was looking at a day of waiting with a little worry mixed in. It wasn't my favorite cocktail.

Without thinking, I found myself turning toward Marnie Lundquist's house. Wallis might say it was because I'd been thinking like a prey animal that I caught myself pondering the missing brown bunny. I thought it was something more. For all of her worries, Marnie Lundquist was a calming presence, with the kind of down-to-earth kindness that would calm my nerves, as it did Henry's. I told myself as I drove that it only made sense for me to follow up. Marnie was a steady client, and would be until her granddaughter reclaimed her pet. And while she had relaxed on seeing the evidence that Henry was not only alive, he was still somewhere nearby, I didn't like to leave her hanging. If I couldn't use my sensitivity to find one house rabbit, then I wasn't only not much good as a behaviorist, I was useless as any so-called animal psychic. I had this gift, I told myself as I pulled up in front of her house; I might as well put it to use.

"Why, Ms. Marlowe." The woman who greeted me at the door was as pleasant and tranquil as I could have hoped. "What a lovely surprise."

"Good morning, Ms. Lundquist." I hesitated. I had lost track of time. "I'm sorry to disturb you, but I just couldn't help thinking about Henry."

"What a sweetheart," she said, holding the door open. "Please, come in."

"Has he surfaced?" I asked as I followed her into the warm kitchen. The smell of baking made the room even cozier than I remembered.

"No, not yet." She bent to check the oven. "A few more minutes."

"Excuse me?" The scent was intoxicating, but that feeling of contentment...

"Hot cross buns." She stood, pushing herself up carefully. "They'll be ready to take out of the oven in maybe two more minutes."

"Oh, I couldn't." My mouth was watering. I felt...bliss. I needed to focus. "But, Ms. Lundquist, you're not concerned?"

She shook her head, smiling, as she fetched a cooling rack from the cabinet. "Henry is definitely around here somewhere," she said. "The level of the hay was way down, and, well, I'm not sure I can explain it…"

I waited. The mix of cinnamon and sugar as heady as any bourbon. As warm…

"All I can say is I feel sure that all is well," she said at last. Behind her, a timer pinged, and she pulled a tray of the sweet rolls from the oven. "Now, we'll have to let these cool a bit."

"I can wait," I said. This was a home, warmer than anyplace I had ever lived. The key, I thought, my mind wandering, was that there were no secrets here. Only warmth. Hot buns fresh from the oven.

Something was nagging at me. "Maybe I can do another search?" I roused myself. "Earn that bun, so to speak."

"Of course, dear." Marnie Lundquist was taking plates out of another cabinet. "If you would like."

With a smile, I went past her into the pantry. She had refilled the hay rack, but I knelt and put my hand on it, pretending to examine it for visual clues. As I did, I tried to empty my mind. That wonderful scent helped, propelling me into a dreamlike state as if it were I, and not the kitchen, that was filled with warmth.

"Come on, Henry," I closed my eyes to concentrate better. *"You don't want Marnie to worry."*

Images filed through me. Henry, timid and aware, shying away from my touch and yet meeting my gaze with his large, liquid eyes. Henry shielding himself from me, claiming family. Claiming safety here with this kind, white-haired woman.

I remembered what Frank had said about secrets, about family. What Wallis had said, too.

"They're ready." Marnie Lundquist broke into my reverie. "They'll be hot, but maybe we could break one open and see if they're any good."

"I'm sure they are." I smile up at her, as something close to peace flooded through my veins.

Chapter Forty-seven

"Jim, you've got to come over tonight." I was still feeling mellow when my phone rang, an hour later, my suspicions nearly forgotten. "I've got such a treat for you."

His chuckle broke through my happy haze.

"I mean, baked goods," I explained, emphasized the last words. "One of my clients makes the best buns."

"Your clients can cook now?" I waited while his laughter subsided. "Somehow, I can't see Wallis wearing an apron "

"Forget it, Jim." I hadn't joined in. I don't do domestic. "What's up?"

"Hey, you messaged me." He was calling from his car. I could hear the squawk of his radio and hoped that the access didn't go both ways. "You wanted to know about Ronnie?"

"You've seen him?" The last of the lingering languor fell from me as I sat up straight. With a worried look, Marnie Lundquist offered succor in the form of a refill. I held out my cup, but all my attention was on the phone. "What happened?"

"The usual." Creighton sounded casual. Too casual.

"What?" I snapped. My hostess started, splashing the tea onto the saucer. "I'm sorry." I looked up at her worried face. "Bad news."

She nodded and retreated to give me privacy, and I missed what Creighton was saying.

"Hang on, Jim." I stood and walked over to the front door. I didn't want to bring any sadness into this house.

"I just said, you don't have to wig out on me." His voice faded out as he drove. "But since you're so keen on seeing him, I'm on my way over to The Pines now. I gather he's been staying there, as well as working there."

"He's not there." I could have pulled my hair out. Creighton wasn't listening to a thing I said. "I went by last night. This morning, too, and he wasn't there."

"I know that, Pru." He was speaking slowly now, as if explaining himself to a child or to an idiot. "I know he wasn't there last night. He was at the precinct last night. One of my guys picked him up outside Happy's. He was all over the road. Not the first time, I might add. We cut him loose this morning. Joe gave him a lift over to the impound about an hour ago. I've been in meetings, or I'd have let you know."

"Those meetings, Jim." I leaned against the door, my earlier suspicions rushing back. I didn't want to talk about them here. "Are you working with the Feds, still?"

"Pru." His voice said it all.

I pushed anyway. "Jim, there are things you don't know."

"And there are things I can't talk about, Pru." His voice had an edge to it. "Look, I respect your need for privacy often enough. Can you not do me the courtesy of respecting mine?"

That shut me up. How could I tell him that this wasn't about personal boundaries? This was about life and death.

"So anyway…" He cleared his throat, as if that had been the cause of the silence hovering between us. "I did get your message, and I wanted to touch base. And because you sounded so concerned, I thought I'd swing by and see how our roly-poly friend is doing."

"Roly-poly?" A thought was poking around the back of my mind. Something to do with what I'd discovered about Henry. With what Wallis had said—and Frank and Growler…

"Yeah, don't you think he's kind of like a woodland creature?" Creighton sounded like his jovial self again. "A big bear, one of those that come out of hibernation and gets picked up lumbering around downtown and sent back into the forest?"

It couldn't be. It was too simple. Too simple and—too dangerous.

"Jim, you can't…" I paused. I didn't know how to explain. How to ask. "You don't have to go check on Ronnie right now. In fact, I'm going to head over there myself." I grabbed my jacket off its hook and ducked back in to wave goodbye to my hostess.

"It's no problem," said my beau, oblivious to the tension in my voice. "I just need to swing by the office and pick something up, and then I'll be on my way."

He was making a stop. I had time. I had to have time.

"There's no hurry, Jim." Marnie Lundquist pushed the covered plate toward me. It was still warm. "I'm on it."

"Great," said my heedless sweetheart. "I guess I'll meet you there."

The humor of the situation did not evade me as I made my way to the highway. Here I was, in a controlled panic, while my car smelled like a bakery at Easter. Driving as quickly as I safely could in the heavily populated side of Beauville, on my way to avert catastrophe—or, at least, to keep the men I cared about from a potentially disastrous collision. No, the absurdity of the situation was quite apparent. That, and my blindness through it all.

"Pick up, pick up, pick up." Ronnie wasn't answering, which could mean nothing. If he was that drunk, he'd probably lost his phone or let the battery run out. Maybe he was being a good boy, not using his phone as he made his penitent drive back home. Maybe…

I dialed again.

"Uh, hi." Ronnie's voice. I grabbed the phone. "Is this thing on?"

"Ronnie! It's Pru—" The sound of fingers over a phone. A rustling.

"Leave a message." The beep cut off as he started to laugh. Voice mail.

"Ronnie, if you're at home," I emphasized the last word. I didn't know who would get this message or who was listening as I spoke. "You need to leave there. Now. Come meet me at

Happy's." I paused, unsure how much I wanted to make myself a mark. "It's Pru," I said finally. My voice was probably distinctive enough to identify me, even if my phone number wasn't marked. Besides, all the concerned parties knew how deep I was in this. Even I knew that.

I'd hit the highway by then, and I floored it. I passed a family in an SUV like it was standing still, and did my best to ignore the look of horror on the driver's face as I passed.

"Sorry, Dad," I said to the air. Let him use me as an object lesson for his kids.

The shadows reaching across the road made the next bit trickier. I didn't think we had any more ice, but even damp spots could be deadly if I hit them wrong. I had both hands on the wheel, and I made myself lower my shoulders as I took at turn at ninety. Relax into the road. Just…drive.

I didn't jump, not much, when my phone rang. But I did overcorrect slightly as I answered.

"Ronnie?"

"No." A female voice, slightly confused. "It's Cheryl. Cheryl Ginger."

"Cheryl." I sighed. "I thought you were gone."

"I meant to be." Her voice was low with regret—or could it be shame? "I was going to…well, you know. But then I thought of my brother and…well, everything."

"And you realized you didn't want to be on the run forever?" I was willing to bet that fear of Benazi had more to do with her change of plans than her concern for her brother. But what did I know? I was an only child.

"I realized I had to finish this," she corrected me. "And also, well, I had a thought about the…you know."

"Yeah, I think I do." I wasn't going to say it, either. "Want to share?"

"I just want to end this, once and for all." There was a new steel in her voice, and for the first time I thought maybe she honestly had been an Olympic contender. "And you've been part of this, so…"

"Where are you now?" I had an idea. I wanted to be sure.

"I'm on my way back to The Pines. To Teddy's condo," she said.

"Good." I had plans for the pretty redhead. "I'll meet you there."

I turned off my phone after that. There was only one player left who hadn't checked in with me. One player who had a role in this whole scheme, and I didn't want to talk to Gregor Benazi just then. I half hoped I wouldn't ever have to again, and that I wouldn't find him somehow involved in what was about to happen. Still, as my car ate up the road, I kept one eye on my rearview mirror, looking for a red Maserati with a silver fox behind the wheel.

Chapter Forty-eight

I cut my engine on the path up to the condo. A four-hundred-fifty-cubic-inch has a healthy growl, and I saw no reason to announce my arrival to anyone who wasn't already expecting me. As it was, I had enough momentum to cruise past Teddy Rhinecrest's former love nest and around to a secluded spot in back. Once I'd parked, I sat there, listening to the engine tick, as I played over my options in my mind.

I needed to talk to Ronnie, both for his protection and to end this cycle of violence. What I didn't need was for anyone else to be present—not at first. Cheryl was going to be useful, but she had her own agenda. Maybe she'd gotten hooked into this out of concern for her brother. Maybe that was what was still driving her, I didn't know. I did know that she wanted out, and I suspected that she'd take any deal to make that happen. I had to make my moves before she did.

Creighton's motives were likely to be a lot more pure. And that was going to be a different kind of problem. I was going to have to strike a bargain with Benazi, I suspected, in order to make this all go away. If my boy scout of a boyfriend was hanging around, that could get complicated. For the moment, I seemed to be the only person here. If I was lucky…

I was. In my rearview, I saw Ronnie's truck and, a moment later, the big man himself, a brown paper bag in his arms.

"Ronnie." I got out as he was still fiddling with his keys. "You and I have to have a conversation."

"Not now, Pru." He looked up at me with bloodshot eyes. "I've got the world's worst headache."

"Hangovers will do that to you." I followed him into his office. As he placed the bag on the desk, I looked around. The magazines were still there. The food wrappers. That was it. "So will a guilty conscience," I said.

"A guilty what?" Still standing, he extracted a bottle of aspirin and six-pack from the bag, pulling a can free as he spoke. Before I could answer, he threw the aspirin back, closing his eyes as he washed it down with half the can.

"Conscience, Ronnie." I sat behind the desk and pulled open the top drawer to find some paperclips and about thirty cents. "That little voice inside you that says you've done wrong." The next drawer held a bottle of lotion and more magazines. I closed it quickly.

"Pru…" He looked around, as if he didn't know the place, finally settling on the couch/bed. "I'm really tired."

"I bet." I wheeled the chair up to the side of the desk. The place was a mess, and I was getting a little worried. "But before you take your nap, I need you to tell me where it is."

"Where what is?" He looked around as if seeing the place for the first time. "Honest, Pru…"

"The bear." I was losing patience. "I know you were spying on Cheryl, but you must have seen more than you bargained for. You figured out what Teddy Rhinecrest was hiding—and you took it."

"Pru." He shook his head. "I don't know…"

"Do you mean this?"

I turned. Cheryl Ginger stood in the doorway. She was holding a small plush teddy bear. The red heart in its arms was still bright, but the toy's white fur was now brown and dotted with what looked like coffee grounds.

"Where did you find it?" I asked, even as Ronnie stuttered. "I didn't—honest—"

"You did, you creep." Cheryl stepped in, and for a moment I thought she was going to take a swing at Ronnie. "I knew this place was bad news. I didn't think you'd break into our condo."

"It wasn't…" He was sputtering. "I had to fix the wall, you know. By the door?"

"That doesn't make it right, Ronnie." I reached over and took the bear from Cheryl. "This was yours?"

She nodded. "It was one of Teddy's stupid gifts. I think he picked it up at a gas station or something. I recognized it on the top of the trash. "

I turned it over in my hands. Brushed the grounds off the fur, off the red satin heart. "When did he give it to you?"

"About a week before…" She stopped. Swallowed. "We had a fight, the morning he was killed. He couldn't believe I'd lost it."

"I bet." I was looking for something. I didn't know what.

"Hey!" She turned to Ronnie, her voice rising. "You didn't take this when you came to fix the wainscoting. Teddy only gave me that bear that night!"

"It was the next day." He cowered. "I forgot my tools, and I had to go back. I had to. But after what you said…" He looked from Cheryl to me and back again.

She was staring daggers, but that only confirmed it. I turned the bear over again. Plucked the heart from his arms, and pulled out my knife.

"What are you doing?" Cheryl whipped around, hands on her own chest.

"Teddy wasn't angry at you for losing a present," I said, as I examined the back of the red satin heart. The stitching there was loose. Amateurish, and my blade made quick work of it.

"He was angry at you for losing this." I held up the key. It had a number on it, like you'd find on a locker. "And after he'd been so smart about hiding it—hiding it again, I should say. Your repairs, Ronnie. They made him jumpy, only he was looking out for the wrong people."

"So that's what all the fuss has been about." As Creighton stepped in, we all turned. "My colleagues have been pretty close-mouthed about the details."

He held out his hand, palm up. "Pru?" He was watching me. Waiting.

I had no choice. I gave him the key.

"Looks like it came from the Hills," he said, turning it over. "Maybe one of those lockers big enough for skis. Tell me, Ms. Ginger. Was it your idea that you two take a ski vacation here?"

She shook her head. "No, Teddy's. He knew I skied, and he said he didn't want to fly."

"Don't blame him," said Creighton, with a smile. "Not with close to a billion dollars' worth of stolen art hidden in his car."

"A billion?" A voice chimed up behind us. We'd all but forgotten Ronnie.

"You didn't know, did you?" I actually found myself smiling at him.

"I just…" He looked down at the floor, but even that didn't hide his blush. "I thought it was sweet."

I looked over at the redhead, expecting more fireworks. After all, Ronnie was a voyeuristic creep who'd used his job to steal love tokens. To my surprise, she was blinking away tears.

"It *was* sweet," she said. She turned toward me and Creighton. "He could be…Teddy was always insisting I keep his presents. Keep them to remember him, even if something happened to him. He said he wanted me to have something—something of my own."

"Pity it wasn't his to give." The dark-haired man—the one from the woods—stepped in, his broad shoulders silhouetted against the morning light. I heard Cheryl gasp as my own heart began to race. "But you're right, that is what we've been looking for. Federal agent Brian Dalehy." He handed a billfold to Creighton, who glanced down and handed it back. "I've been undercover on this operation since Day One."

As the newcomer pocketed his credentials, my beau just stared. I had the feeling he was sizing up the dark-haired man, his blue eyes narrowed slightly against the glare. What he saw, I couldn't tell.

"Detective?" In a move that echoed one Creighton had made only moments before, the dark-haired man held out his hand. When my guy had done it, I'd hesitated because of the backstory.

Because I knew Benazi was involved, and that the agent who was supposed to be Cheryl Ginger's contact on the case was really working for the old gangster.

Now it was Jim's turn to pause, appraising that outstretched hand. Maybe it was professional jealousy. The Feds had taken over his case. Maybe it was some cop instinct. I'm not the only one with heightened senses.

The room was silent. The dark-haired man's face unreadable against the brightness of the open door. I looked up at Creighton, saw the creases around his mouth. The tension in his eyes.

And then he handed it over. The man had identified himself as a federal agent, and at heart Jim Creighton is a boy scout.

"Good." Brian nodded once at Creighton and turned to take us all in, and then he left. Was I relieved? Sure. I didn't want any bloodshed, particularly mine. But I knew what would happen if Creighton discovered the truth. I knew what it would cost him, and a little part of me died.

"Jim?" I didn't know what to say.

"I've been working with him," Cheryl interrupted. "He's why I've been here. With Teddy." In her rush to explain—to exonerate herself—she spilled out the story I'd so painstakingly put together. Her brother. The undercover operation. Even her adopting the spaniel as an excuse to go for walks. To meet with Dalehy, the collar a way to pass messages—the signal that she never got to give. As she told it, I could see how it started as an honest operation. Maybe even a good one.

"That's quite some story." Creighton didn't look comfortable. He still had some qualms about Brian, I could tell. But my chance to tell him had passed. I hadn't heard Brian drive away, but I had no doubt he was gone. I didn't think he'd be reporting to the Feds. "But I..." He rubbed his face, as if he could shed some feeling that was nagging at him. "There's going to be paperwork."

"Go," I said. I looked around at Cheryl, who had collapsed against the desk, and Ronnie, who sat up, more awake than ever. "I'll...clean up."

He raised his eyebrows at that, but with a nod he left. I turned toward Ronnie.

"Ronnie, you are not to tell anybody about this." I pitched my voice low. He needed to understand. "Nobody. Not even Albert."

He nodded. The night in jail had scared him. Maybe not as much as the truth would, but then again, if he knew about Benazi—about how Parvis had gotten killed—he might not have been able to function.

"Cheryl?" She was pulling herself upright. Pulling her bag up onto her shoulder. "You okay?"

She nodded. "They cleared me this morning. That's why I came by."

"And your brother?"

She shook her head. "I don't know. I'm supposed to hear from Brian…" She looked out the door.

"I'm sure you will," I said. I was lying. Then again, hope isn't a bad thing.

"Yeah, well…" She looked down at the floor and then up at me. Maybe she knew. Maybe she had done all she could. She held out her hand. "Thanks, Pru."

"My pleasure." I thought of those twenties. I wasn't offering her another refund. "You're taking Stewie?"

"Stewie?" She blinked, a hint of a smile making her cheek dimple. "That is a better name than Pudgy, isn't it? Yeah, I am." Her smile broadened. "I think we both deserve a fresh start."

I followed her out and closed the door behind us. I doubted that Ronnie was going to get much sleep after that, even with five beers to go. Better he mull the morning over here, though. With any luck, by the time he got to Happy's tonight, he'd have decided most of it was just a bad dream.

Cheryl's silver Honda was parked right outside, the window slightly ajar, and I leaned in to give Stewie one last pet.

"How you doing, boy?" His ears were warm and silky, and his flag of a tail thudded against the seat as I rubbed them at their base.

"*The master was here.*" His voice deep in my head.

"I know." If Cheryl were listening, she'd think I was talking endearments. Nonsense to an animal I'd grown fond of. "I know, Stewie."

"He said he's leaving." This startled me. *"That I'm to protect her from now on."*

"Because you're such a good boy," I said. It was the truth. "You're such a good boy."

I stepped back from the car and waved as Cheryl drove off. Then I turned and walked a little way into the woods. I knew he would be waiting.

◇◇◇

"Pru." Benazi stepped out of the shadows as silent as a panther. "And how are you this fine morning?"

"Well, thank you." I looked at him. "I gather your associates—the ones whose methods you don't approve of—have moved on?"

He ducked his head slightly, as if to hide his wolfish grin. "They were quite rash, and their methods simply inefficient."

"And Martin Parvis?"

The grin disappeared. "He shouldn't have been pushing as hard as he did." He shook his head. "It's one thing to ask questions. Another to threaten people."

I nodded. I had the feeling one of those underlings would confess to the private investigator's murder. No matter who was truly behind it.

"And the painting?" It seemed so silly that something I had never seen could be so important. "What's going to happen to that?"

"Certain people have made an investment," he said, one eyebrow arched. "You could say they have always only wanted the return of their property."

"*Their* property?" Somewhere, a thrush began singing. A small bird, but his song had a sense of place and propriety. "This isn't money we're talking about. This is a national treasure." The song trilled, cutting through the morning air like a clarion call.

"That's a bit extreme, wouldn't you say?" He took a step closer.

"There's a lot I wouldn't say." I didn't know where this was coming from. That thrush. Creighton. I didn't want to let him down. "And I won't, but…"

I left the sentence unfinished, as I looked up into trees. Somewhere up there, the thrush sang on and was joined by other birds. A chorus of small creatures, all exclaiming their right to life and beauty in their own lands. The sun had broken through. And that, it struck me then, was how my sensitivity worked. This was how I trained—no, *communicated*—with other creatures. Not through tricks or fear, but by understanding them, and asking them to understand me, in turn. What worked for me—what had always worked—was clarity. Enlightenment. I needed to be honest. To be direct. To be clear.

"The painting has to go back," I said. My voice was level and low. My command voice. Right now it was simply the only way I could speak. "You know that, and so do I."

I had turned toward him, and now I looked him in the eye. He looked old, then. Old and sad. But not, I thought, as distant as I had once believed. We stood there silent, and then he gave a small, almost imperceptible nod.

"My colleagues won't be happy about this." Benazi tilted his head back, breaking away, but still watching me.

It didn't matter. It was my turn to smile.

"I'm sure you can make it right," I said, and then I turned and walked away.

Chapter Forty-nine

On my way home, I stopped off at Marnie Lundquist's house. No business, and I wasn't needed. I simply couldn't resist going back. Piecing together the clues the little leporid had left for us, I had finally found the missing pet before Creighton's call had caused me to run off, a little more than an hour before. The bunny had indeed been working on that hay, largely to drag it down to a corner of the basement, warm and safe behind the old house's boiler. That's where we had found Henry—and her day-old kits.

"How precious!" Marnie Lundquist had blinked away tears when I showed her the nest. She had enough sense not to try to touch the tiny bunnies. Instead we'd both crouched there, on the basement floor, watching as Henry nursed and then washed the little blind things. When I'd gone back up, to bring both food and water closer to the nursing mother, I'd fetched a pillow and stool for Marnie to sit on as well. I had a feeling she'd be down here often in the days to come. I had a feeling I would be, too.

◇◇◇

Marnie Lundquist didn't look surprised to see me return. "Poor Cara," she said as I followed her back to the basement. "She's going to be quite taken aback."

"Because she wasn't here?" The low rumble of contentment coming from the new mother was as intoxicating as bourbon. "Should we take some photos for her?"

"Oh, yes!" Marnie clasped her hands together—and held them. We'd both been speaking softly, and clapping might have been disruptive. "But, no, my dear. I meant that she might feel rather foolish. To have missed something so, well, basic."

"She shouldn't." I shook my head. "She's been a vet tech. She knows how hard it is to determine the gender of some animals." I could have gone into how breeders measure the anal-genital distance and still often get it wrong, especially with a rabbit as young as Henry. "Except, of course, to other rabbits."

The white bun bobbed as the old lady nodded, somewhat ruefully. "Perhaps Cara will agree to a veterinary visit now," she said. "After all, my house is only so big."

"Good idea." I had been wondering what would happen to the kits. I didn't know their odds out in the wild with a semi-domesticated mother. I needn't have worried. "You can bring the babies in, too, in a few months."

"I gather I should change her name to Henrietta," said the old lady after we'd sat there for a while. "But perhaps I may still call her Henry, for short."

"I'm sure she'll be happy with that," I replied.

From deep inside the nest, I got the only confirmation I needed. *"Family, safe...safe and warm."* The bunny had finally let me in.

Chapter Fifty

The unveiling was held in the city a few months later. A spokesman from the FBI was joined on the podium by a representative of the museum as they drew back a curtain to reveal the restored painting, *Berkshire Forest*, ready to go back on display. Creighton and I watched it on my mom's old TV, which he'd cajoled back to life when we heard the news.

"No mention of Agent Dalehy." My guy grumbled as the camera focused in on the woodland scene, the shaft of sun between the trees. "Only that claptrap about an anonymous tip."

"Well, he was undercover." I watched him out of the corner of my eye, doing my best to keep my voice casual. The bunny had come to light. I didn't think the full story ever would. "I wonder if it's true that they have no lead on who stole it or where it's been?"

"That's what they're saying," he said, frowning. But then he opened his beer, and I realized I'd been holding my breath.

"Make it a little obvious, why don't you?" Beside me on the couch, Wallis paused from her bathing.

"I'm just glad they caught the guys," I said, to shift the subject. "The ones who killed Martin Parvis. I mean, he was a jerk, but really all he was doing was asking questions."

"And I'm glad I took you out to lunch while they were on the loose." Creighton shot me a look. "I can't believe you thought I'd do an illegal search."

I shrugged. "Hey, I'm my mother's daughter." He put his arm around me. In lieu of an apology, I snuggled in.

On the TV, the mayor began making a speech. I watched without listening, looking at his suit and thinking I'd seen better.

Benazi, of course, had never come up in the investigation or in the trial that was just now winding up. But his colleagues— the ones he'd warned Cheryl about?—they'd been apprehended roughing up one of the regulars behind Happy's.

It hadn't been difficult to link them to the private investigator's death: they were out-of-town muscle. Bad guys with known ties to organized crime. I didn't know what Parvis' greatest sin had been—poking about, looking for the painting, or disobeying the widow's direct orders. As I'd noticed, she had clout.

For a week or two, the two goons seemed likely to take the fall for Teddy Rhinecrest's murder, too. Only the timeline didn't work out. They actually had alibis, and once the painting had been recovered, the Feds lost interest in the grumpy old man as a victim. Maybe the trail went cold. At any rate, once they'd backed off, Creighton had been able to do his job. As he'd suspected all along, the murder had nothing to do with the stolen masterpiece. Nothing except that by coming to Beauville, Teddy Rhinecrest had left his territory, the home base where he was known, respected, and feared. Out here, he was no longer an alpha predator. Just another rich tourist, one with a smart mouth who liked to gamble but didn't want to pay his debts.

"Don't you know who I am?" It might have been the last thing he said.

Vince was probably lucky that Creighton picked him up when he did. Rhinecrest's former associates had figured out what had happened, too. They knew how the old man could be, and they'd been trolling for whoever had taken him down, with their high-stakes card games and the free food. The regular they were kicking around probably would have given them Vince's name, if he'd known it. It was just a matter of time.

The DA had said Vince would plead to manslaughter, in the hope of getting into protective custody while inside. I didn't know if he'd make it, even then. The Feds would never admit it, but Creighton told me how annoyed they were that Vince had cut the phone lines they'd spent so much effort tapping. Cut them with the same knife he'd stabbed Rhinecrest with, when he had the old man cornered and he'd still refused to pay up. When you piss off both sides, the mobsters and the FBI, you don't tend to live long.

The image on the TV flickered as the camera panned from the mayor back to the masterpiece. Creighton leaned in to toy with the makeshift antennae.

"I guess everyone was after the same thing," said Creighton, once he'd gotten the image stabilized. Reaching for his beer, he paused, squinted at the TV. "The billion-dollar bunny. I still don't see it." He looked over at me. Saw my smile. "The rabbit, I mean."

"He's right out in the open," I said, thinking of another bunny. "But you have to know where to look."

◇◇◇

Later, when Creighton had fallen asleep, Wallis jumped on the bed.

"*You don't have to treat me like a kitten, you know.*" She began kneading the pillow, purring like a bellows. "*Or him for that matter.*"

"Hush." I shifted over to make room. "*He'll hear you.*" The thought came unbidden, and I shook my head to disperse it. Of course he couldn't. Only I could. Only, when I glanced over, I found myself looking into those blue eyes. My beau was awake.

"I'm not a fool, Pru." He leaned over. I braced myself. For what, I wasn't sure. "I know about you."

I began to compile excuses. Benazi had threatened me. He'd threatened Wallis. At that, my tabby looked up at me, her green eyes unreadable.

"I know you have some kind of special…" If he said "relationship," I was going to deny it. Benazi and I weren't friends. We certainly weren't anything more.

"Sensitivity," Creighton said after a moment's pause, "with animals. I've seen it, again and again. How you seem to understand not just what they're doing but why."

I had no answer. I had no thoughts left, and it was with an effort that I closed my mouth at all.

"I am a detective, you know," said my sweetheart, with a chuckle. "I think it's part of what makes you special."

"Special?" I choked out the word.

"Yeah," he said, as he drew me close. Beside us, Wallis kept on purring.

Acknowledgments

Big bunny thanks go to Janie Matocha of the House Rabbit Network. She answered all my questions, and any errors are mine not hers. As always, huge thanks to my agent Colleen Mohyde and to John McDonough, for his police expertise, as well as to my editor Annette Rogers and copy editor Beth Deveny. I cannot thank Shell Welles, Brett Milano, Lisa Jones, Lisa Susser, Vicki Croke, Karen Schlosberg, Frank Garelick, and Sophie Garelick enough for all their support and encouragement, but please know how vital you are. Last but far from least, Jon S. Garelick for everything.

To receive a free catalog of Poisoned Pen Press titles, please provide your name, address, and email address in one of the following ways:

Phone: 1-800-421-3976
Facsimile: 1-480-949-1707
Email: info@poisonedpenpress.com
Website: www.poisonedpenpress.com

Poisoned Pen Press
6962 E. First Ave. Ste 103
Scottsdale, AZ 85251